Time Travel for Love and Profit

Time Travel for Love and Profit

SARAH LARIVIERE

Alfred A. Knopf
New York

Library of Congress Cataloging-in-Publication Data is available upon request.
ISBN 978-0-593-17420-3 (trade) — ISBN 978-0-593-17421-0 (lib. bdg.) —
ISBN 978-0-593-17422-7 (ebook)

The text of this book is set in 11.5-point Fairfield LT.
Interior design by Ken Crossland

Printed in the United States of America
October 2020
10 9 8 7 6 5 4 3 2 1

First Edition

Dedicated to my children,
Laszlo and Adèle Mapp

PART I

CHAPTER 1

My Miserable Destiny

The day my best friend, Vera Knight, dumped me, I didn't know what happened. We were sitting in the cafeteria right after winter break. I was eating my usual burrito. Vera was eating her usual six jelly beans and a bagel. I said, "My current favorite mathematical concept is fractals. Not only do they make psychedelic patterns, they also describe infinity."

Vera nodded, and nudged a white jelly bean across the table with her index finger.

"What's your current favorite mathematical concept?" I asked. "You're probably still obsessed with square roots."

Vera kept nodding and looked over her shoulder. I looked where she was looking and saw nothing but Ramsey Schultz, with her bored facial expression and her multitude of extraneous accessories. The dangly feather earrings, the metallic boots, the table of worshippers who shadowed her every move like spy drones.

"Square roots," I said. "I knew it."

Vera stood, said "I'll be right back," walked to Ramsey's table, sat and didn't say another word to me for the rest of the year.

Of course, at the time, I didn't know Vera was ghosting me. Sure, I knew that Vera and Ramsey had been taking ballet together, and that Ramsey, according to Vera, was "actually supersweet." But Vera said she'd be right back, and I believed her. So I enjoyed the remainder of my burrito, ignorant of my miserable destiny. The icy shivers I would get when Vera passed me in the hallways and looked through me like I was transparent. The dizziness that would hit when I realized she was never going to answer my texts. The misery of overhearing my peers describe a party at Vera's house, during which there was a kissing game, where actual kissing happened. Vera and I had sworn we'd tell each other every single detail of our first kisses. Did Vera kiss someone? Who was it? How was it? The loneliness of knowing she'd never tell me.

Things only got worse from there. When I walked down the hallway, Ramsey and her minions hissed. I guess they were supposed to be snakes, and I was the prey or something? Whatever it was, it worked; I felt like a moving target. Other kids pretended not to see me, as if looking at me might get them sent to Outcast Island, too. Then one day, someone shouted, "Neffa-Freak!" And the insult caught on. Perhaps because it's easier to pronounce than my name, which is Nephele, after a cloud nymph from Greek mythology who is so obscure I was pretty sure nobody but my mother had ever heard of her.

NEH-fuh-lee rhymes with especially is what Mom used to tell me to tell people, but you'd have to be alarmingly adorable to pull that off. Alarming I could do. Adorable? Not so much.

And then there was Valentine's Day. Oh, how I loved Valentine's Day. The one holiday a year when a dashing stranger might parachute into Redwood Cove out of nowhere, march up to me with a rose between his teeth and kneel, holding a sign above his head that said, *Nephele, your beauty may be complicated, but it is unmistakable,* while a chubby baby with hot-pink cheeks shot an arrow made of sunbeams through my heart. I was sitting on the redwood stump outside the school, imagining other things my valentine might proclaim, such as *Nephele, let's go to the beach together and contemplate irregular polyhedrons until the sun plunges into the deep blue sea,* when Youki Johnson fist-bumped Kyle "Dirty Dog" Jones and started walking my way.

Youki had the face of a superhero, and he was a straight-A student like me. And he was coming to talk to me—*on Valentine's Day.* My head hummed. My tongue tingled. I was so excited that I almost forgot how to breathe. Looking back, my reaction was irrational, but at the time, I couldn't think straight. I'd been fantasizing about a moment like this for years.

When Youki stopped in front of me, he handed me a pink razor tied with a droopy red bow. "This is for you, Woolly Mammoth," he said. "Shave those hairy arms."

Kyle fell all over himself laughing in this strangled way, like he was choking on a chipmunk. Other kids also laughed. A few frowned; a few looked at their feet.

5

I looked at the pink razor dressed up in its bow tie and wondered where Youki had gotten the red ribbon. Did his mother keep a roll of it for presents? Had he asked her for a piece of it that morning? Had she smiled when she'd handed it to him, proud that her son had found a valentine?

Then I looked at my arms. Thousands of thick black hairs crawled over each other like headless, skinny, wiry blind worms. I was hairy. My mother was hairy. Our relatives in Greece were total furballs. Our hairiness was fascinating, and I knew this. I wished someone would explain the rules to me about what constituted an attractive person and what did not. It made zero sense, mathematically.

"*Omigod*, she's talking to herself," said someone, and I looked up. Behind Youki, Ramsey was wiping tears of laughter from her eyes. She said, "That girl is, like, *aggressively* weird."

Beside Ramsey, Vera was frowning, playing with a droopy branch of a cypress tree. "It's not her fault," she said. My ears perked up, and my heart pumped a woozy, hopeful beat. Was my former best friend finally going to defend me?

Vera went on. "My mother says all prodigies develop abnormal personalities after puberty."

I closed my eyes and concentrated on the black static pattern of the galaxy. Inner space. I liked inner space. It was safe in there.

After Valentine's Day came spring, with its bursts of rain, and its dewy flowers, and its rapidly multiplying bunnies—and a rapidly multiplying crowd of people who yelled "Neffa-Freak!"

when I walked by. I felt more and more lonely and desperate, like the world would just keep turning while I spiraled down a rickety roller coaster that was one earthquake away from collapsing.

When the last day of freshman year was finally over, I walked directly to the Big Blue Wave. My loose plan was to hide in my parents' bookshop until I died of a rare used-book disease, such as paper-cut plague or word poisoning.

The foghorns moaned low and steady as I crossed Highway 1 and turned onto Main Street. The wind was tugging my hair out of its bun and tying it in knots. I put up my hood and shoved my hands deep in my sweatshirt pockets.

The Big Blue Wave used to be a fish-canning factory. It's brick with tons of windows and two floors crammed with used books, with a special section on California History for the tourists. Sometimes birds slip in through the skylights and flit around, pooping on the cement floor. The front door was propped open, and from Main Street I heard Dad spinning jazz saxophone.

My parents are tragically analog. Fact: One milk crate full of records weighs as much as a baby sperm whale. Dad has more than a hundred crates, and he keeps the bulk of his collection in the shop. I'm always offering to digitize it. I think I do it just to see the face Dad makes when I use the word "digitize." It's disturbing.

Dad was standing behind the checkout counter, wearing his usual outfit of a band T-shirt, a flannel button-down and jeans. Recently he'd grown a mustache. It was puffy and red, as opposed to his hair, which was curly and black, which created a clashing situation that Mom and I couldn't decide how we felt about.

When he saw me, he called, "Congrats, Fi! Another year bites the dust."

My parents were the only ones who called me "Fi." It's pronounced "fee," as in when you have to pay extra.

I leaned on the counter. "Well, it bites, anyway."

"It's like that?" said Dad. "What's up?"

I sighed. I didn't know what to tell him. That I'm destined to spend eternity alone? Dad would only try to reassure me. Ignore the haters, this too shall pass, get that dirt off your shoulder, etc.

"Where's Mom?" I asked.

"She's in the back, whittling."

My mother was in a whittling phase. "Spatula?" I asked.

"Spoon," said Dad. "Maybe this'll cheer you up. Came in today."

Dad handed me a hardback book with a glossy cream cover that was torn around the edges. The title was written in faded purple calligraphy: *Time Travel for Love & Profit*. That was it; just text. No illustrations of futuristic vehicles, no calendar with the dates swirling in a tornado. No Civil War soldiers dancing in a 1970s New York City disco. No half-naked alien draped over a cowboy with perfect teeth. Oh well. It would probably be pretty good anyway. I turned the book over and read the back cover out loud. "The author, Oona Gold, lives in the beautiful cosmos."

Dad said, "If it gets your stamp of approval, would you mind shelving it?"

"Sure, boss," I said as Dad saluted me and turned to help a customer.

The Science Fiction section is on the second floor of the bookshop, nestled between Math and Poetry. Dad had appointed me its manager, which meant I got to decide which books were worth stocking. Which was, of course, all of them. I'd never met a science fiction book I didn't get mildly obsessed with. But I did enjoy reading new additions before we made them available to the general public.

I flopped on the ratty yellow couch that faced the window to Main Street and cracked open the book. It exhaled a puff of mildew that made me sneeze. One of the alley cats who sometimes strolled around the shop leapt into my lap, and I stroked its silver ears.

Introduction

Can you pinpoint the instant your life turned from hopeful and promising into a depressing pile of horse poop?

Have you dreamed about getting a do-over?

Do you want love?

9

Do you want money?

If the answer to any of these questions is
yes, there is only one solution to your problem:
Time travel.

Time Travel for Love & Profit will teach
you to borrow the power of your future self
to make the current you a better you by
renovating your past.

Don't be trapped in your pathetic, hopeless
and completely avoidable future. If you
change the you of yesterday, you will not be
the same sad you tomorrow.

I looked up. Main Street was invisible, swallowed by a thick cloud of fog. The bookshop swirled with the shimmery sound of the saxophone. The cat looked at me, and I looked at the cat.

Huh.

I looked at the cover again: *Time Travel for Love & Profit.*

Was this book sketchy? Yes. Self-published? Most likely. Should it be shelved in Self-Help instead of Science Fiction? For sure.

Did I love it? Were my arm hairs quivering with anticipation? Was I going to read it immediately, cover to cover, in one sitting?

Does an octopus undulate squishily?

I held the cat's pointy face in my hand. "This is it," I said.

"The solution to my problem. It's so obvious I can't believe I didn't think of it before."

The cat yowled and leapt out of my lap and rolled on the floor in a crazy cat stretch. I looked out the window at the blobs of car headlights and the shadowy pedestrians passing through the fog.

Okay, okay—it wasn't *that* obvious. But now that I was thinking about it, why not? Why not go back in time and give myself an epic do-over? Only this time, I wouldn't end up a friendless freak. New Nephele could be anyone I imagined. Someone Vera wouldn't want to abandon. Someone cute boys would make elaborate plans to kiss, not to humiliate. Sure, building a time machine had never occurred to me before, but that was just because I'd never needed one. A time machine was basically a complicated math problem. Wasn't math my one superpower?

Right. It was decided. I was going to test the limits of my mathematical talents. To stretch my infatuation with science fiction to the breaking point.

I, Nephele Weather, was going to build a time machine, and use it to do freshman year over. New Nephele would be sassy, like a superstar singer with a skimpy, sequined bodysuit and a team of synchronized dancers behind her. Stylish and sleepy and bored with the world, like a mall mannequin with pointy boobs and no teeth. The new me would be saucier than a truckload of barbecued beans, hotter than a blazing hunk of coal.

No: wait, not coal. Coal was what you got instead of gifts when you'd been naughty. On the other hand, I kind of loved the idea of being associated with the word "naughty." I flipped through *Time Travel for Love & Profit* feeling hopeful.

It's amusing now, sort of, to think about it. Back then, people were always referring to me as a "child prodigy." Supposedly, I learned things ridiculously quickly. So, I figured, how hard could it be to avoid Outcast Island and make the whole world love me?

With Oona Gold's help, one more shot at freshman year was really all it should take. I squinted into the fog and saw my future gleaming like a newly discovered planet, twinkling in the center of a telescope.

Round. Reachable. Perfect.

CHAPTER 2

Dirk Angus Is Born

That afternoon at the bookshop, I read *Time Travel for Love & Profit* twice. That night, when I crawled into bed, I read it a third time to be sure I hadn't missed anything.

It's a good book. It's one of those books that keep you turning the pages, even though there are no actual characters, and you can't explain what it's about, and you wouldn't recommend it to anyone because they might not like it as much as you do, which would spoil the beauty of it, especially if they pointed out any logical flaws or sketchy theories or pseudoscience, which you were of course completely aware of, but happy to ignore temporarily for personal reasons.

And it didn't explain how to build a time machine—which wasn't too surprising. If Oona Gold knew the secret to time travel, she'd be so busy winning the Nobel Prize that it probably wouldn't occur to her to write a self-help book.

That was fine. I could handle the technical part.

There was one legitimate reason my peers thought I was aggressively weird. It's because I am aggressively, weirdly good at something, and I didn't do anything in particular to get that way.

Mom says she first noticed it when I was three years old. My bedroom quilt is white with patchwork stars made of black and blue diamonds. One day, I told her, "There are 4,320 diamonds." Mom said, "What?" I said, "There are 4,320 diamonds in the stars. If we had 392,050 diamonds, we could cover the whole house with stars," and she spilled a box of macaroni on the floor.

My own first memory of being different from the other kids was in kindergarten. While the rest of the class sat on the circular carpet counting how many pennies were in a nickel, I did my own set of calculations. When the teacher called on me, I said, "This carpet is approximately 7.3 square meters."

The teacher scrunched her nose like I'd used an off-limits word, like butt crack or fart. "Who told you that?" she asked.

"Nobody," I said. "It's only a rough estimate."

"Lying is naughty, Nephele," she said. "And we don't teach the metric system in this classroom."

I told her that if what she meant by "metric system" was the International System of Units, I, like most scientists, preferred it, and that I was telling the truth, and recited the formula for calculating the area of a circle, along with the first thirty decimals of pi.

She looked at me like I was a talking koala bear.

Meaning, she looked scared of me. Which scared *me*. After

school, I asked Mom, "Am I scary? Like a monster?" And she called the principal. I don't know what they said exactly, but I started spending part of every day with a tutor from the University of California named Starla. Starla had purple hair, a belly button piercing and several toe rings (Starla preferred to tutor in bare feet). Supposedly, Starla was teaching me geometry. In fact, she mostly talked about her boyfriend, Rob, a "smoking hot slob" who was "totally inconsistent" and "a master of the mixed message." Starla had a very sophisticated social life; it contained many logical contradictions. As for geometry, she was decent. She got most things more or less right.

Fast-forward to second grade. By that time, I was reading college-level math books like comic books. Calculus? Number theory? Algorithms? Bring 'em on.

Math made me happy. Like, insanely happy. I loved seeing the patterns all around me. Math described the waves of the ocean, the light of the constellations, the rings of the redwood trees. Math made sense to me the way nothing else did. I felt like I knew how to communicate with the universe. I understood its language.

As for the language of my fellow humans?

I didn't think much about it. I had Vera.

When Vera and I met in first grade, we had the exact same sense of humor. I would pretend to fall down, she would pretend to fall down. She would be a rat and chase me, I would be a rat and chase her. We both hated sparkles. Our friendship was meant to be.

In middle school, Vera and I ate lunch together every single day. After school, we'd go to one of our houses to continue the epic saga of Amazingland, our imaginary city where the laws of physics didn't apply. We'd be weightless and jump on my bed until it broke. Pretend we were trapped inside a two-dimensional cave and slither like slugs across the floor.

We laughed so hard. Vera was quiet, but her laugh was loud, like . . . I don't know. A broken blender or something. Her laugh made her self-conscious, but I liked it.

After I finished my third reading of *Time Travel for Love & Profit,* I set it on the floor beside my bed, feeling uncertain. I didn't need a book to teach me how to build a time machine, but I did wish Oona Gold had been more specific about how I was supposed to "tap into the fabulousness of the future me" to "gut-renovate my pathetic now" other than by subscribing to a series of online videos for $49.99 a month (card will be charged automatically at the end of each billing cycle).

I curled up under my star quilt and looked toward my bedroom window, which was open a crack. My white curtains fluttered, and I inhaled the chilly salt breeze.

Well, the first step in gut-renovating my life was building my time machine. That, I was excited about. It would be an epic mathematical challenge. The thought of all the formulas I'd need to cook up made my mouth water. For the first time in months, I couldn't wait to wake up the next morning.

The more I thought about it, the more excited I got. The practical applications of a successful time machine would be endless. It wouldn't just fix my social life; it would be a mind-blowing scientific achievement. *Humanity itself* could get an epic do-over. We could undo global warming and save the ocean, its kelp forests and coral reefs. Prevent sea levels from rising and destroying creatures' habitats; reverse the epidemic of lethal storms.

Time travel wouldn't save just me. It might just save the planet.

And when it did?

The world would have Vera Knight to thank. Which was, I decided, perfectly fine. When I became a popular, highly kissable mathematician whose discovery had changed the course of human history?

I'd be more than happy to share the credit.

That night, I dreamt I was walking on a gust of wind, folding an inflating balloon. In the morning, I woke up laughing like a maniac. I was dying to tell someone about my time machine, and given the circumstances, that someone would have to be Chicago.

I threw on my usual T-shirt, hoodie and jeans, shoved my long mess of black hair into a bun and checked myself in the mirror. Same eyes as gold as a bat, same three-millimeter gap between my two front teeth, same ears sticking out like a dog who is listening carefully. I raised my thick black eyebrows at myself and ran downstairs.

I was running out our front door when Mom yelled, "Fi! Where are you going?"

I spun around. "Bookshop."

Mom was sitting at the green kitchen table with a speckled mug of coffee, reading a magazine called *Modern Axe Worker*. With her wavy red hair and wide turquoise eyes, I used to pretend my mother was a mermaid Dad had met on the beach. Actually, she's a freelance tax consultant. According to Dad, Mom's talent with numbers saved the bookshop when it almost went under. "She was magic," said Dad. "I had to marry her."

Mom asked, "What about breakfast?"

Breakfast would have been nice, now that I thought about it. But I had to build a time machine that would save me from my future self, and I didn't want to waste a single second. I said, "The clock is ticking on my destiny, Mom. Toast is eternal."

"Well, at least take some fruit," said Mom as she tossed me an orange.

I covered my face. The orange thunked on the floor and rolled into the vestibule. "What was that?" I asked.

"Sorry, sugar," said Mom.

I yelled, "See you later," leapt over the spherical object and sprinted out the front door.

I skipped down our warped red front porch steps and ran down the hill past my neighbors' wind-battered houses and overgrown yards. At the bottom of the hill I pulled up my hood and turned onto Highway 1.

To Redwood Cove locals, Highway 1 is just another road we take to work or to pick up groceries. To the tourists snapping photos, Highway 1 is a giant living postcard. The roller-coaster ride of twists and plunges, built into the rocky cliffs beside the Pacific Ocean, ribbons all the way up the California coast. On any given day you might see surfers catching gnarly waves, schools of leaping dolphins or spouting whales silhouetted against a blazing sunset. Near Redwood Cove, wildflowers ramble along the edges of forests of coastal redwoods, the oldest, tallest trees in the world. Some live for hundreds of years. Some for thousands. Many people put driving all 650 miles of Highway 1 on their bucket lists, the things they want to do before they die. I think bucket lists are morbid, gruesome and hopelessly romantic.

I walked toward Main Street, inhaling the minty scent of eucalyptus trees until my chest felt warm and my head buzzed. Swollen flower buds were packed so dense with energy I could almost hear them ready to sing out. I felt the cheeps and gargles of birds prickling my skin. Baby birds, mama birds, hunting and mating birds, their songs created a geometry in my brain, the place where the world became patterns, and patterns became glorious numbers. Numbers that would build me a time machine.

I went into the Big Blue Wave and breezed past Dad, who was lugging a crate of records onto the checkout counter. As I clomped up the wooden stairs to the second floor, I looked over my shoulder. "Seven thousand albums, weightless in the cloud! Every song title, alphabetized!"

Dad shook his head. "Nephele Ann, the music is in the grooves. It's in the *heft*."

Then he muttered the word "digitize" and made the face.

Chicago hangs on the second floor of the bookshop in a black metal frame on a blood-red wall. Her full name—her title, actually—is *Chicago, 1955.* She's a picture of two women walking past each other in opposite directions on a sidewalk that looks nearly white against a city that looks nearly black. But the way they're lined up, you see one two-headed woman, walking in both directions simultaneously. Half of her has one foot in the air, like she's heading home to cook dinner. The other half looks less rushed. Like she's thinking, or daydreaming, or remembering something she lost. Around her, the atmosphere is hazy; the sky bleeds into the ground. I liked to imagine that if I stared long enough, other creatures would step out of the mist. Dad told me that the photographer who took the picture was named Harry Callahan, and that he was dead. Which was hard to believe, because Chicago felt so alive.

Below Chicago, there's a carved wooden table with stuff for hot beverages, plus some melty mugs Mom crafted in her ceramics phase. I grabbed a mug and tore open a packet of green tea. "So I'm walking on a gust of wind, folding an inflating balloon."

"Hello to you, too," Chicago answered.

I sighed. "Aren't we beyond chatting?"

"Chatting is what normal people do," she said. "You should practice."

"Who's normal, Chicago? You? Whatever. How are you?"

"Same as always," she said. "Thanks for asking."

"Stupendous," I said. "Now I feel normal."

I started talking to Chicago after Vera dumped me. Something about the photograph of the two-headed woman made me feel better. She was a freak; I was a freak. Chicago made me feel less alone.

"So I'm walking on a gust of wind, folding an inflating balloon," I repeated, "and I realize I'm walking through a tunnel. Only it isn't a balloon I'm folding, and it isn't the wind I'm walking on. It's time. I've got it, Chicago."

"Got what?" she said. "An overactive imagination?"

"No," I said. "A blueprint for my time machine."

Stories about time travel tend to share a basic premise: if you could fold the fabric of time to make two points touch, poke a hole there and pass through it, you'd come out on the other side. That is, at a different point in time. The question is, can you fold time? Or is time folded already, and you just have to find the place where now meets then, and go?

I loved this question. It made me think about how time connects with itself every day. You see this person, you remember that conversation. You hear this music, you remember your father doing that silly dance. You inhale a scent that knocks you back to someplace you visited once, long ago. Time is folded into all kinds of shapes inside our heads.

"So you're going to build a spaceship out of balloons," said Chicago.

"No," I said. "I'm going to build a smartphone app out of code. A timeship app, let's call it."

Real time-travel research shares more or less the same premise as science fiction. But instead of setting off on thrilling adventures in rockets and falling into tragic love stories with people who've been dead for centuries, time-travel researchers spend their days working on mathematical equations.

Math is the heartbeat that gives life to tons of amazing scientific discoveries. Isaac Newton used calculus to show how the planets orbit the sun. Albert Einstein's equations describe how gravity warps the fabric of space and time. Ada Lovelace wrote calculations for the world's first computer program.

Now it was my turn to use math to make scientific history. My dream had given me a theory about how time travel could work mathematically, and it boiled down to two of my favorite words:

Quantum foam.

Have you ever looked through a microscope and screamed? You think you're looking at some eensie-weensie, harmless little eyelash, and instead you see wriggling *Demodex* mites with claw feet and fangs, and it hits you that your whole face is a universe, a landscape teeming with minuscule organisms eating and making out and laying eggs and oozing and living and dying on you like you're an organic farm.

Sorry. Not trying to ruin your face for you.

I'm just saying.

Now imagine you can shrink and hike around the landscape of your terrifying face with your magnifying glass, studying the atmosphere, and you find even teensier organisms squirming with life—bacteria and fungi and viruses—and you shrink again to investigate those, and then again, and again, until you're a bazillion times smaller than the nucleus of a hydrogen atom.

You're floating in the infinitesimal mathematical bubble bath known as quantum foam.

And it's chaos. A spinning maze of warped funhouse mirrors where the only thing you can count on is uncertainty. Some scientists believe that at such a small scale, space and time follow their own rules, fizzing and popping frantically, like bubbles in root beer. In the foam, math gets freaky—which is, of course, why I'm kind of in love with it.

Quantum theorists believe that quantum foam is everywhere. In outer space. In your living room. In your brain. And in my dream, I could mold it, stretch it, inflate it—and fold it, and poke a hole in it—creating a tunnel through time.

In theory, it was beautiful. Now all I had to do was write the equations: the equations that would form the backbone of the code for the world's first time-travel app.

"So your time machine is gonna be an *app*?" said Chicago.

I put my hand on my heart and sighed. "Isn't it elegant? In an instant, my humble smartphone simultaneously de-encrypts every wireless device on earth and harnesses their power to measure the state of the quantum foam, then sets up a resonance that effectively *folds time* and shakes open a *wormhole* in it—"

"Hang on! You're going to power your timeship with a bunch of strangers' shoe-shopping stereos and thinking thermostats and self-driving cars?"

"I know it sounds nuts, but when you get a billion artificially intelligent appliances working on the same project—trust me, Chicago, you can do some serious . . . well, I don't want to use the word 'damage,' but—"

"Where are you even drilling this wormhole? The North Pole? What happens when some poor penguin stumbles in and lands in a dinosaur's dinner bowl?"

"That won't happen!"

"How do you know?"

"Because the wormhole will be located in the quantum foam inside my body! I think I'll drill it right behind my belly button."

Chicago struck me as looking particularly thoughtful, her foot lingering mid-step, like she'd paused to seriously consider this. After a few seconds, she said, "Which is . . . safe?"

"Well, I mean, naturally I'll program the app to concentrate me with enough negative energy density that I don't disintegrate when I'm sucked through the wormhole and pop back out again—"

"In the same place, at a different time," said Chicago. "Like you're turning yourself inside out."

"It's beautiful, Chicago, isn't it? And the whole thing happens instantaneously. Nobody will even lose their internet connection."

In fact, my time-travel solution was more than elegant. To me, it felt inevitable.

"And you can make this happen with a bunch of numbers and symbols," said Chicago.

"If I described it to you mathematically, it would bore both your heads off," I said. "Although it's not boring. It's so not boring. Anyway, I don't know all the details yet—the equations will take me a while to work out, and the coding will take the rest of the summer. Of course, I'll need to figure out how to synchronize the topology of hyperspace across devices, not to mention the issues I'll have with electromagnetism—blah, blah, blah—the point is, it's totally doable! The crucial thing now is that I give my timeship app a name."

"Clearly, the name of the app is the most important part," said Chicago.

I said, "I agree wholeheartedly."

Yes: I was aware that having conversations with a black-and-white photograph was aggressively weird. But I needed Chicago more than ever now. Sure, I could've told Mom and Dad that I was inventing a time machine. My parents would've been happy for me. They'd have hugged me and told me they believed in me. Because they did believe in me.

But they'd never *believe* me.

When you're destined to do something that's widely considered impossible, you need one person to believe you unconditionally, even if you have to invent that person yourself.

"I can't wait to see what name I pick," I said. "I'll bet this is what it feels like to be pregnant."

"I'm not going to respond to that," said Chicago, and I headed for Romance.

*   *   *

I was sitting in a beanbag, sipping tea and flipping through the pile of books I'd gathered from the Romance section for timeship app name inspiration. The character names in Romance are far superior to the ones in Science Fiction. I mean, who wants to name their baby Astralflork or Mxylprlf 782?

After a couple of hot-and-heavy hours evaluating the biographies of potential candidates, I had a short list: Dr. Carissa Silk, Thor Jackson, Friar Ubu, Antonio de la Noir, Soleil Zesati and Candy Buttons. All of these names had their strengths; all of them had their limitations. Dr. Carissa Silk sounded like someone who wore lacy pink lingerie and a stethoscope. Which is, in fact, exactly what she does in her book, *The Sordid Sacrifices of Dr. Silk*; her healing methods are highly unorthodox. Unorthodox was a plus, but the lingerie uniform seemed needlessly provocative for my purposes. I wasn't quite sold.

Thor Jackson was a solid name, but in his series, Nordic Nocturne: Nine Naughty Tales of Endless Night, Thor is plagued by nightmares, owing to his past life as a murderous Viking. I liked that he had a conscience, but I didn't want my timeship app to be burdened with a heavy backstory.

I really loved Friar Ubu, the monk with ripped abs and a secret desire to be a go-go dancer. He was a contender. And the rest of the names had potential, too. Yet I felt unsatisfied. Nothing was making me drool. I was about to call it a night when I opened one last book: *Thirsty for Thrills*.

On the cover, a shirtless man is crawling across a desert toward a woman holding a pitcher of water. I'd read *Thirsty for Thrills* before, and recalled a few technical problems—like, who could "drift into a blissful sleep under the stars" in the same place where she'd been battling rattlesnakes and tarantulas? But when I opened it that day, something else jumped out at me. The name of the love interest is Dirk Angus.

"Dirk Angus," I said. "Dirk Angus." I busted out my romance-novel-heroine voice, which is husky yet vulnerable, and said, "Dirk Angus, how would you like to be a timeship app?"

Dirk Angus flashed a brutish smile and replied, in a voice that was throbbing yet vulnerable, *I'd love to, Fi. And while we're on the subject, there are a few other things I'd like to do—*

"Hey, Nephele. Sorry to bother you."

Who said that?!

I shoved *Thirsty for Thrills* under my thigh and looked around; nobody else seemed to be upstairs. Then I noticed Wylie Buford standing in Graphic Novels. He was doing the thing where he cleaned his ear with his pinky finger and looked at the wax.

"Oh," I said, relieved. "Hey, Wylie. You're not interrupting."

I'd known Wylie since kindergarten. He reminded me of a bruised apple. Round red face, constantly apologizing (that was the bruised part). He was wearing his usual T-shirt, the alien with a million eyes.

"Sorry," said Wylie. "You can get back to your reading. Looks scintillating. . . ."

Immediately, I realized that although I had hidden *Thirsty for Thrills,* I was surrounded in the beanbag chair by books whose covers featured humans with their clothes falling off.

"It's, uh," I said as I gathered them into a sweaty, heaving pile, "it's fine."

"Oh, okay. So, first day of summer vacation," said Wylie. "What a relief, eh? I'm not going to say I was counting the days until we were freed from the torturers, but . . ."

Wylie pulled a handkerchief out of his pants pocket. When he blew his nose, it sounded like the horn of a semitruck. I looked around again. Thankfully, we still seemed to be the only ones upstairs. Since Vera had abandoned me, I'd been avoiding Wylie. Not to his face or anything. Just quietly. Wylie was the only freshman who got bullied worse than me. I was terrified of spending the rest of my high school career stranded with him on Outcast Island.

When Wylie was done wiping, he held up his handkerchief. "Eco-friendly alternative to tissue. My grandfather has a whole drawerful."

"That seems like a grandfatherly thing to have," I said.

"The elderly are unintentional environmentalists," said Wylie. "When they were young, there was less to throw away. Waste not, want not."

I looked around again; we still seemed to be alone. "My mom is like that," I said. "She pulled a table off a street corner a few weeks ago and painted it green. Like, shamrock green. Now we eat all our meals off it."

Wylie giggled. And giggled. In this high-pitched way only Wylie giggles. "Beware of bedbugs and *E. coli*! Seriously. That's economizing. Scrupulous."

Scrupulous. Wylie was the only kid I knew who sounded

more like an adult than I did. He stuffed his handkerchief in his pocket. "So. What are you up to this summer, Nephele?"

I shifted in the beanbag, feeling uncomfortable. Was Wylie going to ask me to hang out? "Just . . . you know, I'm gonna be super busy. Doing stuff. I'm working on, like, a project."

"Oh?" said Wylie. "What sort of project?"

Wylie's brown eyes were warm behind his glasses. The sun shining through the skylights made his hair look rusty and full of shadows, like sequoia bark.

That was such a nice thing to ask.

I had a sudden, inexplicable urge to tell Wylie about my time machine.

But I hesitated. I mean, if I became friends with Wylie Buford, I'd *never* get Vera back.

I was watching the barn swallows fight over a perch on the rim of the skylight, trying to figure out what to do about Wylie, when I realized he was gone. I got up and went to the railing, where I could look down on the first floor. Wylie was leaving through the back exit, the one that leads to the alley where the cats hang out. The screen door smacked shut behind him.

Shoot.

Well, I thought, I could follow Wylie. I should follow him.

But did I *want* to follow Wylie Buford? When I was on the verge of pipe-bombing my mortifying past so I could give birth to my spectacular future?

I did.

But I didn't.

CHAPTER 3

Hungry Like a Black Hole

The cold wind blowing inland from the ocean makes Redwood Cove the kind of place where you always keep a sweater on hand, even in the middle of July. All summer, I sat at the desk in my bedroom, bundled in my hoodie, scribbling out the equations that would show Dirk Angus how to turn the wireless devices of the world into a gazillion-headed Hydra that would activate the quantum foam and send me to the past for my do-over.

People say teenagers need exercise. Fresh air.

Nonsense.

June happened. July happened. In the blink of an eye, it was August.

The day before my first day of sophomore year, a sharp chill blew through my window, ruffling the pictures of quasars taped to my wall. I'd torn them out of the moldy old *National*

*Geographic*s that people were always donating to the Big Blue Wave.

Quasars are the brightest objects in the known universe. Super-massive black holes that devour everything that comes near them, spitting out only their light. As if the light is bones.

Any massive object has the power to warp time, thanks to its gravitational pull; Einstein taught us that. And a quasar is the definition of a massive object. The problem is, you can't go inside one without getting devoured. So I considered quasars pretty useless as time machines. But I loved them. Quasars were so beautiful. And they made me wonder, where does something go when its light is gone?

Luckily, smartphones weren't known for devouring people. Dirk Angus wasn't ready yet, but at least he wouldn't eat me alive and spit out my bones.

There was a soft knock at the door before it opened.

"Cheese sandwich?" asked Mom.

I didn't turn around. "Just leave it on my bed."

When Mom cleared her throat, I put down my pencil. I knew what was coming next.

"Wanna take a walk with me?" she asked.

"No," I said.

"How about a movie?"

"No, thank you."

"I ran into Vera Knight's mom on Main Street again. She said she wishes you'd stop by. . . ."

I dropped my pencil, leaned back in my chair and groaned.

"What, Fi?" asked Mom.

If I told Mom the truth about Vera ghosting me, she'd call Mrs. Knight. She'd say she wouldn't, but then she would, and it would be humiliating. I did not need my mother making my life more complicated than it already was.

"What happened with Vera, sweetie?" Mom asked for the zillionth time.

I turned around. "Mom! Quit worrying about me."

Mom started to say something and stopped. She crossed her arms. "Whatcha workin' on?"

I sighed. "I'm super busy right now. Could I get some privacy, please?"

Mom smoothed her mermaid hair, gave me a thumbs-up, slipped out the door and quietly shut it behind her.

I picked up my pencil and dropped it again, feeling guilty. I didn't mean to be *mean* to Mom. I loved Mom. But why should I put myself through the humiliation of explaining what had happened with Vera? Soon, it never would've happened in the first place.

This was something I had to handle alone.

When I woke up, my bedroom was dark and my face was resting on my desk in a pool of slobber.

"Ew," I said, wiping my cheek with my hoodie sleeve. Through my window, I saw a sliver of a mustard-colored moon. I yawned and pressed the space bar on my laptop, which was also napping, and felt a surge of panic. It was almost nine o'clock! The first day of sophomore year was tomorrow, and I absolutely could not be there.

I mean, sure. If Dirk Angus took me another day or week or month to finish, technically, it wouldn't matter. But I preferred to avoid prolonging the agony. I really didn't want to face the wrath of my peers the next day if I didn't have to.

"Come on, Fi," I mumbled. "You can do this."

In the soft blue glow of the laptop, I reread the code for Dirk Angus. When I got to the last line, I read through the whole program again, more carefully.

And again.

And then I heard a ringing in my ears. It was high-pitched without being painful, and it got higher and louder until it morphed into a whooshing feeling that made my whole body shiver and my arm fur stand on end.

I could not add or remove a single line of code. The universe was curling up around me, hissing, *Yessss*.

Dirk Angus was ready. I could put the timeship app on my phone and use it to go back to my first day of freshman year *right now*.

A breeze blew my white curtains; an owl hooted a few short, serious hoots. A foghorn moaned a long, low note and another moaned back, a song that felt like a prayer. The world outside my window was announcing itself and I needed to answer. I wanted to say, "Here I am, universe! I'm about to rewrite the laws of physics!" But I couldn't. I felt like I'd just met a stranger, someone I couldn't be sure I wanted to get to know.

I leaned on my elbows and closed my eyes. Was I doing this?

Should I do a test run?

A test run would give me one more chance to find any bugs in the app. The problem was, I'd worked until the last minute. For all I felt sure about, there was so much I couldn't predict. Such as, how would time travel affect me physically? Would I be exhausted? Dehydrated? Get a headache? Amnesia?

I didn't know what I'd feel like doing or not doing after hurling myself faster than the speed of light backward through time. I might not want to try it again right away. I might not be able to.

No. No test run. Couldn't risk it. Tonight, Dirk Angus would strut his stuff on the big stage. We'd go back to my first day of freshman year, or we'd go nowhere at all.

I stood at the top of the stairs watching my parents, who were sitting at the green kitchen table. Mom was rubbing oil on a bowl she'd carved from a log. Dad was munching peanuts. They were listening to an opera. Of all the records Dad played, opera had the strangest effect on me. No matter the language—Italian, German, Hungarian—certain voices singing certain notes made my eyes fill with tears. As I stood there teary-eyed, I thought about how music didn't need language to do its job. It was pure feeling that could sail through the air and touch your soul. Not that I knew what a soul was, exactly. It just felt like that's what the music touched to make the tears.

Dad looked up. "Fi!" he said. "You got a hug for me?"

I swallowed my tears and went downstairs.

Dad's hug was snuggly and comforting, like always, but when I hugged Mom, I felt a wave of misery. I said, "I'm really sorry, Mom."

Mom pulled me back to look at me. Her eyes sparkled silently, like the sun on the sea. "For what?" she asked.

"For . . . I don't know."

"Listen," she said. "It's gonna be okay, Fi. School, and Vera, and— it's just, girls can be so—" She shook her head.

"So what?" I asked.

"So *mean*," she said. "But it's going to be okay tomorrow, sugar. You know that? It really is."

I hugged Mom again, feeling slightly better. Mom was right. It would be okay; it had to be.

The math was flawless.

I waited until my parents fell asleep. And longer, until our house moved through quiet into too quiet. No more creaks and clicks. Mom's occasional alarmed-sounding snore was the only disturbance beneath the surface of a still and inviting darkness.

It was time.

The night breeze made my curtains float gently. I was

sitting on my neatly made bed with its quilt of shadowy stars, wearing my backpack and holding my phone, which contained Dirk Angus. I flipped to a page I'd bookmarked in *Time Travel for Love & Profit*:

> Dear reader, don't delay your rightful fate.
> Wipe away the future that's so wrong for you.
> Look in your heart, turn back time and unwalk
>   your tragic path.
> I have faith in you.
> Now you have faith in you.
> Can you give yourself this gift?
> Will you take the plunge?

Time travel was my rightful fate. I believed that.

But now that the moment had arrived, I was hesitating. I mean, I'd read enough science fiction to imagine some fairly gruesome things that could go wrong.

Such as I make it back in time, disturb a butterfly and accidentally cause an avalanche.

Or I make it back in time, learn that time travel already exists, and there are time police who are twisted thugs who put me in jail for infinity for breaking some nonsensical intergalactic law I couldn't possibly have known about.

Or I accidentally travel too far back in time and somehow meet my father when he was my age, and he falls in love with me instead of Mom and I can never be born (ew, ew, *ew*). That happens in a science fiction movie I'd considered highly amusing until recently, when I determined that I couldn't rule out being un-born as a mathematical possibility.

The question is, how can you be sure you're doing the right thing until you do it?

I didn't know.

I felt close to tears again, sitting on the edge of my bed in my hoodie, holding my phone. I had to admit the risk that when I opened my timeship app and pressed GO, the consequences could be far worse than being locked up by the time police.

Dirk Angus might just kill me.

I didn't know how that would happen exactly, but it seemed possible. There was so much I wouldn't know until I tried. And it wouldn't be worth it to devastate my parents for a science experiment.

But I couldn't ask someone else to go first. And I couldn't stand in the way of a groundbreaking mathematical discovery I might have been born to reveal.

If I did that?

Well. I wouldn't be a scientist at all.

I took a deep breath and opened Dirk Angus. As I started to type in my destination, I noticed that my hand was quivering. I shook it out and kept typing. "We're doing this, Fi," I said. And before I could talk myself out of it, I took half a breath and pressed GO.

• • •

I'm shooting like a bullet through a pulsing, sticky liquid, breathing so fast I'm almost hyperventilating. It's hot; it smells like burning leaves. Rough shells with squishy insides attach themselves to my skin like barnacles. I try to pull them off with my fingers, but my hands are slippery, like fish fins, and I can't grasp them. My mouth fills with tangy smoke. My ears are ringing. My tongue is swelling. Something tastes metallic. Is it blood?

My bones are stretching in every direction simultaneously, like I'm the sun's rays—but I don't hurt.

Now I'm shattering into billions of tiny pieces, spinning and spiraling away from myself.

I am pure light, sleeping on a log in the redwood forest.

I sleep for a hundred years, or a thousand.

Time can't touch me anymore. I'm a memory. The memory of microscopic particles swimming through the galaxy.

I am nowhere, with fire all around me.

I'm a dark night brimming with shooting stars.

I am everything and nothing at the same time. I am the universe, being born and dying, being born and dying, again and again and again, forever.

• • •

CHAPTER 4

I'm Here! Wherever That Is . . .

Something punched me in the gut.

I gasped, drinking in air. It tasted like rainwater. My heart squeezed, then squeezed again. I had a body and it was pulsating. I felt the softness of my pillow under my head and the weight of my star quilt.

I remembered two faces.

"Mom?!" I yelled. My voice was tight and scratchy. "Dad?!"

My legs felt heavy as I scrambled out of bed, desperate to find my parents.

Gold light filtered through the fog outside the window and made the kitchen bright. So it was morning. Had I slept? That explained it. Like a movie with an eye-rolling cop-out of an ending, the incredible part had only been a dream.

On the other hand, I was pretty sure I'd died in that dream.

When I saw Dad with his mess of curly hair and his blue band T-shirt, scuffling in his socks and plaid pajama pants toward the coffee pot, I bolted downstairs and hugged him so hard I almost plowed him over.

"Whoa!" he said. *"Guten Morgen!"*

"First day of freshman year! Look how excited she is." Mom was wearing her white sweater over her yellow sundress, pouring orange juice. "Horace, can you believe our baby is all grown up?"

"I can, Maddy. Our Fi, freshman in high school. Take that, world. She's coming for you."

I let go of Dad and leaned on the green kitchen table. My body felt like it had been cranked through a pasta machine, and my brain felt mealy, like an overripe tomato.

What did he say?

"Remember, Fi," said Dad as he shook a skillet on the stove, "don't let those upper-class cats mess with your head. Everybody has to be a freshman once."

"A freshman?" I said.

"Best freshman ever," said Mom, tweaking my cheek and taking a seat.

I looked at the faucet, which was dripping—*drip, drip, drip*—and knew this wasn't a dream. I did something. I went somewhere.

"I did it," I said softly. "I'm doing it."

"Did what?" asked Dad.

I covered my mouth so I would not scream I JUST WENT BACK IN TIME! *And I'm not dead!* I LOVE YOU, DIRK

ANGUS! I was patting my back pocket, looking for my phone, when I realized I was wearing the same hoodie and jeans I'd had on the night before, and started laughing. I felt delirious as I pulled out my chair and sat beside my mother at the kitchen table—the kitchen table my beautiful, wonderful mother had dragged in from the street last spring like a beautiful, wonderful maniac and painted bright green!

No—not last spring.

Next spring.

Wait.

"Eat this," said Dad. A plate of scrambled tofu slid onto the green patch of table where my eyes were glued. "Freshman fuel."

"Wait," I said. "Wait, wait. Dad, when did we get this table?"

When Dad looked at Mom, his eyes flickered like someone was playing with their on-off switch. "When did we get this table?" he repeated.

Mom's eyes were crackling, but not in their usual mermaid-y way; it looked like they were freezing over. Her body swayed. "You'd think I'd remember." Her voice sounded waterlogged, like she was sinking to the bottom of the ocean. "We did acquire this table at some point."

Dad smoothed his mustache; his lip was twitching. "That we indubitably did."

What was happening? Did my parents remember rescuing this table from the street and painting it, or didn't they? How could they remember something that hadn't happened yet?

And what was wrong with them?

Mom blinked hard several times, like there was a lash in her eye, and stopped swaying. "Hustle, Fi," she said. "Don't want to be late for school!"

Dad's lip quit spazzing, and he took a seat and stabbed his tofu scramble.

I watched my parents for a few seconds; they seemed totally normal again. It was like a powerful spell had possessed them, but then, just as abruptly, had worn off.

Or maybe I was imagining things. If I was sitting at the green kitchen table—which I totally was—I must've misheard my parents about it being the first day of high school. My parents weren't malfunctioning; I was.

I'd failed.

I frowned at my breakfast. "Sophomore year is gonna blow."

"Language," said Mom.

"Blow *bubbles*," I said. "You interrupted me." I took a bite of tofu scramble but didn't have the energy to chew it. Zingy spices dissolved in my saliva.

"Don't get ahead of us," said Dad. "Freshman year gets to blow bubbles first."

"Freshman year," said Mom. "Time flies."

I dropped my fork and it clattered on my plate. Well, had I gone back in time, or hadn't I? I scooted out of my chair and marched upstairs to look for my phone so I could find out, in private, what year it was.

My phone was lying on my star quilt. When I grabbed it, it felt warm to me, like a pet. A pet I couldn't quite trust not to pee on the rug. I unlocked it and looked at the date.

Okay, so it wasn't one year ago; it was tomorrow. I mean, today. The day *after* I'd attempted to travel through time. But if that was the case, why had my parents said it was my first day of freshman year? It was my first day of *sophomore* year— wasn't it?

I looked at the button I'd created for the Dirk Angus app. To amuse myself, I'd snapped a photograph of Dirk Angus's head from the cover of *Thirsty for Thrills* and cut-and-pasted it on a backdrop of cartoon bubbles. Get it? Quantum foam? Now the image struck me as sinister. Like some decapitated mannequin was mocking me from a nice hot bath.

I spotted my backpack on the floor and rushed to unzip it. *Time Travel for Love & Profit* was still inside. So Oona Gold had come here with me. The question was, where was here, exactly? And were Oona Gold and I the only ones who'd made the trip?

Redwood Cove High School is tucked in a grove of coastal redwoods on a cliff overlooking the Pacific Ocean. Tourists sometimes mistake it for a cute seaside hotel and turn off the road, looking for a place to check in. I crossed Highway 1 and went down the path toward the school feeling sicker with every step.

I'd lingered at home as long as possible, interrogating Mom and Dad about my first freshman year. Did they remember my fifteenth birthday? "Your fifteenth birthday?" Mom had laughed. "Let's get through your first day of high school." What about New Year's Day, when we'd gone line-dancing at the VFW hall on Main Street and Mom had kicked her leg in the air and thrown her back out? Dad's eyebrow had convulsed like it was being prodded by a Taser as he'd said, "Now, there's a picture." I'd asked about big things, little things, any and every memorable thing I could think of that had happened last year.

My parents remembered nothing.

I'd only meant to poke a hole in the fabric of the universe. Had I accidentally hacked off a year-long hunk of it?

Meanwhile, between demonic glossy spells, Mom had been getting more and more panicked about me being late for my first day of high school, so finally, I'd decided, fine. I need to figure out where Dirk Angus sent me, and this is my logical next step. Go to school, see what happens.

The first person I recognized was Youki Johnson, standing with his friends under the cypress tree beside the bike rack about seven meters away. My jaw started trembling. I was looking for someone else, anyone else I knew, when Youki looked at me.

For a fraction of a second.

Then looked away.

No rude gestures. No references to woolly mammoths. No yelling "Neffa-Freak!" Did that mean no one had invented the nickname yet? That was a good sign, wasn't it?

I kept walking through the mob of students, with their backpacks and their hairstyles and their music blasting from their phones. Redwood Cove is a fraction of the size of the wing of a fly that lands on the corner of a postage stamp; there was almost nobody my age I didn't at least sort of know, and almost nobody who didn't at least sort of know me. Whenever I caught someone's eye, I raised my eyebrows and tried to look non-threatening—the We-know-each-other-but-we-don't-have-to-chat face—but everyone looked through me or away. It wasn't the same sort of ignoring as last year, when it had felt like people didn't want to be associated with me. It was the way you look past someone you don't recognize.

I was trying to figure out what to make of that when I saw Vera. She was standing with Ramsey Schultz near a patch of orange poppies by the picnic tables. Her long, straight black hair was parted down the middle, and she was wearing almost the same outfit as Ramsey but in different colors—a plastic-looking dress and beige knee-high boots with treacherous platforms. If it *was* the first day of freshman year, Vera was already friends with Ramsey from dance class—but Vera and I were still *best* friends. Which would mean she hadn't dumped me yet. I felt a pang of hope. How I longed to hear her broken-blender laugh again.

I was heading in Vera's direction when Ramsey whispered in Vera's ear and Vera smiled this twisted smile, like she'd just heard some extra-juicy gossip. Then the wind caught Vera's hair and it flew straight up like she was electrified. A thought popped into my head that stopped me cold.

What if Vera *wasn't* happy to see me? If it turned out that

45

Dirk Angus had sent only *me* to the past? If today was Vera's first day of sophomore year, she'd still avoid me, like my aggressive weirdness was contagious.

Which would be crushing.

I was standing on the blacktop, staring at Vera, when the bell rang and everyone swarmed inside.

I looked toward the forest and spotted a squirrel darting up a redwood tree. I was tempted to follow it. All I needed was a harness. Ropes. The proper footwear. A tent, so I could sleep in the canopy.

I shoved my hands in my hoodie pockets and sighed. Unfortunately, fleeing to the treetops wasn't an option. It was my scientific duty to continue my investigation into what the hell I had done.

Last year, we'd checked into third period first to get our schedules, so I headed to Mrs. Saint Johnabelle's science-slash-homeroom, dreading what would happen next.

I must admit I was also semi-dreading having Mrs. Saint Johnabelle again. The good thing was that she'd taught me how to run a proper scientific experiment. "Be thorough, be organized, and never settle for mediocrity." She never treated her students like freshmen—more like employees she was training for NASA.

The bad thing was that in addition to having Mrs. Saint Johnabelle for science, I had her for sixth period, which was Advanced Placement calculus and all seniors except for me. Last year, I'd naturally assumed I'd be free to work independently. Every teacher I'd ever had before had been fine with that because it meant I needed zero attention. Leaving me alone with a four-hundred-page dissertation on parabolas was like a parent plopping their kid in front of cartoons. I'd sit quietly and contentedly until somebody tore the thing out of my hands.

But Mrs. Saint Johnabelle had forced me to participate in the class discussions and help the other kids, which had bored the living crap out of me. Plus, unlike all the other math teachers, Mrs. Saint Johnabelle had never seemed remotely afraid of me. Which might have been why I was still semi-terrified of her, even after being her student for an entire year.

I took my usual seat in the back of Mrs. Saint Johnabelle's classroom and watched my fellow students pour in, which confirmed my growing fear.

Every single freshman was a year younger than me. I recognized them all from middle school.

I was starting to panic when Mrs. Saint Johnabelle strode into the room wearing one of her crisp pastel suits and sized us up. Her short white hair, her clear plastic eyeglasses, her brown complexion that glowed sort of coral. The look in her eyes that said she was paying attention; the feeling you had that she'd never let you off the hook.

Suddenly I felt a little more confident. Didn't Mrs. Saint Johnabelle always tell us that uncertainty was a necessary part of a science experiment? When you got results you hadn't predicted, you recorded them, returned to the scientific method and got back to work. Progress happened in small increments, not overnight.

"Nephele Weather?" called Mrs. Saint Johnabelle. Hearing her stern voice say my name, I felt relieved. I even smiled at her. She did not smile back. She kept looking around the classroom, and asked again. "Is Nephele Weather here today?"

"Right here, Mrs. Saint Johnabelle," I said, waving.

When she looked at me, sparks flashed in her eyes like fireworks and then fizzled. She checked her paper. "Nephele Weather. Did I pronounce your name correctly?" It took me a second to nod. She said, "Fine. Welcome to Redwood Cove High School. Camille Walters? Is Camille Walters here?"

I looked around once again for signs that I was dreaming. Melting faces or mythological animals, or maybe I wasn't fully dressed?

I checked: Normal faces. No centaurs. And thank the goddesses of mathematics, I was wearing pants.

This was happening.

Mrs. Saint Johnabelle didn't remember me.

Between classes, I rushed through the hallways in a panic, looking for Vera. I passed Youki and his friends again, pumping their fists and making dog grunts, and again, they all ignored me. I spotted a cloud of strawberry-blond curls bobbing in the crowd and made a beeline for Ramsey Schultz.

When she saw me looking, Ramsey stopped walking and flashed her trademark pink lipstick smirk.

But she didn't insult me. She just thought I was some

freshman who was admiring her, and was humoring me by acknowledging my existence. Weirdly, I felt sort of flattered.

Then Ramsey waved at someone behind me, and I looked.

Vera was waving back. When I caught her eye and smiled a cautious smile, Vera nodded and smiled a vague smile like I was anyone, just some random someone she maybe did and maybe didn't know. A smile that deleted our entire friendship.

Vera didn't remember me either.

When the bell rang for second period, I stood in the emptying hallway, feeling like I'd fallen through a galactic trap door. What was happening to people's memories of me? Had they disappeared into black holes? Could there be black holes in inner space? *Brain holes?*

And if nobody else remembered me, why did my parents?

The harder I tried to make sense of what had happened, the more confused I got. Time had gone from a circular clock ticking tamely at regular intervals to an animal I'd dredged up from the quantum foam, writhing and snarling and snapping at my hands. It was like I'd made time *mad.*

I took my phone out of my hoodie pocket and looked at it. "Dirk Angus," I said, "we have a problem."

Seventh period was French, and unfortunately, time travel, or pseudo–time travel, or whatever the hell I'd just done, had not improved my accent.

"*Répétez-vous,* Mademoiselle Weather," said Madame LeBlanc. "*Un, deux, trois.*"

"Uhhn, doo, twar," I said.

"C'est horrible!" she said, and then she snorted.

Orr-ee-bull, I thought. Sounds about right.

When the final bell rang, I decided to go to the Big Blue Wave. There was only one person I could talk to about what was happening. She had two heads but no brains, which made it physically impossible for her memories of me to get sucked into an inner-space vortex.

Outside the school, the wind was scooting rotting leaves around the blacktop. I was zipping my hoodie when I noticed someone sitting on the redwood stump, hunched over a comic book and wearing his dark green T-shirt with the alien with a million eyes.

"Wylie Buford!" I said. "You wouldn't believe how happy I am to see you."

Wylie looked up, his eyes confused behind his glasses.

I was as surprised by my reaction as he was. It had just sort of slipped out.

"I apologize," said Wylie. "Have we met?"

Of course Wylie didn't remember me either. "It's Nephele Weather," I said. "We've been in school together since kinder-garten. . . ."

"Ah. I do apologize. Nothing personal, Neffrey. Sorry: Neffro, was it? Only, I think you're confusing me with someone else."

"I'm not confused, Wylie," I said, feeling suddenly confident. "We know each other."

Wylie gave me an awkward smile. "Ah . . ." He laughed nervously and looked at his lap.

50

I did not laugh. I took a step closer to him and touched his arm. Maybe if I pushed Wylie I could force him to remember all the years we'd spent sitting in the same classrooms together, surrounded by the same peers. "Wylie. Concentrate. Look in my eyes. Look at me."

Wylie laughed a dry laugh that caught in his throat. Then he licked his lips and pulled his arm away gently, like if he made the wrong move, I might attack him. He checked his wristwatch. "Oh, wow. Is it late. Best of luck there, Neffro. Cheers."

As I watched Wylie run toward the path to Highway 1, I had an inspiration. If I wanted to go back in time for real, I was obviously going to have to upgrade Dirk Angus. How, I had no clue—but somehow. If I got started on Dirk Angus 2.0 right away, it'd probably be ready in the next few weeks. And when it was ready—

When I went back in time for real, and escaped from Outcast Island—

I would take Wylie Buford with me. When I became popular, I wouldn't be cruel and exclusive. I'd welcome the whole world into my gigantic circle of friends.

As I watched Wylie disappear into the redwoods, I felt a glimmer of hope. Maybe it was okay that my first time-travel experiment had skidded me into a parallel universe where everything was blurred and out of sync. If it hadn't, I might've forgotten Wylie. How normal it felt to talk with him somehow.

Saving Wylie Buford was a great idea. My timeship wasn't a selfish (not to mention illegal) invention that had seriously malfunctioned, drilling memory-chomping quasars into people's brains. It was simply a fun new app with a glitch. As soon as I fixed the glitch, I could go back to saving myself, and Wylie, and the planet. Hawks screeched overhead; I watched them sail in graceful loops. For the first time that day, I felt optimistic. Dirk Angus 2.0 would put things back on track.

Upstairs at the Big Blue Wave, I leaned against the red wall. "Someday we'll look back and laugh about this, Chicago."

"About what?" she asked, sounding skeptical.

"About how my first time-travel experiment went awry," I said.

"*Awry?*" she repeated. "Like a goofball plan in a romantic comedy? No way. Dirk Angus is evil and must be destroyed."

"Don't be melodramatic. I made a minor mistake, which I will find and un-make. Meanwhile, I'm living in a parallel universe where I don't quite exist. It's comical. The expression 'wacky hijinks' comes to mind. Now I just need a boy I can engage in some witty banter with."

"What," said Chicago, "I'm not witty?"

"Of course you're witty, Chicago. I'm writing your dialogue. But I wouldn't mind having a real person to laugh about all this with. Preferably a boy with a rare and spectacular brain who recognizes immediately how kissable I am."

"I'm hurt," said Chicago. "If I only exist in your imagination, why do you bother coming to visit me?"

I was about to say, "Because you believe that I'm going to build the world's first functioning time machine. Didn't I explain this already?" But I stopped myself, because that wasn't entirely true.

I mean, yes: I was personifying a black-and-white photograph and confessing the details of my life to her because I needed to talk to someone who wouldn't think I was bonkers. But it was more than that. I could've picked a stuffed animal or a picture of a famous mathematician or adopted a dog if all I needed was a friend who wouldn't judge me.

There was something about Chicago, specifically. She felt alive to me. I didn't have the same thoughts when I was away from her as I did when I was standing there looking at her. Maybe the photograph had its own soul. Was that possible?

"At this point, anything seems possible," said Chicago.

I looked at her two heads and sighed. "Is that a good thing or a bad thing?" I asked.

"Maybe it's both," she said.

Both. That's the kind of answer you get from a woman who is walking in two directions at once. Clever, but confusing.

"Why don't you find your birth certificate," said Chicago. "See if it has the right date."

"I should also check my medical records," I said. "And my school records."

"Don't forget photographs," said Chicago.

"I wonder if I'll be able to find any evidence of my missing year. Or if the universe has forgotten me like everybody else did.

Anyway, I've decided that as long as I'm stuck here, I'm going to test New Nephele. Work out the bugs in the new me with a fresh batch of freshmen before I go back in time for real."

"*New Nephele?* Are you serious? Is that the best way for you to spend your time right now?"

"Of course it is," I said. "Becoming un-rejectable is the whole reason I invented Dirk Angus."

"Huh," said Chicago. It seemed like one of her heads was trying to look at me.

"What, Chicago?" I asked. "You can't just say 'huh' in a suspicious voice without elaborating."

I swear I saw the two-headed woman shrug. "It just seems like if New Nephele was that important to you, you would have worked on her all summer instead of having a private math party."

Hmm. Chicago had a point. I'd spent the entire summer developing the timeship app without thinking once about how to become the new me. "I did the math first because it was the easy part," I said. "Now I'm ready for the hard part. Gut-renovating my entire personality."

"Right, the math was the easy part," said Chicago. "Dirk Angus should be a snap to fix, then."

I tugged on my hoodie sleeves. It *would* be a snap to fix—once I figured out what the problem was. The problem was, I didn't know what the problem was. The code for Dirk Angus was as clear and sharp as a killer icicle. The app had done precisely what I'd asked it to do. Apparently, I'd just asked it to do the wrong thing.

"I need to rest my brain before I dive back into the math. Meanwhile, becoming New Nephele will be . . . funnish. I assume. Zany and, you know, liberating, once I get into character."

"If you say so," said Chicago. "How will you do it?"

That was precisely the question. *Time Travel for Love & Profit* was full of exciting statements, such as "Now is the moment to reconstruct your past in your true image," but it was awfully light on specifics.

"I guess I'll have to improvise. Act like Ramsey Schultz without the mean parts. You know: be sassy, wear a stylish outfit, get some backup dancers . . . all that."

"What stylish outfit would that be?" asked Chicago. "Your fancy hoodie?"

Hmm.

"I'll ask Mom to take me to the mall tonight," I said.

"The mall? Seriously?"

We both shuddered. "Got any shopping tips?" I asked.

"Don't ask me," said Chicago. "I'll be wearing the same outfit forever."

On the ride to the mall that night, I watched the sky. It was a paler shade of gray than it had been that morning; less intimidating, like it was giving up on the day. Orange clouds blew across it in feathery streaks. I needed to ask Mom where she kept my birth certificate, but I didn't want to risk it while she was driving. I couldn't predict precisely how she'd react—which was the problem. I felt guilty enough about the brain holes without potentially morphing my mother into a swaying, glossy-eyed highway terror.

While Mom listened to the news, I wondered about Chicago's lack of interest in my popularity project. Did the photograph know something I didn't? But what?

Mom parked near the mall's entrance. After she dropped the car keys in her purse and twirled her hair into a topknot, I decided it was safe to ask my question.

"Hey, where do you guys keep my birth certificate?"

"In the file," said Mom, chirpily.

"Which file?" I asked.

"The file with the birth certificate," she said, smiling.

She wasn't swaying, but the smile was bad. People don't smile about files.

"Where is that file, though?" I asked. "In your bedroom? At the bookshop . . . ?"

Mom nodded, still smiling, like she was reliving some long-ago kiss. "It's right there where it always has been," she said, dreamily, as she unbuckled her seat belt.

Okay: so Mom was avoiding the birth certificate question just like she and Dad were avoiding conversations about my first freshman year. Did the legal documentation of my birthday still exist? Did *I* still exist? I was beginning to wonder.

I rested my head on the headrest. Headrests should be everywhere, I thought. I should start walking around with one.

"C'mon, Fi! Back-to-school sales beckon," said Mom, and I grunted in resentment. "This was your idea," she said, and I grumbled, "Purportedly," in a bitter tone that I do realize was inappropriate. Nevertheless, we both got out of the car.

Inside the mall, I was immediately distracted from the birth certificate question. The lighting was green and blinding. Music was thumping and fountains were drooling and it smelled like new shoes and soy sauce. People were eating cinnamon buns the size of their heads. From every store window, mannequins with painted-on eyeballs stared at me like they were challenging me to make a fashion mistake. I would've bought anything to get out of that hellhole.

Mom put her hands on her hips like we were going into battle. "Our mission is school clothes," she said.

"And accessories," I added.

That's when I saw her: the mannequin in the window at a store called Teen 2 B U 'n' Me. I said, "That's her."

"Who?" said Mom.

"New Nephele. I want it."

"You want what?" asked Mom.

"All of it," I said as I went to get a better look at my future self.

The mannequin's silver pants made her butt look dazzling. Her tight black cropped shirt made her boobs gleam like they were dipped in glossy paint. She was wearing a furry white cardigan and a long string of silver beads that dangled over her belly button. One lavender sock, one green. To top it off, her hair was electric blue and several different lengths, like she'd taken a lawn mower and zoomed it across her head and ended up accidentally adorable. And she was frowning like she was mad at the world for looking at her.

She was everything I'd never wanted to be but was absolutely going to become, starting now.

It's not like I thought the outfit would do the work of becoming the new, insult-proof me for me. A new look would simply kick-start the process. That was the point of a makeover, wasn't it? To boost your confidence? There were entire television shows devoted to this concept. Yes, I used to think those shows were shallow, but I also used to think that there was nothing wrong with me. Now anything that made me resemble someone different from the miserable human I was seemed like a stroke of damn genius. The different-er, the better.

Inside Teen 2 B U 'n' Me, the bass was pumping as Mom and I walk-danced to the beat. But when Mom spoke with the saleswoman about the outfit in the window, she stopped dancing and swung her purse over her shoulder in a way I found impressively spunky, and made a mental note to imitate.

"Sorry, sugar bun," she told me. "I'm not ready to live in the Subaru."

"What?"

"Hon, they want eighty bucks for those pants and sixty dollars for that junky little necklace. And she's only wearing half a shirt—"

"I LOVE that necklace."

"Yes . . . I mean, I understand. We can find you something very similar—except for that shirt; it looks like a bandage."

"I don't want something very similar," I moaned.

Mom sighed. As we stood in Teen 2 B U 'n' Me with the bass thwacking our heads, I felt guilty. People loved the Big Blue Wave, but my parents' business would never make us wealthy; it wasn't meant to. It wasn't some Silicon Valley tech start-up that throws expensive parties where people eat artisan artichokes rolled in diamond dust and drink liquid gold straight from the bottle—the kind of business that was driving up rent all over the California coast, including the rent my parents paid for the bookshop. And I knew this.

"Sorry, Mom," I said. "I guess just . . . something similar like what?"

"I don't know, Fi," said Mom. She looked toward the saleswoman again. I recognized the focus in her eyes. She was getting ready to negotiate.

Fact: There is a compass inside my mother that analyzes every situation and points to the most embarrassing way out of it. So I quickly said, "Do you smell caramel corn?" and dragged her out of the store.

To make a long story short, sometimes a girl must use fancy shops as style inspiration. With help from the caramel corn sugar rush, Mom and I found something similar at the discount place on the other side of the mall, and the grand total was, in her words, "something we can live with."

New Nephele may have been a fashionista, but current

Nephele had sensory overload. It was only one outfit, but it was a start.

That night, as I lay curled under my star quilt, a fog of fear settled over me. I felt like a small nocturnal animal surrounded by invisible predators. Thinking about the way the lights in my parents' eyes had flickered on and off while their memories flew out the windows. Thinking about sitting in Mrs. Saint Johnabelle's classroom, feeling like a ghost. Somehow, people's missing memories had to be related to the reason that my time machine had failed. But how? And the fact that people's memories were inconsistent—my parents remembering me but forgetting my first freshman year, Mrs. Saint Johnabelle and Vera and Wylie forgetting me altogether—it had to be a clue. Saving Wylie Buford was the only good idea I'd had that day, but I couldn't do that until I fixed Dirk Angus, and I didn't know where to begin. I felt helpless.

So I concentrated on the one thing I might be able to control tomorrow: pulling off that very conspicuous outfit. I decided to imagine myself wearing the silver pants while kissing a boy. Specifically, I pictured myself as a younger version of the romance-novel heroine Dr. Carissa Silk. She would definitely wear metallic pants if she ever got dressed. I didn't have a crush on a specific boy, so I went with a younger Thor Jackson. On the cover of *Delirious in Denmark*, book one of the Nordic Nocturne series, he's writhing on the concrete floor of his jail cell, having a nightmare about his true love, who jumped off a Viking ship and drowned. I loved the way he was gritting his teeth like he couldn't bear to open his mouth without her. I fell asleep drowning in Thor's imaginary kisses—the type of kisses where one person is basically eating the other person's neck. "Thor Jackson, are these metallic pants too conspicuous?" I asked while he devoured my clavicle, and he growled, "New Nephele, you're irresistible. Get used to it." As I drifted off to sleep, I almost believed him.

CHAPTER 5

New Nephele's Dress Rehearsal

When I woke up the next morning, my limbs felt like sand-bags and my brain felt gooey, like it was clogged with slime. I yawned, which flooded me with oxygen, and everything came rushing back.

Dirk Angus. My second freshman year. My parents' brain holes. Vera and Wylie and Mrs. Saint Johnabelle forgetting me. I felt panicky, like I was trapped in a fishing net.

When I glimpsed my silver pants and clingy shirt draped over my desk chair, I moaned. What was I thinking with that outfit? And, I mean . . . what was the plan? Act sassy and spunky? How the hell would I do that?

I rested my fists on my eye sockets. I had a very strong feeling that I should skip school and concentrate on fixing my timeship. I mean, my parents had *black holes in their brains.* I didn't know if they'd get worse or spread or what. I grabbed my phone and scrolled through the code for Dirk Angus once again, slowly. Still flawless. I had hit a mathematical wall. I felt like there was a cloud of evil time particles hovering in the quantum foam around me, and if I took a deep breath I'd choke.

I tossed my phone on my star quilt and thought, Okay, okay. Something will come to me. For now, I just need to focus on New Nephele.

Time Travel for Love & Profit was on the floor beside my bed; I picked it up and flipped through it again, hoping in vain for some last-minute inspiration about how to use the sex appeal of my future self to squelch my furry and repugnant actual self. The best I could find was this:

> You're not alone, time traveler. Every creature
> in the cosmos is fumbling its way toward its
> rightful fate.

"Fumbling" was definitely the word. I had one new outfit, a vague idea of who I wanted to pretend to be and I had to be at school in an hour. Well, a girl had to start somewhere.

I got out of bed.

When I asked to borrow Mom's hair dryer, she practically wept. "You're growing up so fast," she said, which she did not realize was ironic.

I stood in the bathroom blasting screaming hot wind into my hair until it was so slick and shiny that my ears poked through it and I felt like Santa's helper. The only makeup Mom had let me buy on our mall adventure was lip gloss, which made me look, I don't know . . . wet?

But easily the most disturbing part of the morning was when I shaved my arms. The black hair filled the bathroom sink. It looked like someone had sheared a yeti. Then I made the idiotic mistake of turning on the faucet to wash the hair down the drain, which clogged it.

Have you ever seen a sink burp fur? It's exponentially more vile than it sounds. Things come up from the pipes with the fur, if you know what I'm saying. Think spit bubbles. Islands of mossy toothpaste.

On the other hand, my arms were bald! Which was . . . hot? I had no idea. But I looked different, and different had to be better, because it definitely couldn't have been worse.

In the kitchen, my parents were sitting at the green table. Dad was sipping coffee and Mom was sharpening her carving knives. I said, "Bye, guys," and Mom said, "Look at you," and set down a knife to hug me.

When I let go of her, I noticed that her eyes were extra turquoise. They were full of tears. She rubbed my arms, smiling. "You know, I did this once."

"What?"

"Shaved my arms."

"Mom!" I said, glancing at Dad, who hid his face by pretending to gulp down coffee.

"I get it, Fi," Mom said in a gentle voice. "But you're Greek, you know? We're hairy people. We have hairy arms and hairy eyebrows, and mustaches—"

"Mom."

"I just want you to know that you're beautiful exactly the way you are. And also, please remember—"

I didn't catch the rest of Mom's mortifying sentence, which she'd probably lifted from some pamphlet full of stock phrases they give mothers when their daughters start their periods.

Yet, as I ran down our warped red front porch steps, part of me knew Mom was right—which was also annoying. I felt frustrated, like I was doing something preposterous and couldn't stop. What did I expect to happen today, exactly? The new batch of freshmen were going to fall in love with me because I had a metallic butt? I knew better than this. I wasn't an idiot.

But that's the thing. I *wasn't* an idiot. I'd had this idea because, sometimes, makeovers work. Vera was into stylish clothes now, and Vera wasn't an idiot. And, you know, clothes were—they were fine. They wouldn't change me in a bad way. They'd just . . . What did they say on those makeover shows? They'd enhance my assets. That's what I needed; I just needed to concentrate on showing off the parts of me that resembled my peers, so that they wouldn't think I was some aggressively weird child prodigy who had nothing in common with them. Besides, there was no reason *not* to have a metallic butt. Was there?

In the sunlight, I squinted to inspect my blinding costume. Well, there were a few reasons. For starters, my outfit would never decompose. Someday global warming would be so extreme that the only things left on earth would be supersized scorpions, swarms of flying cockroaches and these pants.

But I couldn't stop now. I mean, I *wanted* to try my social experiment. To attempt to be a non-prodigy version of myself. And my time-travel failure had given me a chance to practice with a bunch of kids who had zero memories of me raving about the beauty of parametric equations or explaining stellar parallax or pondering the distribution patterns of mycological spores at recess, and see what happened. To prove to myself that I *could* be like them, if I wanted to. I wasn't *entirely* abnormal. I could be other things, too.

A flock of seagulls were cawing above me, flying in a jagged rhythm, like they were bouncing on the wind. Fumbling their way toward their rightful fate, I thought, just like me.

Where our street meets Highway 1, the houses are replaced by sand dunes dotted with orange poppies and a stretch of redwood trees. The hill is especially steep there, which might have been why the sandals I picked to show off my mismatched socks started slicing into my ankles. Meanwhile, gusts of wind kept blowing my hair into my face and sticking it to my lip gloss. Every time I un-stuck it, it whipped right back into my face and got re-stuck, so finally I just left it and crossed the highway. This is when I noticed that my silver pants were itchy around the waistline—but you know what they say: fashion kills.

Do they say that? They should.

Outside the school, I saw two girls from my new homeroom standing near the honeysuckle vine and felt a jolt of fear. One had a halo of curly black hair and a complexion like speckled autumn leaves, and was wearing reflective sunglasses. The other had bleached-blond hair, a long, thin nose and a creamy leather jacket with tons of zippers.

These girls were stylish. They were sleepy. They were bored with the world.

They were Coco Livingston and Lara Black—the Vera and Ramsey of my second freshman year.

I looked down at my beaded necklace and made a split-second decision to remove it. I was shoving it inside my backpack, feeling relieved that Mom hadn't let me buy a crop top, trying not to bump into anyone as I headed in Coco and Lara's direction to introduce myself, when I noticed someone else from my new homeroom sitting alone on the redwood stump, reading a book and laughing. She was wearing an oversized Berkeley sweatshirt, and I was pretty sure her name was Marla. What was she reading? What was she laughing about? I made a mental note to ask later. For I, too, had an excellent sense of humor. Maybe the girl was this year's Wylie, and after New Nephele stole everyone's hearts, Marla and I could team up and share witty observations in a podcast.

But first things first: I needed to pass as normal with Coco and Lara.

The closer I got to them, the more my jaw quivered. There was no need to be nervous. This was only a dress rehearsal for when I went back in time for real. I had absolutely nothing to lose.

The pep talk helped; I could breathe again. Then the new Vera and the new Ramsey noticed me staring at them and started staring back. Immediately my jaw stopped quivering because my face turned to stone. I couldn't even make myself blink.

Loosen up, New Nephele, loosen up, for the love of Dionysus, I told myself as I threw them a flirty wave. My hair was still glued to my lips. I removed it and said, "Hey there," in what I detected was a slight New Zealand accent. Not sure where that came from, but I decided to roll with it.

The girls looked at each other.

The stiffness came back with a vengeance. Every muscle in my body felt tight enough to chisel a diamond. I had to force my lungs to expand and then force the air back out. When I moved to fluff my hair, which was going to be one of my flirtatious quirks, I saw my bald arm, which shocked me and made me remember the burping bathroom sink, and I accidentally made a strangled noise, like a hiccup.

My mouth tasted funny. My eyes itched. I felt like I was losing my balance.

Someone yelled, "Excuse me!"

Mrs. Saint Johnabelle was rushing past the students. "This young woman is going to be ill," she said, wrapping her arm around my shoulders. "Someone help me escort her to the nurse's office."

Did anyone admire my metallic butt while I hurled scrambled tofu on my homeroom teacher's shoes?

I didn't know. My eyes were scrunched shut and I was never going to open them again.

Not the first impression I was going for.

*　*　*

The nurse's office was silent. The nurse was shorter than me and had one of those faces that looked like she was both highly suspicious of and totally uninterested in me at the same time. She had me lie down on an examination table, where I instantly fell asleep on a rock-hard pillow that was smaller than my head.

I slept for a long time and dreamt my fingertips caught fire from touching a star. Or was I the star? I didn't know, but it felt too vivid for me. When I opened my eyes, I was staring at a rectangular ceiling light that was blinking and buzzing like it was being electrocuted. I said, "Excuse me, do you have any spare pairs of pants?"

"No," said the nurse, suspiciously yet disinterestedly. "Feeling better, then, are we?" When she cleared me to go to lunch, I put on my backpack and reluctantly left the quiet room.

I'd only been going to introduce myself to those girls. Why would that make me sick? Was it truly *that* difficult for me to act normal? My footsteps echoed in the empty hallway as I walked past the sad green lockers to the cafeteria.

As soon as I stepped over the cafeteria threshold, I got hit with the smell of a hundred thousand years of lukewarm meat. At a table near the door, Coco leaned over to Lara and said, in a voice that wasn't trying not to be heard, "Look. It's Psycho Socks."

I spotted an empty table with a crumpled napkin on it,

took a seat there and put my head down on my arms. My belly gurgled, and it didn't mean I was craving a burrito.

If I didn't fix Dirk Angus fast, it was going to be another long year.

At dinner, my parents and I had a conversation that sounded like a comedy sketch from an old-fashioned radio show. "But where's the file with my birth certificate, Dad?" / "With all the other files, Fi." / "But where's that?" / "Where's what?" / "The place with the files!" / "It's where we keep your birth certificate." / "But where *is* that?" / "Where's what?" / "My birth certificate!" / "Your birth certificate? It's in the file." I rolled my eyes and excused myself from the green table.

The only way I could escape from time's underwhelming comedy routine was to upgrade Dirk Angus, so I spent the rest of the evening in my bedroom, determined to find the flaw in my equations, trying not to think about New Nephele's epic fail, and epically failing. If I couldn't bust out my assets with a bunch of strangers, I'd never be able to pull it off with Vera. Did I have any assets? I *felt* sassy and spunky. Somewhere inside me, a rock star was ready to sing. Maybe I was delusional. Maybe Chicago was right about the New Nephele project. Even if I could figure out how to act more like my peers, my mission felt selfish and idiotic now that my timeship had hurt Mom and Dad.

Dozens of tabs were open on my web browser, and my desk was plastered with books about quantum theory, topology, theoretical physics—all the books that had gotten me into this mess in the first place. In fact, rereading them only reassured me that I had made the best damn time machine a girl could possibly make. The missing memories were my only clue about where Dirk Angus had gone wrong.

That night, a full moon shined through my window. My quasar pictures glowed softly on my wall. As I lay in bed breathing the cool night air, I imagined micro-quasars forming out of the quantum foam in my parents' brains. The fountains of light shooting out of the quasars were their memories of my first freshman year.

What even *is* a brain, I wondered? A glob of neurons, fat and water whose entire job is to make sense of the world. When a brain encounters something that *doesn't* make sense, it collects information, analyzes it and develops a reasonable explanation. For instance: if I look in the mirror and my nose is green, my brain doesn't jump to the conclusion that I'm becoming a frog. Instead, it assumes I touched my face while helping my mother paint a certain kitchen table. If I *am* becoming a frog, my brain will require compelling evidence to be convinced of that.

By that logic, for most people, it must've made more sense to forget me than to remember me and wonder why I was still a freshman. Not that forgetting me made sense—it didn't. But what I'd done made even *less* sense. I wasn't important enough in most people's brains to justify questioning their entire concept of time. Which, when I thought about it like that, I could hardly take personally.

But my parents loved me. For fifteen years, I'd been the center of their world. And they'd been the center of mine. For my parents, forgetting me made no sense. Their brains refused to do it. Yet their brains couldn't deal with my time loop either. Not only was the concept illogical, it was probably terrifying.

Huh. Maybe that's why they seemed paralyzed whenever we got too close to the subject. My parents were frozen with fear. Their brains were trying to protect them from the horror of what was happening. I mean, I was petrified too, wasn't I? Weak and woozy and shivering with silent screams—like the Sphinx in Greek mythology, beaten at my own game, ready to devour myself—

I took a deep breath. Back to logic:

For my parents, it made the most sense to remember me but forget the previous year. In both cases, people's brains were using some version of autocorrect. But what did that have to do with the design for my timeship?

My own brain was boiling over like some rabid mathematical potion, but I was stumped. Luckily, the next day was Friday. After school, I could spend the whole weekend swimming in brains at the Big Blue Wave.

In the morning, I didn't bother to blow-dry my hair; I shoved the mess of black tangles in a bun and threw on my hoodie and jeans. Dress rehearsals would have to be postponed. New Nephele was too distracting. It was imperative that I devote all my energy to developing Dirk Angus 2.0.

On day three of my second freshman year, as I plopped into a seat at an empty lab table in Mrs. Saint Johnabelle's classroom, Coco and Lara smiled at each other with a look in their eyes like Let's-see-what-stupid-thing-Psycho-Socks-does-next. Give me a break, I thought. All I did was say hello in a sassy accent, wave flirtily and puke. I didn't insult your mothers and kidnap your pet geckos.

When third period ended, everybody got up from their lab tables to go to lunch. I got up, too. But as I watched kids congeal into groups, joking and whacking each other and checking their phones as they headed to the cafeteria, I couldn't join them. I couldn't bear the thought of sitting alone yet again at an empty table in a room full of my peers.

So I lingered in Mrs. Saint Johnabelle's classroom, hovering awkwardly near her desk, wondering what to do.

When everyone was gone, the door slowly shut itself and Mrs. Saint Johnabelle looked up. "Can I help you, Ms. Weather?"

"I don't know," I said. "I mean, maybe. I just wondered . . ." Mrs. Saint Johnabelle was peering at me through the thick lenses of her clear plastic glasses. I knew what I wanted to ask, but I also knew she'd say no, and I didn't know what I'd do then, so I was stalling. "Could I maybe, like, I mean today. For today only, possibly eat lunch in here with you?"

"Sure!" she said, waving her hand back and forth over the classroom, like I could take a seat wherever I damn well pleased.

I felt like I'd just slipped off a lead jacket. "Really?" I said. "You don't mind? I won't bother you. I mean, I have a book to read."

Mrs. Saint Johnabelle pulled a giant bag of potato chips out of nowhere and ripped it open. She said, "Read away."

I started for my usual lab table in the back row, but it felt rude to choose a seat so far away when we were the only two people in the room. So instead I sat in the front row, directly across from her desk.

Unfortunately, the only book I'd brought with me was *Time Travel for Love & Profit,* which was definitely not going to help me fix Dirk Angus. I wished I'd planned ahead and brought something useful—neuroscience or astrophysics or knitting or jousting or pretty much anything except Oona Gold's exceptionally vague book of advice. But I didn't want Mrs. Saint Johnabelle to feel like she had to entertain me, so I took the book out of my backpack and opened it to a page at random.

> Time travelers are wanderers. They resist progressing through life along a marked path. They prefer to forge through the jungle of human emotions armed with the razor-sharp machete of their intelligence, whacking away their illusions, and—

"Theoretical physics!" said Mrs. Saint Johnabelle, and I looked up. She nodded at my book. "Time travel belongs to a branch of science called theoretical physics. Scientists in that field perform something called thought experiments. They're a wonderful way to flex the muscles of your mathematical imagination."

Um, yeah; I was familiar with theoretical physics. Theoretical physics and I had serious beef—beef that had just gotten personal. But I was surprised that Mrs. Saint Johnabelle was so enthusiastic. I watched her eat a handful of chips. Was that her whole lunch? I didn't see anything else.

"You don't think science fiction is a waste of brain cells?" I asked.

Mrs. Saint Johnabelle took her time chewing before she answered. "Not at all. Scientific questions inspire human beings in fascinating ways. The things that make you curious are a gift, Nephele. Pay attention to your questions. By the way, have you ever seen the television program *Star Trek*?"

I shook my head.

She grinned like she knew something dangerous. "I'll loan you the DVDs. You'll love them."

That fall, I called the county courthouse on a weekly basis, trying to track down my birth certificate. The person who answered the phone always said the same thing. "So sorry for the delay. Please visit our website and complete our online form." Which I did. Repeatedly. My birth certificate never arrived.

Same thing with my school and medical records. Whenever I tried collecting them in person, every administrator I met smiled the same off-key smile, something between a clown and a compulsive arsonist, and said they'd be happy to help me, while they didn't. My parents became animatronic ghouls whenever I asked to see a photograph of myself or had any questions about my missing year.

From a scientific perspective, it was awe-inspiring. Everything that placed me at a particular moment in time was lost. The universe was staring right through me, just like my so-called peers. The fact that I'd stumbled into such a spectacular math problem almost made the experience less devastating.

I spent my free time at the bookshop reading anything that seemed remotely relevant to the Case of the Missing Memories and taking tea breaks with Chicago. Unfortunately, the bookshop didn't have many books about neuroscience, except a few that promised to teach you how to master something, like playing golf, or asking your boss for a raise. And those were shelved in Self-Help—a genre that had gotten me into enough trouble already. On the other hand, *Time Travel for Love & Profit* came the closest to describing what was happening to me:

> No one will recognize that you've changed
> your past except your future you, who will be
> aligned with your rightful fate. Everything
> that's different about you will be quietly folded
> into people's current understanding of who
> you are now. The people around you will do
> the work of hiding your time travel for you.

Which was, more or less, my autocorrect theory. And it still didn't explain what had gone wrong with my timeship.

Meanwhile, autumn turned into winter, my arm hair grew back thicker than ever and Dad sprouted a long, wiry beard with silver streaks that made him look exactly like the devil. New Nephele's metallic pants collected dust on my closet shelf, and I spent every lunch period talking theoretical physics with Mrs. Saint Johnabelle.

Then came the holiday break, and our annual video call with our relatives in Greece, including my mom's cousin Penelope, who didn't want to go to her mother-in-law's house for Christmas dinner, and didn't want to stay home alone eating *yiaprakia* just like last year. And just like last year, Mom replied, "It sounds like you're caught between Scylla and Charybdis," and they laughed, and just like last year, I cringed and made a mental note to avoid referencing Greek mythology in casual conversation so I wouldn't become my mother. You don't need to do loops in time for certain conversations to repeat themselves endlessly.

It was on New Year's Day at the Big Blue Wave when something significant finally happened. I was sitting cross-legged on the threadbare Turkish rug in the Art section when the skylight flew open and I was showered in a rainbow of confetti.

In other words, I had a revelation.

CHAPTER 6

Optical Illusions Are Not Just for Those Wacky T-Shirts They Sell in the Tourist Traps

Serrafin Saint Johnabelle reached into the giant foil bag, pulled out a single sour-cream-and-onion potato chip and took a delicate bite. As she chewed it, she looked drowsy and content, like she was dreaming of her blissful childhood on a sour-cream-and-onion farm.

We'd been having lunch together for four months, and I'd never seen Serrafin eat anything but sour-cream-and-onion potato chips. No protein. No beverages. I didn't know how the woman stayed so energetic. But she was a grandmother, so she was healthy, apparently. Maybe when she wasn't at school, Serrafin was all about green smoothies.

Incidentally, Mrs. Saint Johnabelle never let me call her by her first name. I just liked to pretend that's how we rolled.

"So, Nephele," said Serrafin as she dusted crumbs off her lapels, "tell me you made progress on your time-travel thought experiment over the break."

I said, "Something did occur to me."

"Oh?"

I unzipped my backpack and took out a collection of prints by an artist named M. C. Escher. On every page there was an optical illusion—an image of something that should be impossible, but in the picture isn't. For instance, there was a staircase in the shape of a square where every flight appeared to be going up, like you could climb up the stairs forever without going back down. There was also a hand that was drawing itself and a snake swallowing its own tail. I opened the book to the page with the snake and handed it to Serrafin, who wiped her fingertips on a tiny wet wipe before taking it.

The fact that Serrafin taught her students to take their ideas seriously made it especially easy for me to talk with her about Dirk Angus. Instead of saying, "In theory, my app should do *this,* but instead, it's doing *that,*" I could say, "My timeship is pulverizing my life in a cosmic blender and I don't know why," and she'd calmly nod like that was the sanest sentence a girl could ever utter.

Serrafin's eyes darted over the picture of the snake.

I said, "So you know how I went back in time while the rest of the universe kept going?"

She nodded.

"My new theory is that my timeship app folded time and poked a hole in it, but it didn't pull the rest of the universe through the hole with me. The snake didn't swallow its own tail. It only swallowed me."

"So your wormhole in time is more of a snake mouth," she said.

"Exactly. My time machine should work correctly if the universe swallows itself through the wormhole in the quantum foam inside my body. The snake has to swallow its own tail."

"Fascinating. So you began by shaking open a hole in the cosmic foam, aided by a planet-wide simple harmonic oscillation, thanks to the internet of things."

"Right. Talking toasters and self-guided delivery drones, united for the advancement of science."

"Okay. Let's set aside the ethical issues here, for the moment. Now, you want to extend the impact of your timeship universally. You want to magnify its resonance. Theoretically, it's an idea worth pursuing."

"It is?" I asked. I mean, I knew it was—I hoped it was—but I sorely welcomed outside confirmation that being inspired by an optical illusion wasn't a symptom of some time-warp illness I'd contracted in the quantum foam.

"Of course it is." Mrs. Saint Johnabelle removed her eyeglasses and half smiled. "Do you know, Nephele, that I've often wondered whether our entire universe might be located within a wormhole? Or perhaps a black hole."

"Whoa," I said. "You've often wondered that?"

"Mathematics suggests all manner of interstellar oddities," she said. "Your imagination is the limit."

"So you think maybe we're lost between two places," I said. "Born into a black hole, living our whole lives inside a tunnel.

And when we die, we go out the other side. Like light from a white hole."

Serrafin's half-smile turned into a wide grin. All at once, I had a vision of Serrafin as a teenager surrounded by math books, grinning about wormholes. I wished I'd known her then. I wondered if she'd ever felt as alone as I felt. Full of ideas so thrilling you want to share them with the whole world, and knowing that if you do, you'll be ridiculed. I wished I could figure out a way to ask.

Serrafin stood. "I admire how seriously you're taking your thought experiment, Nephele. It feels very vivid. By the way, how did you like *Star Trek*? I keep meaning to ask."

I'd sort of been avoiding getting back to her on that. I mean, I'd watched a few episodes months ago, when she'd lent me her DVDs, but that show is . . . How can I put this? Totally implausible! The acting is cringe-y, and for some reason, everybody is wearing a wetsuit. Plus, the rules of space and time are constantly changing. My life was less of an illogical soap opera than that spaceship.

Don't get me wrong: I love science fiction. Books, television, movies, whatever. But I'd hoped Serrafin had given me something that would genuinely help me—something based on the actual laws of physics.

Then again, now that I was drowning in space-time quicksand, I probably needed to pay more attention to science that made zero sense.

Mrs. Saint Johnabelle was looking at me with a mischievous glint in her eyes, like we shared the password to paradise.

I said, "Phenomenal," and tried to look stoked.

"Right?" she said, and sighed.

After lunch I went into the hallway and saw Vera leaning against the green lockers, kissing Youki Johnson.

Kissing. Youki.

Vera. Youki? Youki, Vera? Youki?

Fact: Youki Johnson looked like Superman and, yes, he was very intelligent. But he wasn't Superman! He used his powers for evil when he could have been saving the world. And plus— Vera was kissing someone. Even if it was Youki, I couldn't help it. I was jealous.

I was walking toward fourth period, wondering whether Dr. Carissa Silk had ever been jealous of her former best friend who had left her for dead in a ditch, when I noticed Wylie Buford wandering in my direction, scrolling on his phone. When we made eye contact, I smiled and waved maniacally, like I always did nowadays when Wylie caught me looking at him, and like always, he forced a smile, turned around and ran the other direction.

Before I had a chance to kick myself for continuously freaking out the one person who wasn't supposed to be freaked out by me, I spotted Marla, the new Wylie, the freshman with the Berkeley sweatshirt. As usual, she was read-walking. Snickering and reading as she walked. She wasn't even looking up; she was so used to everybody going around her. Which they did.

Maybe it was all the rest I'd gotten over the holiday break.

Maybe I was feeling confident from my lunch with Serrafin. I stayed put and waited for Marla to bump into me.

Which she didn't. When she was about seventeen centimeters away, she dodged me without taking her eyes off her book, *The Merriest of Murders.* I scooted to get back in her path.

Now Marla looked up.

"Whatcha reading, Marla?" I asked.

"A book, you idiot," she said, walking around me.

Wow.

Okay: Marla was *definitely* not the new Wylie. Maybe she was a misanthrope. She wasn't laughing to herself because her murder mysteries were amusing. She was laughing because she was, like, amused by murder.

I was so over this year. Thankfully, Serrafin had given me the thumbs-up on my snake-mouth theory, so I felt confident about developing equations inspired by that theory to rebuild my timeship. The missing memories were a side effect I could relegate to the . . . I want to say "the toilet of history." That seems harsh—but honestly? That's what I wanted. I wanted this stinky, poopy, accidental side effect of my failure to disappear forever into the sewer of science-gone-wrong. I figured I could have Dirk Angus 2.0 fully coded and ready to launch in three weeks.

Soon my first time-travel screw-up would be a distant memory—and I'd be the only one who remembered that memory, which would be absolutely fine.

* * *

Did I say three weeks? Make that eight months.

Late in the afternoon on the last day of summer, I walked down the winding trail through the cypress grove that led to the empty beach. When I got to the sand, I put my hands in my hoodie pockets and listened to the ocean's roar. The background of my whole life was that shushing noise, that sound like the breath of the planet. I loved walking over wet sand, lifting slick seaweed with my sneaker toe. I loved the way the light glinted off iridescent spiral shells and watching baby hermit crabs scuttle through the tide pools in their portable cabins. The ocean was always in motion, always making something new. Full of life, and death, and whatever happened in between. The ocean was the friend who didn't remember me, but hadn't forgotten me either.

It had taken a lot longer than I'd expected to upgrade Dirk Angus, but ever since my New Year's Day revelation that to truly go back in time, I needed the universe to swallow itself along with me, I'd felt oddly happy. Happy discussing my "thought experiment" at lunch with Serrafin. Happily absorbed in my new set of equations; happy swimming through my second freshman year as a total unknown.

Fairly happy, anyway. Happier than I'd been before, for sure.

I mean, yes: Mom and Dad were still missing an entire year of memories, and whenever I encountered their brain holes I felt like I was sliding down a crumbling cliff.

But soon they'd go back to normal.

Meanwhile, I'd become a space cowgirl. I was a genuine

scientist in the middle of a groundbreaking experiment. I hadn't made it to the past yet, but I'd definitely made it somewhere, and I wasn't going to quit until I got where I was meant to be.

I sat facing the ocean on a bleached log near a burned-out fire pit, adjusted my backpack and opened my timeship app. "We've got this, Dirk Angus 2.0," I said. My hair blew in my face as I typed in my destination: my first first day of freshman year, two years ago.

Dirk Angus could only send me through time, not space; in the morning I'd still be on the beach. Last year I'd fallen asleep immediately after emerging from the wormhole, and hadn't woken up until the next morning. I assumed that would happen again, and didn't want to risk being gone when my parents got up. I wanted to wake up before they did and walk home. That sounded peaceful to me, strolling home from the beach at the crack of dawn. I looked forward to feeling some peace. I programmed my phone's alarm to go off at five-thirty a.m.

"It's been a trippy ride, eh, Dirk? Our wacky relationship? But everything is clicking now," I said. "Just like that scene in *Thirsty for Thrills* when you and Sheena Firestorm make out on that threadbare rope bridge above the nest of scorpions and poisonous cacti. Ready, set . . ."

I bit my lip, said a prayer to the math goddesses and pressed GO.

There is a sonic boom. The forest sprouts a brassy halo and dims with a silver flare. The sun rises. The sun sets over the ocean in a blinding flash. The sun rises, searing pink and hopeful while the blue earth spins. The sun drops like a bomb, smashing the day, and rises like a rocket, attacking the night. The sun rises, sets, rises, sets; the earth spins, the sun rises sets rises sets risessetsrisessets. . . .

Thousands of voices like colorful ribbons twine into an effervescent braid, a song that vibrates so hard it shatters my own throat and sears my veins.

I am dripping and reconstituting, sucking myself back together like a cloud after a storm.

I rise from the ocean, a girl.

I feel like I've been here before.

• • •

CHAPTER 7

Older & Wiser & Younger & Worser

I woke up on my belly, my cheek pressing into the damp sand. Electronic chimes pealed quietly. When my head stopped spinning and my eyes focused, I turned off my alarm and watched the gray waves, kissed by the early-morning sun, sweep the wet shore and slide back out again. The ocean whispered, *Good morning, Fi; good morning again,* and I smiled. I felt as cool as an echinoderm, like a starfish or a sea cucumber, quietly shimmying across the ocean floor. As happy as a clam buried in the sand beneath high tide, deep down where no predators could reach me. This time I'd made it back for real.

I stood and stretched my arms above my head. "I am a supernova!" I yelled, and the ocean roared back, and a great blue heron with its long, curving neck swerved past me toward the cliffs. I shook out my rubbery limbs and found the path through the cypress trees that leads up to Highway 1.

I couldn't wait to be home.

As I walked, I rolled my stiff shoulders. I had exploded in an iridescent rainbow; I remembered it. I had erupted like a volcano; I felt my own heat. I had blasted apart and reassembled; I felt the remnants of a tingly song, painful and sweet, in every one of my blood cells, in my eyeballs and my elbows and my teeth.

I was also drowsy, but it was a lovely drowsy. I was ready to get on with my life. I said in my flirty New Zealand accent, "Dirk Angus, we are superstars," and started to take my phone out of my pocket.

But no; I didn't want to see the date. I'd confirm my success the fun way.

I crossed Highway 1 and started running up the hill toward home, where I could check the kitchen table. After a few steps, my whole body flinched and I stumbled. My legs felt numb, like I was in shock from splashing in a freezing cold sea—yet I wanted to keep running. I remembered this from last year, the giddy sensation of being simultaneously exhilarated and exhausted. I decided to slow down a little.

For the rest of the walk, I imagined founding my own start-up—but not to get rich and waste money on parties while the people around me struggled to pay rent. My company would use time travel to heal the earth.

Naturally, we'd start with the ocean. I'd read somewhere that every nine minutes, a hundred metric tons of plastic makes its way into the ocean. And those plastics never entirely break down. Most seabirds have stomachs full of plastic.

If we went back in time and stopped plastic from becoming part of every single thing—shopping bags, toys, clothes—we could begin to restore the ocean's food web. How amazing would that be? As I passed a clump of sunflowers, their heads seemed to nod in agreement.

I was so glad I'd failed the first time around and gotten New Nephele out of my system. Acting sassy and spunky had been a terrible idea. *Orr ee-bull!* It seemed so obvious now. Oona Gold had said to remake your life in your true image, not to pick someone else's image and try to become that. My aggressively weird talent for math was exactly the thing that was going to make people love me.

After a few minutes envisioning the boy who would kiss me when I won the Nobel Prize—his grin would be roguish yet genuine, and he'd be into rhombicuboctahedrons the way other people are into the Golden State Warriors—I walked up our warped front porch steps, unlocked the front door and sashayed down the hallway and through the archway that led to the kitchen. I said, "Hello, kitchen table!"

The kitchen was silent.

The table was green.

Gold light poured through the window over the sink and pooled in a puddle on the floor. The radiator clicked quietly. I stared at the green table for so long it turned red. Everything turned red.

"Morning, Fi!" called Mom, and I turned to look. At the top of the stairs, my mother was finger-combing tangles out of her hair, which glinted with silver streaks. Silver hair? Had she had that yesterday? "Up early, dressed and everything!" she said. "First day of freshman year. You must be so excited."

Behind Mom, Dad appeared. *Devil beard.* They started to come downstairs.

No.

No.

No.

My heartbeat was pounding louder and faster and taking up too much space, like a jackhammer. I fumbled to pull my phone out of my pocket and unlocked it: it was the next day. I yelled, "Where is my birth certificate?!"

My mother stopped halfway down the stairs and swayed like her feet were planted in ice. My father's body twitched like a squid tossed live on a grill.

I yelled, "You guys!" and ran up the stairs and grabbed their arms, afraid that they'd tumble down. Mom's wrist felt cold and bony. Dad's arm shook, which made my arm shake. This was *bad.*

"Dad?" I said, feeling the tremor from Dad's body rumbling inside me, a tremor of terror taking my organs hostage and assuring me that I had made a grave mistake. I didn't know what to do. I heard myself stammering the same questions that had stumped me last year—the questions that had come back stronger than ever to stare me down and let me know that the universe was ready for a fight. "Where are my medical records? How old were you when I was born? Where are the photographs of me from last . . ." It hit me that I could not remember a single photograph that my parents had taken of me the previous year. "Why do we never take photographs of each other? Why is our entire family malfunctioning?"

Dad's free hand moved, which startled me. In a nerve-racking slow motion, he stroked his devil beard and said, "Cameras don't understand my face."

Mom's voice was unusually high-pitched, like she was singing a breathy lullaby. "I took pictures of you on a *daily basis* from birth to kindergarten. After that, I may have slacked off a bit."

I looked in my father's eyes. I was afraid to push him, but I had to know how deep this brain hole went. I had to know exactly what I'd done. I said, "Dad, what year was I born?"

Dad froze. As in, stopped moving altogether.

"Dad?" I said. He was looking at me, but when I leaned to the left, he was still looking in the same spot.

I couldn't believe it. My modifications to the code had done nothing. Nothing, that is, but drill two new quasars in the quantum foam inside my parents' brains—and *paralyze my father.*

I was no child prodigy; I was evil.

"Fi?" said Mom. I looked into her turquoise eyes and silently pleaded for help. But how could my mother help me? I was the one who needed to help her! "Fi, where did your father go? I didn't see him leave."

I looked at Dad, then back at Mom.

Mom couldn't see Dad.

Mom started to say something else, and then she froze.

I rubbed Mom's cold wrist, looking frantically for her pulse. When I found it, I almost wept. "It's okay, Mom," I said, although it was anything but.

A minute passed. Two minutes.

What do I do? What do I do? I had to call 911. And say what?!

Suddenly, Dad was locking arms with me; Mom's hand slid into mine. She was leading us downstairs.

"How kind of you to escort us to breakfast," said Dad. At the bottom of the stairs, Dad tweaked my chin and followed Mom into the kitchen. Mom opened the refrigerator and took out a basket of raspberries. I stopped in the archway and watched them. Was that it? Was the spell broken?

Mom was washing berries and humming. Dad was shaking coffee beans into the grinder. They seemed to be back to normal. Shiny and morning-y and breathing in regular rhythms.

I, on the other hand, was anything but normal. I was wrecked. I'd shot through the quantum wormhole and slammed into a brick wall. How old was I supposed to be now? Sixteen?

Sixteen, halfway to seventeen.

I definitely did not feel sixteen. I still felt fourteen, halfway to fifteen. What did that even mean? Did I look sixteen? I needed to check. But first I needed to collapse against the kitchen wall below our cuckoo clock, which had been broken forever, a fact that now felt like an omen or a curse. I looked up at the clock and resisted the urge to gesticulate rudely in its general direction.

Dad noticed me looking and nodded at the clock. "Gotta figure out how to fix that thing. Clocks have their own whole deal. Right now I need a record." He cut through the kitchen into the living room. "What do we feel like listening to?" he asked.

I closed my eyes and said, "Something tragic."

"Ah," said Mom. "To be a freshman."

After breakfast I went upstairs to take a hot shower. There was sand in my fingernails and I smelled like seaweed and salt.

The scalding water felt good on my skin. It reminded me that I was real. Dirk Angus 2.0 hadn't taken me where I wanted to go, but it hadn't killed me. And if I was still alive, I could still fix this.

I *had to* fix this.

But first, the question that had occurred to me downstairs was nagging at me. Was I aging? I dried off and confronted my naked self in the full-length mirror.

My face was still round, and so was the rest of the round stuff, like my boobs and my butt and all that. My eyes were still the same nefarious gold, and I had my same pointy chin. Hair galore, I still had: the black mane down my back, plus the fur on my arms and the shadow above my upper lip that I have always liked because it makes me look like a gentleman who smokes a pipe while wearing a paisley silk jacket and sitting in a leather armchair, which probably makes sense to nobody except me. My legs, which I shaved sporadically, were spiky, which made me think of a ghost spider grossly inflated by a scientific experiment gone awry.

Awry. Like a goofball plan in a romantic comedy.

If only. What I would've given for my world to be resolved in ninety minutes or less and fade out on an epic first kiss.

My point is that standing there naked, inspecting myself, I had many thoughts, but it was difficult to detect from the outside whether or not I was aging.

But on the inside? I really, truly felt like I totally wasn't. I just didn't *feel* older. Like, at all. On my second fifteenth birthday, last March 11, I'd felt like a deceptive creep.

Sure, I fantasized about kissing boys, which was mature, I guess. I'd even tried to imagine myself kissing a girl. Both years during our unit on biological reproduction, Mrs. Saint Johnabelle had said, "I stand in awe of the beauty of the spectrum of sexuality across species," and I'd loved how that sounded, and had tried to figure out where I fit into that spectrum, but how would I know for sure until I actually got kissed? And I wasn't making any progress in the kissing department, or any other department. I wasn't *growing up.*

"You think you're pretty clever, don't you?" I said to the naked, forever-young version of myself in the mirror, and the girl looked like she wasn't sure. "What are you going to do now, clever girl?" I leaned forward and peered into her eerie yellow eyes. As we inspected each other, we both looked highly suspicious.

* * *

Standing outside the school before the morning bell rang, I bounced on my toes to keep warm. A few seagulls fluttered near the forest's edge, collecting the muffin chunks some boys were tossing that way. *Eat up, scavengers,* I thought. *The universe will spoil you today and starve you tomorrow.* I should've been thinking about where I'd gone wrong with Dirk Angus, but I was still preoccupied with the aging question. Last year's freshmen would be sophomores now, and the freshmen from my first year would be juniors. Some girls from my first freshman year—juniors now—were huddled in a circle. Were they older than last year? Presumably. How would I know that if I didn't know them? I didn't know.

When I spotted this boy named Terrence Jack, I swooned internally. I'd developed a huge crush on him during my second freshman year. Terrence Jack had a lip ring and a nose ring, and he was pretty much always snarling. He'd looked about thirty to me even when he was a freshman. But he'd definitely grown over the summer. He was thicker around the neck, or something. I was launching my Terrence Jack fantasy, wherein we save each other from a hungry pack of turkey vultures on a moonlit night by hiding together in the back seat of someone's car, when I noticed Vera standing near the dumpsters.

She'd cut her hair short, which looked sophisticated. And she was holding hands with Youki, who was . . . Okay, Youki was *extra* tall, no doubt . . . and he was wearing glasses. The glasses were new.

Then I noticed Marla the misanthropic read-walker near the school's front doors, leaning back to back with a girl with a single blue hair extension. They looked genuinely bored with the world—the look I'd once imagined New Nephele cultivating. I sighed. I would never have pulled that look off.

Serrafin was milling around the crowd in a cream-colored suit, keeping an eye on things. She looked extra old. But she'd always looked extra old, with her white hair and her wrinkles. Unlike my mother, whose mermaid hair seemed to have sprouted silver stripes overnight. I mean, it must've been silver before. I was just hypersensitive today.

I headed for Serrafin. At least now that we were friends, I'd be important enough in her brain for her to remember me. Like my parents, she'd remember me and forget my first two freshman years.

True: Vera hadn't remembered me, and we'd been best friends forever. But last year I'd read that humans' brains aren't fully developed until they're, like, twenty-five years old. Vera's brain was still forming; it needed all its energy for that. She'd forgotten me because it took less juice to autocorrect me out of existence than to remember me and forget the previous year. Serrafin's brain had been fully developed for decades; she wouldn't have that problem. As long as my teacher remembered me, I could live with her forgetting our theoretical physics research. I just needed her to see me, to show me the secret smile hiding in her eyes—and possibly I needed to collapse, sobbing, in her arms.

When I reached her, I said, "Serrafi—I mean, Mrs. Saint Johnabelle?"

Serrafin looked at me over her eyeglasses. "Good morning, young lady. May I help you find something?"

Young lady? That wasn't promising. "It's me," I said. "Nephele Weather. From your homeroom."

Serrafin nodded in a formal way and looked over the crowd. "Welcome to Redwood Cove High School, Nephele. What a unique name. Might it be Greek?"

My heart collapsed like a parachute, crash-landing. Serrafin didn't remember me. Which meant . . . I wasn't as important to my teacher as she was to me. I was one of thousands of students she'd taught in her long career. Just another utterly replaceable freshman.

"I look forward to making your acquaintance," said Serrafin. Then she hurried away, yelling, "Excuse me? Excuse me, you there: students are not to ride electric scooters in the schoolyard."

I was about to unleash a primal scream to call forth my Greek ancestors from the sea—Stheno and Euryale and Medusa, the shrieking semi-immortals with hair made of serpents that had *totally refused to swallow themselves*—when I noticed a cluster of upperclassmen standing near the redwood stump and did a double take.

One of them was Wylie. His reddish-brown hair was chin-length, and he was wearing a T-shirt with a skull on it with a bloody knife going through it. Beside him, a guy wearing a black cape was telling a story with his whole body.

And then I noticed the girl in the combat boots.

She had super-short bleached curly hair and bright amber-brown skin and chunky gold earrings that dangled to her shoulders. She was laughing. They were all holding paper coffee cups.

I just stood there watching them. At one point, the girl in the combat boots poked Wylie in the belly, which made him giggle like . . . I didn't know what. A rubber duckie? I doubted ducks giggled. He was still Wylie, though. That's what I mean. Something had happened to him over the summer, but he was still Wylie. He was *in* there.

The bell rang, and Wylie and his friends went inside. I felt fragile, standing on the blacktop alone, like a sand dollar exposed to the tourists on a busy stretch of beach. I could not fathom getting through that day.

After school, at the Big Blue Wave, I made my cup of tea in silence. The opera Dad was spinning was working its way into my soul, and I felt the tears coming. Mrs. Saint Johnabelle didn't remember me, and there was a whole new class of freshmen I couldn't begin to deal with. I was genuinely hurting my parents. And I'd never been lonelier in my life. I was doing everything wrong.

"Maybe it's time to give up on time travel," said Chicago.

"And leave my parents like this? Like short-circuiting robots? No way. The only solution is to upgrade Dirk Angus, *stat*. Dirk Angus 3.0 has to be *flawless*."

"Where are you going to start?" Chicago asked.

"How should I know?" I clutched my mug and let the warmth seep into my hands. I wished it could make me feel better.

Chicago almost looked at me, but didn't quite. "And you're sure you don't want to practice New Nephele while you try to figure out what happened? If you get stuck here in the wrong future, you may need to crank up the sass."

"Are you kidding? New Nephele is dead. All I care about now is fixing Mom and Dad. And, you know. When my scientific revelation saves the earth too, I mean, yeah. I'll take it. Anyway, I'm an idiot, Chicago. I should've been Wylie's friend when I had the chance. I should be the girl in the combat boots."

"Says who?"

"Says me. When I go back in time, I'm not going to save Wylie from Outcast Island. Hopefully, Wylie will save me by being my friend, even though I am a colossal idiot. Until then, Chicago, I have you."

"But I'm imaginary, aren't I?"

She was. I mean—she was and she wasn't. I couldn't review my equations yet; my brain was still too mealy from last night's time travel. However, I needed something to distract me from the mess I was making, so I decided to conduct a new investigation.

I'd always wondered if Chicago had a soul. Her own soul, separate from mine. If a photograph could have a soul, maybe I could figure out how it got there.

Yes, it was a bizarre idea, and no, it had nothing to do with time travel. Which was exactly why I felt like thinking about it. I took my tea and headed for Photography.

Harry Callahan made *Chicago, 1955* before digital cameras existed. He used film. With film, you can create the illusion that two things are happening in the same place at the same time by taking a photograph, rewinding the film and taking another photograph on top of it. It's called a double exposure. In theory, there's no limit to the number of exposures you can make, but if you aren't careful, you'll cram so many pictures on top of one another that the final result looks like mud. That idea got me thinking.

The next day, I asked to have lunch with Serrafin, and when she said yes, I dived right into my "thought experiment." After I brought her up to speed, I posed my new theory.

"What if it isn't just the universe and me who need to pass through the wormhole in time?" I asked. "What if I need every version of myself that could ever exist to pass through the hole? All of the choices I could ever have made, or could ever make."

"The set of all possible Nepheles?" asked Serrafin as she munched her chips.

"Exactly. Any and every Nephele I could possibly be."

Serrafin crumpled her chip bag and tossed it toward the garbage can. It landed a few feet away on the floor. "Shoot," she said, standing. "So you want to combine all possible outcomes in a single superposed state. A single wave that's a collection of all the possible waves that describe Nephele Weather."

"Precisely," I said.

"Fascinating, Ms. Weather. Where did you get that idea?" she asked.

I told her about my research into old-fashioned photography. "I think I rewound the film of my life and am imprinting myself on a universe that keeps moving forward. Like I'm a multiple exposure of a photograph. And every time I go back, the universe gets blurrier. If I send back every version of myself that could ever exist, maybe I'll solve the problem."

"Intriguing concept, Ms. Weather. This conversation brings me back to my days as a graduate student." Mrs. Saint Johnabelle held a hand on her lower back to brace it as she bent to grab the chip bag from the floor.

I jumped up to get it for her. "Graduate school," I said. "You mean, to become a teacher?"

"No. To become a physicist. I only teach because—well. Being a woman scientist when I was young was certainly possible. But I didn't like being around all those men. They were bullies, Nephele. Don't fret, however; thanks to girls like you, things are changing and will continue to. I do miss having this kind of conversation with my peers. For me, science is the skeleton of the universe. It is a profound way of making sense of the world."

"I wish my thought experiment made more sense. Sometimes I feel like my ideas are all over the place," I said. "And I keep failing. It scares me, how wrong I can be. And it's like, why am I even doing this in the first place? Honestly, Serra— Mrs. Saint Johnabelle—I'm feeling like . . . not like giving up;

I mean, I can't give up now. It's just, I'm like, so like . . . I don't know."

"Overwhelmed?" Serrafin sat again and looked out the window. Pine needles whirled across the blacktop. "In graduate school, I sometimes felt that way. And when I did, I made sure to tightly control every variable in my experimental model except the one I wanted to modify. Right down to the seemingly extraneous details."

"Extraneous like what?"

"For instance, I'd eat exactly the same breakfast every morning. Wear exactly the same outfit. Listen to the same music on my way to the lab, et cetera."

"Those *are* extraneous details," I said. "You're superstitious?"

Serrafin shrugged. "I liked the idea that nothing would change except what I wanted to change. Then, when I ran the experiment again, I felt clear-headed, as if I were controlling the chaos."

"Hey, is that why you eat the same lunch every day? To control the chaos of us? Your students?"

Mrs. Saint Johnabelle swept sour-cream-and-onion dust off her desk into her napkin. "I don't eat the same lunch every day."

I tried not to smile.

"But that's beside the point," she said. Then she leaned back in her chair and looked at me like she was considering whether or not she should tell me something. I was starting to feel fidgety—the woman's glare could make you confess to sins you didn't even want to commit—when she said, "You mustn't give up, Ms. Weather. Remain confident and persist. Science needs women like you."

Her voice sounded a little different than usual. It wasn't friendly or unfriendly. It was reaching for me. Asking for a promise.

"I won't give up," I said.

Serrafin nodded. "So. How will you create the universal wave function for your timeship?"

"Well, I was thinking I could teach Dirk Angus 3.0 to predict what choices I would make in any given situation," I said. "Although there's a bunch of AI stuff I'll have to learn. . . ."

"Artificial intelligence," said Serrafin. "Wonderful. I've been considering taking an online course on the subject. This gives me the kick I need to go for it. We can tutor each other. Have you ever seen the television program *Star Trek*?"

I said, "Yup."

She lowered her voice and smiled like we were breaking the law together. "Don't you just love it?"

I believe it is wrong to lie—and I felt evil enough already. But it would've felt even crueler to tell Serrafin my true feelings about *Star Trek*.

"I sure do," I said. "I really do love *Star Trek*."

Serrafin laughed a scruffy laugh and nodded.

My third freshman year passed in the usual way. I ignored my peers before they could reject me, spending lunchtimes doing theoretical physics with Serrafin and my free time at the bookshop or in my bedroom, learning everything I could about artificial intelligence and developing Dirk Angus 3.0. By mid-July, the code was finished and I was ready to run the experiment again.

But I was inspired by what Serrafin had told me about controlling all of the variables except the one that she had to change. My life felt out of control. Serrafin had said that a routine had helped her stay focused, and I wanted to try it. So I decided to leave on precisely the same day I'd run my previous time-travel experiments: the night before the first day of the school year.

To kill time until my departure, I programmed a simple animation for a cute screen that would pop up when I opened the Dirk Angus app. It looked like you were shooting through a black-and-magenta galaxy, dodging asteroids and comets, and the soundtrack was "Twist and Shout" from one of Dad's Beatles albums. Something about the song's dips and swings reminded me of how I felt when I torpedoed through the wormhole. Strong and weightless and happy and free. Should it feel phenomenal to dive into the quantum bubble bath? I didn't know. But I found myself looking forward to it.

When the last day of summer finally arrived, I was sitting on my star quilt, holding my phone and wearing my backpack, which contained Oona Gold's useless, aggravating book, *Time Travel for Love & Profit,* to which I was now inexplicably, sentimentally attached. As I waited for Mom and Dad to fall asleep, the wind blew through my window and the foghorns sang their mournful song.

When I opened Dirk Angus 3.0, I felt a very specific type of relief. Like when you're hiking a trail in the redwoods and you take a wrong turn right off the bat, and go super out of your way, and run out of drinking water, and hours pass, and your thoughts stop making sense, and you're on your way to being a meal for a mountain lion or a pack of coyotes or a dinner party that includes multiple species of wild carnivores, then you fall on your hands and knees and crawl around the corner and realize, Wait a minute, this is it! The trailhead! Somehow you made it back to where you started. However, if you want to reach your destination, the view you came all that way to see, you still have to do the whole hike.

That was okay. Time was one thing I had plenty of, apparently.

No offense to Oona Gold, but if I ever write a self-help book, I'll be sure to mention that fulfilling your rightful fate requires a high tolerance for colossal face-plants and can cause significant collateral damage.

Anyway, this was it. My moment of truth. You know that part in the science fiction book when the heroine says, "I was born to complete this mission. I've come too far to turn back," and you're like, *Um, you're kind of a chaos machine, maybe you should actually turn back,* and there's a description of the heroine's eyes, and they're all zingy and devastating because she sees a future only she can see? And she finally gets kissed by the international man of mystery who believed her all along? In my story, this is that part.

I would never become a sassy, spunky social media queen

who could take a flattering selfie. I knew that now. But I could certainly fulfill my rightful fate as a mathematician. At this point, if I wasn't a brilliant scientist, what was I?

I'll tell you what.

Nothing.

As for getting kissed by that international man of mystery—someone who was cute, but not in a cutesy way; funny, but not in a jokey way; someone who appreciated situations that were highly abnormal—I'd concluded that that outcome was impossible. As a scientist, I accepted this. When your whole world is falling down around you, you absolutely must stay realistic.

PART II

CHAPTER 8

Immortal Beings Are Never Not Evil

The redwood trees kept growing. In their canopies, mosses spread creepily and hairy rodents scampered and millipedes scuttled with their minuscule feet. Clouds of insects swarmed and ferns unfurled and berries ripened and dangled from thorny shoots and fell a hundred meters, spinning down, down, down, where they splatted and rotted and stank while the trees kept stretching to the heavens, and they, and the life in their canopies, and the sky and sun and moon they were reaching for, all looked down on me and laughed, because nature is insufferable and the universe is obnoxious.

I was slumping down the sandy hill toward the highway, listening to the bloated foghorns call each other in their groan-y language. A squadron of pelicans sailed past me looking prehistoric, like pterodactyls. The cypress branches that had fallen in last night's storm were already dripping with seagull poop, and the wind that never stopped wouldn't leave my hair alone. Nature was mocking me, and I was lost in its chaos, patterns too complex to understand. The universe was punishing me for trying to decode it. Its never-ending-ness was scratching out my eyes.

I crossed Highway 1 and trudged down the stupid path covered in stupid wildflowers toward the stupid, stupid high school, kicking every twisty blue eucalyptus leaf, trying to forget my parents' wrinkled faces as they wished me luck that morning, trying to forget that abominable green kitchen table.

I could hear the ocean just beyond the highway. The ocean, my fellow semi-immortal.

It was my tenth first day of freshman year.

But who was counting?

As I approached the school, I thought of one of Dad's Eagles albums, this creepy lyric in the song "Hotel California": *You can check out any time you like, but you can never leave.* Redwood Cove High School was my personal Hotel California. I was tied up in a tangled nightmare of time.

How did I not anticipate this outcome? How had I been so overconfident? If this was how child prodigies thought, no wonder people called us abnormal. Clearly, I wasn't. It's not like my best friend was a black-and-white photograph or anything.

I was a failure as a scientist, and my life made less sense than *Star Trek.* It was definitely more boring. By now, I should've at least concocted a body double out of discarded laptops, a pouty mannequin with gravity-defying boobs and a joystick, to go in and do freshman year for me.

As I cut through the crowd, my peers' eyes iced over like a sped-up time lapse of hundreds of freezing lakes. Every memory they had of me was getting sucked down their inner-space whirlpools, stretching and spiraling and disappearing into nothing. The new batch of freshmen didn't have brain holes because we were strangers. It was up to me to ignore them before they discovered my aggressive weirdness and fled. It was a new feature I'd developed over the past few years, the opposite of New Nephele. I called it my force field. It was impenetrable.

In a decade of time-travel failure, I'd nailed one thing, anyway. I'd gotten surviving freshman year down to an art.

I plopped into a seat at the lab table directly across from Serrafin's desk. Kids shouted over each other about which reality television character was the hottest. Television. What would it be like to care about that? It sounded fun. Fun. What would it be like to have that? I couldn't remember. Even math sucked now. Math sucked . . . almost. Not quite. Just . . . math was still . . . okay, fine. I still loved math.

But it was on warning.

By the chalkboard, three girls wearing animal-print leggings were doing a dance step in sync with a hologram projected from someone's smartphone. My phone didn't have that feature; I needed a new one, probably. I needed a new one every year, practically. Even technology was growing up without me. Other kids did other things; the commotion blended into static. I just sat, silently swirling with aggressive weird-ness. My force field was in full effect.

Then Serrafin strode into the room, wearing her pink suit and her royal-blue orthopedic shoes. For a decade, we'd been eating lunch together every single day, sharing her sour-cream-and-onion potato chips, chatting about her grandchildren, looking at pictures of her wearing pointy ears and a giant grin at *Star Trek* conventions, and working out the kinks in my "thought experiment" as Dirk Angus gave birth to disaster after disaster and my life spiraled into insanity. Whenever I felt like giving up, Serrafin had given me hope. She'd made me feel like I wasn't deluded for being obsessed with the time-travel question. Like maybe, just maybe, the answer was still out there, waiting for me to find it. Just because I was the only one who ever remembered those conversations didn't mean they didn't happen.

Or did it?

I couldn't think about that particular question right now.

Serrafin said, "Good morning, class," and doubled over in a coughing fit.

I jumped up. "Are you okay?"

"Thank you," she said in a gravelly voice. "I'm fine. Please take your—" She started hacking again. It sounded like a wicked troll was camping inside her lungs. "Pardon me. Please take your seat. My name is Mrs. Saint Johnabelle." She looked at me. "Young lady, let us continue our introductions with you."

When I looked into my teacher's eyes, I felt like I was being swallowed by a cosmic death worm. I mumbled, "Nephele Weather," and looked away.

"Lovely to meet you, Nephele," she said. "Now—"

"Sorry I'm late!" A boy with a booming voice ran into the room. He was wearing a tuxedo jacket over a royal-blue soccer shirt that said ITALY in huge letters. "Just buzzed in from Los Alamos. . . ." The late kid stumbled backward. His backpack snagged on the door. His jeans were torn clear across both knees.

"Los Alamos," said Serrafin, looking at one of her papers. "And you are . . . ?"

The late kid unsnagged his bag. "Sorry! I meant Las Vegas. Man, am I tweaked to be here. And also nervous." His black curls fell into his eyes. He swung his head to get them out, which worked for half a second, and then they fell again. Although there was only one of this kid, it felt like there were at least three.

"Your name?" asked Serrafin.

"J. J. Shipreck."

"Fine, J.J. Please find a seat—"

"Actually, it's Jeremiah Jackson."

"Fine. Jeremiah, please take a seat—"

"Call me Jazz. I can't believe I said Los Alamos. Los Alamos is a laboratory in the desert where they design nuclear weapons," said . . . What was this boy calling himself? "Definitely not that desert. Different desert."

While the late kid bubbled with random factoids, he re-tied

his shoes, which were made of light blue velvet, or possibly suede.

"We're off to an odd beginning," said Serrafin as she guided the late kid to the empty seat at my lab table.

When I looked at him, he winked.

I cranked up the levels on my force field. It was going to be another long year.

As I walked into the Big Blue Wave, a fat black alley cat leapt out from California History, arched its back and hissed at me. I made claw hands and hissed back so hard I saw spit fly. The cat darted past me and ran out onto Main Street.

Dad was standing behind the counter scratching the same snow-white neckbeard he'd had yesterday. A style that has never looked good on anyone, I thought. Then I thought, *Bleh.* That was supposed to be a joke, to improve my mood. But thinking rude things about my parents, even true rude things, just made me feel more evil. At least he was spinning death metal. Death metal singers sound like they're barfing hot eels. The way my life was going, that was a skill I wanted to acquire.

"Fi!" called Dad. "How's high school?"

I didn't have the energy to lie. "High school is sheer, un-adulterated hell. Hell, I tell you."

Dad said, "Your honesty always gives me a boost."

I wanted to curl up in my father's arms and bawl. Instead, I heard even more truth slipping out despite myself. "My life is a cautionary tale about a girl who bakes a magic pie and then she eats it and her face falls off."

"It's like that?" said Dad, in a sweet voice. "What's wrong with your life, Fi?"

I didn't know what to tell him, so I just leaned on the counter and watched him scratching his neck, which made me want to scratch mine. That beard could not be comfortable.

"Maybe take a break from thinking so hard," said Dad. "Watch stupid cat videos online."

Stupid cat videos? Every aspect of that suggestion disturbed me. But I said, "Thanks, Dad. I really, really love you."

He said, "Aw, kiddo," and came around the counter and wrapped me in a hug. His band T-shirt smelled like coffee and Dadness. I never wanted to leave that exact spot. "I love you too, freshman," he said. "And hey. Don't stress it. High school only gets better from here."

I looked in his eyes, which were blacker than black, like the eyes of your favorite teddy bear, and I felt incredibly sad. My father didn't know me anymore. He didn't know me at all.

And I hadn't even checked his brain holes yet. I couldn't bear to know how much bigger and more ravenous they'd become.

I let Dad go and clomped upstairs, trying not to weep. Chicago wouldn't tell me I was thinking too hard. Quite the opposite. You never could catch a break with a fellow semi-immortal.

And I didn't need a break. I needed someone to yell at me

for being an epic failure and tell me how to save myself and my poor parents from the mess I'd made instead of expanding it exponentially every single stupid time I tried.

"Look who's back," said Chicago.

"Back and forth," I said, "just like you."

"If you don't fix that meathead Dirk Angus soon, your parents' brains will become two useless blobs of cellular mush. What does Oona Gold say about how to handle it when your botched time-travel experiment annihilates the only people on earth who love you?"

I sighed. I hadn't opened *Time Travel for Love & Profit* in years. I should've shelved that book in Fiction when I had the chance.

"You have no plan," said Chicago. "No past, no future, no nothing. What a disaster."

My best friend was really relishing her inner bluntness today. As I made myself a cup of tea, I thought about how much I used to love Chicago's bluntness. I used to think that with the combination of Chicago's brutal honesty, my love of math and my systematic application of the scientific method à la Serrafin, Dirk Angus would reveal the secrets of the universe.

Of course, Dirk Angus had revealed a secret. A secret I'd been slow to accept. In a decade of time-travel research, I'd gotten on a first-name basis with the universe's dark side. I'd learned that it won't hesitate to throw a wrench right at your head.

I inhaled the steam from my tea. It smelled like the wet forest. I decided to wander.

"What's the plan?" asked Chicago as I walked away.

I said, "Read romance novels until I fall asleep."

"Sounds productive," she said.

"It isn't supposed to be productive," I said. "It's supposed to prevent me from feeding myself to the sharks. They'll be migrating soon, you know. The great whites, the leopard sharks, the Pacific angelsh—"

"You're changing the subject, Fi," said Chicago, and I knew this. I'd decided to wait until tomorrow's lunch with Serrafin to start working on Dirk Angus 10.0. As usual, I couldn't fathom why my timeship app had failed. And I couldn't think about it yet. My brain felt like it had been run through a meat grinder. Any information I force-fed it today would only ooze out in a useless trickle, like nap drool.

I was curled up in the beanbag in Poetry, reading a book called *Dirty Limericks for Every Occasion* ("There once was a young lass called Myrtle / Whose fields were especially fertile / She had taters galore / And parsnips to store / And her melons spilled out of her girdle!"), when I heard a thud and looked up.

A boy was gathering the stack of books he'd dropped on the floor. It was the late kid from my homeroom.

I reinforced my force field, took a sip of tea and kept reading.

"Hey!" he said, and I looked up again. He pointed at me. "You go to my school, right? I'm Jazz."

I said, "I know who you are."

117

The late kid pushed his dark curls out of his eyes and raised one of his eyebrows. That's when I noticed that his eyes were violet-blue and luminous, like watercolor soaking into bright white paper or a rare photoluminescent fish.

He asked, "What's your name?"

It felt strange to still be looking at him, but his purple eyes were locked onto mine, and it was impossible to look away. It was highly aggravating. I closed my eyes to break the lock and said, "Nephele."

"Nephele? Huh," he said. "Like the Greek goddess."

"She's not a goddess," I said. "She's a cloud nymph."

Okay: I had just said the words "cloud nymph" to a boy in reference to myself. Now I was forced to imagine the late kid imagining me as an alluring, supernatural maiden who flew around seducing roaming humans, which was preposterous, because no one would ever imagine me that way. Although with eyes like that, the late kid could definitely get into trouble with some semi-immortals. Not semi-immortals like me, of course. You never see humans getting hypnotized by gap-toothed nymphs in hoodies tweaking apps on their smartphones. Or reading books of dirty limericks, for that matter.

The late kid pointed at me again and wagged his finger. "That's what it is."

It's impossible to feel normal in a beanbag. "That's what what is?" I asked as I tried to adjust myself so I wouldn't be talking to this boy from between my knees.

"You look like someone," he said. "A cloud nymph."

Somehow I sank deeper into the stuffed sack. "Sure," I

said. "I resemble that scampy sprite you used to know who wore a crown made of marigolds and had crystal charms dangling from her bare ankles." It was imperative that I extract myself from the blob of beans. Worst. Chair. Ever.

"Can I help you?" asked the late kid.

Finally I popped out, splashing hot tea on my pants in the process. I said, "Boogers."

As I headed downstairs, I heard the late kid call, "See you, cloud nymph. . . ."

I felt highly annoyed. Leaving the bookshop was not my afternoon plan. I was supposed to fall asleep dreaming about heroes with glorious dreadlocks and kisses like candy until the shop closed and Dad woke me up. Now what was I supposed to do? Go home and obsess about my epic failure? Interrogate my zombie mother about my birth certificate for the ten millionth time? Why was it that every time I made a plan, that plan developed a mind of its own and ran off, wild and free, to do whatever the hell it wanted?

And who had purple eyes?

Purple eyes.

Purple.

CHAPTER 9

Dirk Angus Rips a Bodice

The next morning, Mom was leaning beside the antique mirror in the vestibule by our front door, her silver waves washing over her shoulders, her turquoise eyes boring into me with their usual combination of love and epic worrying, as I attempted to zip my overstuffed backpack. For my tenth second day of freshman year, I was bringing as many books as I could carry to discuss with Serrafin at lunch. The astrophysics textbook that reminded her of late evenings studying in graduate school with her true love, her husband, Alvin, who was her "intellectual equal—almost"; the artificial intelligence books that had helped us teach Dirk Angus 9.0 how to make increasingly sophisticated choices; and a ton of other stuff, too. I didn't know where we'd begin our work this year, but maybe something would inspire us.

"You know, Fi," said Mom, "I read online that Redwood Cove High School has a coding club for girls. Maybe—"

"No," I interrupted.

"Fi," said Mom.

"No thank you," I said, trying not to feel angry at my mother for assuming she knew what was best for me when she had no clue what my life was like anymore—no clue!—and feeling angry anyway.

"You're so wonderful, Fi. But if you don't make an effort this year, people aren't going to chase you down and beg to get to know you. High school is an opportunity for you to make new—"

"Could you please remind me of my birthday?"

"March 11," she said.

"The year! The *year*," I said. "I forgot the year, for some reason."

Mom stopped speaking, stopped moving. She stopped breathing, practically.

The parental petrification would last about seventeen minutes. More this year, I assumed. This was the first time I'd poked the black hole beast since my most recent timeship malfunction. Anyway, it'd last long enough for me to leave the house without being interrogated, like if I didn't make a friend soon, my rightful fate was to become a loner sociopath who lived her whole life in her parents' attic. Believe me, I was aware of the possibility.

And also, yes: I was evil.

Totally.

* * *

I was sitting at my lab table before third period, waiting for Serrafin, when a girl with a blond shag walked into the classroom carrying a pair of roller skates over her shoulder. She was giraffe levels of tall, and she was wearing a hoodie, like me. When she saw me looking, she smiled. I felt like I'd been smacked by a sunbeam. She walked directly to the empty seat at my lab table. My jaw locked. My fists clenched. When she looked at me again, her eyes popped open wider. Her eyes were the color of the sky. Not the actual sky, which on the coast is mostly gray and moody. The blue sky in picture books about bumblebees and chirpy baby chicks.

"Were you saving this seat?" she asked. "I can switch. . . ."

I shook my head.

"Rad. I'm Airika. We just moved here from Sausalito."

The girl with the roller skates looked at me like I was supposed to say something. But this was my tenth freshman year. I knew better than to fall for her trap. I didn't think she was setting a trap on purpose; the roller skater seemed really nice. Everyone seems really nice when they're trying to make friends. I unzipped my heavy backpack and dug around in it like I was searching for something.

"Quiet, all," said Serrafin. "We have an enormous amount of territory to cover this year. Let's get started."

After class, I felt the roller skater trying to catch my eye. I pretended to be absorbed in a book called *Quantum Computing: A Quiet Revolution* until she left. When the room was empty, I went to Serrafin's desk.

"Mrs. Saint Johnabelle, do you have lunch plans?"

Serrafin was shuffling through drawers, gathering keys, putting on her trench coat, exchanging her eyeglasses for sunglasses.

"What I mean is—well, it would be nice to get to know you better—"

"Run along to the cafeteria, dear," said Serrafin, coughing.

"Could I—have lunch with you?"

"How kind of you, Nephele. Unfortunately, that's not possible today, as I have an appointment."

I didn't move. Mrs. Saint Johnabelle nodded at my lab table, at my ten-ton backpack, and asked, "Are you forgetting something?"

I collected it and followed her out of the classroom feeling deflated. Then Serrafin locked the door, gave me a polite smile and left without looking back.

I eyed the cafeteria.

If you go halfway to somewhere, then halfway again, then halfway again, and again and again, you never arrive. I decided it was worth a try, but quickly discovered that it was difficult to cross smaller and smaller distances with feet the size of container ships.

As soon as I was over the cafeteria threshold, I headed for an empty table where I could eat my burrito and pretend to be invisible. On my way, I passed the late kid, who was surrounded by a crowd.

"Can't tell you how it's done. Magicians' code of honor," he said. He was wearing ripped jeans, an orange suit jacket and a checkered fedora. Like a nightclub singer. But not a fancy nightclub singer. One who lived in a repurposed school bus with velvet curtains and a bare-boobed mermaid painted on its door (a housing situation that isn't unheard of here on the California coast).

"Dude, was that magic or science?" asked a boy with a wide face, cool khaki skin and a tie-dyed bandana that was knotted at the back of his head. He was wearing baggy shorts with black long underwear underneath them.

The blond roller skater was standing next to him. "Rex is right," she said. "That magic trick looked like a science experiment."

"True, Airika," said the late kid in a carnival-y way. "Where does science end and magic begin? The miracle of life itself is a great science experiment. Or is it a great magic trick? We've never quite figured it out. We only know it works."

I took a seat and unwrapped my burrito. So Jeremiah Jackson Shipreck fancied himself a scientist. I sniffed.

"Do another trick!" somebody yelled.

The late kid yelled back, "That is precisely my intention."

He asked a volunteer for an object. The roller skater handed him her phone. He whipped off his fedora with a dramatic wrist-flip and used it to cover the phone. Then he whistled a funny tune, something between happy and sad, and said, "Airika, please remove the hat." When she did, everybody screamed. In the palm of his hand, there was a flame.

I squinted. It was a colored flame. A flame that was *changing colors*. Red. Green. Blue.

Jazz Shipreck looked around like he was searching for someone. When our eyes locked, he extended his flaming hand like he was giving it to me. Then he raised one eyebrow and bowed.

As I ate my burrito, I read a romance novel that I'd tucked inside a book about astrophysics. *The Lascivious Life of Lili Lenore* featured buoyant bosoms, beads of sweat, things that were soft, things that were hard, things that got whispered, tongues in places I wasn't sure tongues should be. I was wondering how "lusciously savage thrashing" could take place on the narrow ledge of a miles-deep canyon without the two people involved being preoccupied about accidentally plummeting into that canyon, when I heard, "I've got a magic trick for you," and I yelped.

The late kid glided into the seat beside me. How was it that this boy always appeared when I was reading about writhing and jiggling?

"Did I scare you?" he said. "My fault."

To avoid getting locked into his eyes—did all magicians have mesmerizing eyes? It would help them trick people, probably—I looked toward the salad bar. "I've got no interest in your pseudoscience, Jeremiah Shipreck."

"Pseudo?" he asked.

"Pseudo is a prefix that means *fake*," I said.

"I know what pseudo means. I like that you just drop it into a convo. Wham. Greek prefix. Deal with it."

Don't look in his eyes, I thought. *Don't look in his eyes.*

But I really wanted to look in his eyes.

Blue with purple swirls like your favorite marble. The shocking blue of the ocean on a bright October day. Locked! I was locked! My heartbeat pounded in my ears. My neck was hot.

"So you're into science," said Jazz.

"Into science," I said. "You say that like science is some innocent hobby. Doing magic tricks for children."

The late kid said, "Pick a number."

I sniffed. "Do you want to be more specific?"

"Yes, Nephele Weather. I do want to be more specific. Pick your favorite number."

So he knew my last name now. So what? I said, "Seventy."

He opened his mouth, then closed it. "You—okay. Several questions. Uh . . ."

A familiar feeling was wriggling just beneath the surface of my skin. Like I'd done something wrong and didn't know what it was. "What?" I said. "This is your trick, pal, not mine."

The late kid looked at the ceiling and said, "Pal."

I wrapped the remains of my burrito in foil and shoved my books into my backpack.

"No, hang on," he said. "Wait. So you weren't supposed to tell me the number. . . ." I was about to interrupt him, but he was holding up his hand, like he saw that coming. "My fault. I didn't tell you not to tell me. Far more urgent question: Why is seventy your favorite number?"

I stood. It took considerable muscle to swing my backpack over my shoulder. When I did, I said, "Because it's the smallest weird number."

The late kid made his lips into an O shape. His eyelids lowered like somebody yanked the shades. "What's a weird number?"

I walked away without answering him. This was a brazen attempt to penetrate my force field. What nerve. How presumptuous. What else did people say in a British accent when they were indignant?

Incidentally, where was I going? I didn't know, but when I got there, that's where I'd be. And since lunch period wasn't over yet, it was just gonna have to be the unisex bathroom.

I leaned against the pink tile wall facing the stalls. I was still hungry, but the thought of eating a burrito in a room full of toilets was somehow unappetizing. YOU SUCK was scrawled on the stall across from me. I couldn't tell if the evidence of someone else's bad mood made me feel better or worse.

I unzipped my backpack to find something to read, and pulled out *Time Travel for Love & Profit*. I hadn't read it in forever and I didn't miss it. But I did miss the excited feeling it had given me all those years ago, which is probably why I'd packed it. I wondered if it would be possible to feel that way about time travel ever again. I flipped to the index, to the Failure section.

> *Failure, advantages of:* 23, 44–47, 70, 88–90,
> 127–131
> *Failure, bringing it on yourself:* 1, 3, 5–8, 12, 25–
> 34, 40, 66, 72–85, 87, 99, 101–111, 122–128, 131
> *Failure, coping with:* 3, 12–13, 34–35, 66–67, 89,
> 100, 122–125
> *Failure, deciding to embrace:* 5, 28, 77, 103–105

I shut the book. Who was I kidding? I'd memorized every single thing Oona Gold wrote about failure. Failure was inevitable. Failure was my greatest teacher. Failure was FUN!

I considered flushing my inspirational guide down the toilet.

Instead, I rested my head against the wall and thought about the late kid. Why was he talking to me? What was happening to my force field? Why was I thinking about him, anyway?

It didn't matter. I wouldn't let him fool me—him or anybody. This wasn't my first face-plant. I knew how freshman year turned out.

CHAPTER 10

The Week of the Toilet Burrito

For the next couple of days, Mrs. Saint Johnabelle was out sick. At lunch I skipped the cafeteria and went straight to the unisex bathroom, where I ate my burrito on the toilet. Even then, I knew I had reached a low point. On Friday, when Serrafin was out yet again, I skipped the toilet burrito and went home sick myself.

Our living room sofa is squishy and itchy, like a shaggy hot dog bun. That's why it's piled with extra-firm pillows you can wedge behind you for support and silky blankets to wrap around you for smoothness. If you get the balance right, it's almost like being comfortable. Would buying a new sofa be easier? Perhaps. The easy way is often overrated.

Mom tucked a velvet quilt around my feet and kissed my forehead, her silver waves brushing against my cheeks. "You don't seem sick," she said.

"How would you know?" I mumbled.

"Excuse me, Your Highness," she said. "I'll leave you in peace after lunch."

My mother was leaving? Abandoning me? "Sorry, Mom; I'm sorry. I'm just, you know, sick. Where are you going?"

"There's a reading tonight," she said. "Gotta dig out the folding chairs, hose 'em down."

Of course. The Big Blue Wave hosted readings on the first Friday of every month. The fall season kicked off with the school year.

I asked, "Who's reading?"

"Well, tonight it'll be more of a slide show," said Mom. "One of those old black-and-white photographers your father goes gaga over is passing through town from Chicago."

I perked up. Harry Callahan, who had made *Chicago, 1955,* was dead. But he used to live in Chicago. If this photographer was old, maybe they'd known each other.

"What's his name?" I asked.

"Clyde Watkins," she said.

"I'll be there. If I was feeling better, I mean, I'd be there." I coughed.

Mom squeezed my toes through the quilt. "You'll be okay without me?"

I nodded. But I'd had the same question for years now—a question about Chicago. And Clyde Watkins might have an opinion if I could get up the nerve to ask.

My question was: Could a photograph maybe, possibly, have a soul?

The answer would be as irrelevant to time travel as it had

130

always been, but I'd never stopped being curious about it. If an object could have a soul. Or what a soul was, even, exactly. And Serrafin had taught me to take my questions seriously, so until she came back to school and we got back to work on Dirk Angus, I'd just have to research this one.

Funny. Even during the Week of the Toilet Burrito, I could still get excited about a question. I may have been an evil, friendless failure, but apparently, that part of me was indestructible. It wasn't much, I supposed, but it was something.

If Mom found my miraculous recovery in time for the Clyde Watkins reading surprising, she didn't show it. Of course, me begging to go to a social event on a Friday evening instead of staying cooped up in my bedroom having "screen time" probably didn't exactly break her heart.

"Feeling better, Fi?" called Dad as I walked inside. Near the counter, he was setting up his type of screen—the big white one he used to show slides.

"Kinda," I said, forcing a sniffle. I stretched out on the ratty yellow couch, facing the window to Main Street, and was silently rehearsing my question for Clyde Watkins when a blur on roller skates whizzed by, caught my eye and tipped high on her toes to stop.

Before I could flee, Airika was rolling into the Big Blue Wave. "What a coincidence, Fi!" she said, out of breath.

"What did you call me?"

"Jazzy told us your nickname. He heard your mom yelling

from the car when she picked you up today. And me and Rex were like, yeah. Fi! That fits her. How are you feeling?"

"Hey, Fi!" shouted Dad. "Tell your friend to stay for the reading tonight."

"That sounds rad, sir!" shouted Airika, waving her entire arm.

Dad waved back. "We've got cookies!"

I sighed. Dad was obviously drunk with glee at the sight of me talking to one of my peers.

Airika pointed out the window. "Hey! It's Jazzy with his monster bike! Did you know he builds bicycles out of stuff he finds in dumpsters? He's teaching Rex. It's so rad."

When Airika skated out of the shop, every cell in my body relaxed. I felt like a dog after an intruder has passed.

So the late kid builds bikes out of trash, I thought as I clomped upstairs to hide. Of course he does. Something I've never heard of anyone doing that instantly sounds like the most interesting thing anyone has ever done.

Well, the roller skater and the dumpster diver would make an adorable couple. Although it seemed like she was already going out with that dude who wore the bandana and never smiled—Rex. At school, they were always together. Airika probably had multiple boyfriends. She was the type of girl everybody fell in love with. Confident and smiley and all that. It was only a matter of time until she realized I was aggressively weird and didn't want to be associated with me. I grabbed a mug and a packet of tea. "Ask me if I care, Chicago."

"Obviously," she said, "you don't."

The slide projector was one of those outdated machines Dad loved. As it shot light through each slide and transferred its image to the screen, it wheezed like it was on its deathbed.

Most of Clyde Watkins's photographs were of people. A man with sagging eyes, holding a briefcase that looked ready to burst. A child with a dirty face, peering in a shop window. A woman with a broken heel, frowning at the moon.

The view from upstairs was better than I would've expected. I had to stay up there to avoid Jazz and Airika, who were sitting together in the front row.

Clyde Watkins was sitting in a wheelchair facing the audience. He was stocky with a white mustache, and he wore a scarf and a vest with many pockets. He spoke in a buoyant voice that made me think of a tugboat floating on choppy waves. He didn't sound nearly as old as he looked.

"They called us street photographers. We snapped pictures of life as it was in that moment. People who weren't posing. People in a world lit by the sun. Getting on the subway to go to work. On their way to celebrations, coming home from ugly days. In the city. In the weather. We loved shadows. We loved light. But most of all we loved people. I suppose I'm old enough to speak in the past tense and say 'we' instead of 'I'—especially considering that the fellow photographers to whom I'm referring are mostly dead. What are they gonna do about it?"

The crowd laughed. Clyde Watkins shifted in his wheelchair, like he wanted to find a more comfortable position. Dad hustled to help him.

As Clyde Watkins showed more slides, I thought about how people are like cameras, recording the moments of our lives. If only I could print pictures of the things I'd witnessed over the years. The impossible things you'd have to see to believe. Like once, when I was shooting through the wormhole in the quantum foam, I saw a redwood tree two hundred feet tall shrink in a glittery flash and become a seed again, and then blow away in loop-de-loops on the wind. And once I saw a baby hawk being un-born, its crackling eggshell sucking shut around it.

But even if I could print pictures of my time travel, you'd have to wonder. Photographers could play tricks on you. Like how Harry Callahan had made Chicago with the double exposure. What if I only saw those things because I wanted to see them? What if my mind had made them up? Pictures could make you believe in impossible things. Or maybe they showed you that the things you thought were impossible aren't.

Eventually, Clyde Watkins gave Dad a signal like he was slitting his own throat, and Dad flipped on the lights. The thirty or so people in the audience clapped.

"Clyde," said Dad, "a few of these folks may want to ask you some questions. That okay?"

Again, I silently practiced my question for Clyde Watkins. *Do you think a photograph can have a soul?* And after everybody left, I'd introduce him to Chicago.

I mouthed my question silently, over and over, to be sure I wouldn't clam up. When I tuned back in to the questions, Clyde Watkins's face was even brighter than before, like someone had switched on his whole power grid. "Yes! Photography is a sort of magic. I've always thought that. Young man, what's your name?"

"I go by Jazz."

"Jazz," said Clyde Watkins. "A name that suggests the joy of improvisation. I have an extra camera here in my bag. A digital one I can't figure out how to use. That's an exaggeration, but I hate it. You can take too many pictures, too fast. You think you've got infinite opportunities to get the shot. The constraints of film are a better reflection of the human condition. You get a couple shots, and after that . . . poof! Your moment is gone. Film requires you to pay attention the first time. Besides that, it costs too much and today it's as good as dead, like me. Jazz, after that whopping endorsement . . ." Clyde Watkins fished in a sack and pulled out a camera with a long lens. "Could I convince you to take this digital nuisance off my hands? They tell me it's top of the line."

He handed the camera to Jazz, who smiled in his off-kilter way, like a mobile that shouldn't be balanced but convinced you that it was, while the audience gave another round of applause.

I spent quite a while in the upstairs bathroom, washing my face. I wasn't sure what was bothering me, but something was, and washing my face usually made me feel better. As I dried my chin and cheeks with a paper towel, I decided to ask Clyde Watkins my question some other time. Slip out the back door of the bookshop, cats be damned, and go home.

As I was leaving the bathroom, Airika almost crashed into me. "Fi! I was looking for you. The cookies are by the cash register."

"No thanks," I said, and tried to get around her.

She said, "Aw, really?"

I wanted to scream, "Will you stop being so nice to me, Airika? As soon as you get to know me, you're gonna realize you hate me and flee! Let me save us both some time."

Airika tilted her head. "I'm going to *hate* you?"

I could not believe I had just said that out loud.

Jazz stepped out of the Poetry aisle, holding his new camera. I wanted to—hmm, how should I put this?

Die.

He said, "Hey, Fi."

My neck was on fire. I ran downstairs and pushed through the crowd, passing close enough to Clyde Watkins to notice that he smelled like cigar smoke. When I opened the screen door, I nearly smashed a cat. Its screech seared my ears as I ran through the parking lot into the night. I'd text my parents in a few minutes, tell them I felt like throwing up.

As I hiked up the hill toward home, foghorns moaned their bleak tune and the wind shot through my clothes. I was shivering. My sneakers crunched sand and fallen fruit and foliage. Nature and its garbage in the dark.

Suddenly, I felt incredibly stupid.

Seriously.

I mean, seriously—what was wrong with me? Was this who I was now? Someone who exploded at people and stormed off in the middle of sentences?

But how could I let them be nice to me? How could I pretend to be a normal teenager when I wasn't?

I'd never been normal. That's why I'd built Dirk Angus in the first place. Now I was worse than abnormal. I was the monster my mother had sworn I wasn't when I was little, and my aggressively weird talent for math had made me stand out.

The cats knew.

I walked up our porch steps with their splintery cracks and their peeling paint and inhaled the smells of decaying fish and decomposing wood and watched the Main Street lights shimmer as the fog settled over Redwood Cove. Everything was disintegrating thanks to my enemy, time, plus the wind that never stopped and my next-door neighbor, the sea. The exact things that made my home the most beautiful place I could dream of were the things that would rot it to ruins.

And if my time machine kept failing, I'd never save the earth, and pretty soon humans would suffocate the ocean with plastic bags, and climate change would boil us all to death.

Everything was going to be obliterated. Everything.

I rubbed my arms to keep warm. Was that it? Was I afraid of dying now?

Or was I afraid of living forever? Eternal life in a fog that got thicker and thicker until I didn't care where I was going anymore, because I'd never arrive?

In the fog, I saw a blob of someone walking up the hill, and for some reason I let myself imagine it was Wylie Buford. I remembered that afternoon all those years ago, when we'd chatted in the bookshop. How I could see, clear as a clean picture window, Wylie and me becoming friends. Before my first trip in my timeship. When I'd been nothing more complicated than my aggressively weird self.

How was Wylie doing now?

Yes, I could take out my phone and search for him online. I could find out where he went to college, where he lived, maybe even what job he had, whether he had children, who his friends were. But the types of things people posted online would never tell me what I wanted to know.

Which was: How was Wylie actually doing now? How was he really, truly doing?

How did Wylie Buford turn out?

CHAPTER 11

Just Because a Girl Is Evil Doesn't Mean She Can't Be *Nice*

Monday morning I saw Jazz and Rex outside the high school messing with their bikes, which looked like Frankensteins of lots of different bikes. That must have been what Airika was talking about with the dumpster-diving bike-building thing. Rex's had a huge tire in the front and a small one in the back, and the body was spray-painted gold. Jazz's was blue with chunky tires, and the handlebars were coiled like a ram's horns.

I was still beyond mortified about making a fool of myself at the bookshop Friday night. Jazz must've thought I was a big, fat nutball, or a deep-fried cheeseball, or some other ball-shaped thing it was best to keep at a healthy distance. I pulled up my hood and walked out of my way to avoid them.

When second period ended, I ran past the blur of kids and lockers as announcements rained down from the speakers.

The sound kept blinking on and off, chopping the words and making them incomprehensible. I was desperate to get to third period and see Serrafin, aching for our first lunch together so I could get to work. I was almost there when I heard, "Hey, Fi!"

Jazz was leaning against the lockers, smiling in his uneven way, wearing his signature outfit of tuxedo jacket and ripped jeans. One of his knees was bent; he was tapping his foot on a locker door. His body was long and bendy. He looked like a praying mantis on its way to the insect prom.

"Nephele Weather, your parents' bookshop has an outstanding poetry section. As William Blake wrote, *To see the world in a grain of sand* . . . wait. What's next? I forget the next line. But the rhyming part is, *Hold infinity in the palm of your hand.* Poetry puts personal problems in perspective." He looked at the ceiling and smiled. "Peter Piper picked a peck of personal problems. . . ."

Peter Piper? Before I could stop myself, I blurted out, "Who *are* you?"

He said, "My name is Jeremiah—"

"No, no, I mean, did you just move here?"

He said, "Did you?"

I said, "No."

The late kid ran a hand through his curls. They were so black. Like black licorice. He said, "I totally know you didn't just move here. I was trying for . . . yeah. That was failed banter."

He said that word. "Banter."

I said, "If that was banter, it needs a Brobdingnagian amount of work."

Jazz got this glimmer in the purple pools of his eyes, like there was a fat, gold koi swimming around in them, and he wagged his finger. "Brobdingnagian. Huge. Like the giants in *Gulliver's Travels*." He snapped. "I wish I'd said that." He looked at the ceiling again, shaking his head.

I let myself stare at him for another second or two, felt a wave of something between hunger and nausea, and decided to leave before I accidentally exploded at him for no reason.

There's a scene in *Thirsty for Thrills* when the heroine says, "I'm tired of playing the victim. Sit down and shut up and let me show you how it's done."

And Dirk Angus holds up his hands. "Don't shoot," he says. "I'm only in love with you."

That was banter.

There was no reason for *Thirsty for Thrills* to be in my head right now.

Jazz flinched. "Ah! I remember what I wanted to tell you. A weird number is a natural number that is abundant but not semi-perfect. Seventy is the smallest one. That's why it's special."

Wow. I folded my arms into a tight pretzel. "You have no idea what you're talking about, do you?"

"No idea," said Jazz.

What was I supposed to say? Thank you for researching my favorite number online?

Holy jalapeños. *He did that.* I couldn't help it: I fled. I walked as quickly as possible into Serrafin's classroom. Was he behind me? I would not check. I had to check.

But no. There was no room in my brain to be nervous about the late kid or his mesmerizing eyes or his iffy banter!

Because it was finally third period. Serrafin and I were finally about to create Dirk Angus 10.0 so I could bust out of the present and grow up the way I was supposed to all along.

Poetry?

Peter Piper puked a peck of poetry. Peter Pan poked his purple pupil. Perky people pummeled them with pumpkins.

Pigeons pooped, penguins peed. . . .

Yeah.

So . . .

Right.

When I got to the classroom, the principal, Dr. Bellows, was sitting on top of Mrs. Saint Johnabelle's desk, swinging her legs and talking to a skinny guy with a goatee and glasses. Another substitute? I wanted to weep. And did Serrafin really need the principal's butt print on her attendance sheet? I took a seat at my usual lab table, and Airika sat beside me.

Which was surprising. When our eyes met, Airika didn't do the full sunbeam smile; it was more of a trickle-of-sunlight-through-a-dirty-window smile. I didn't know how to react. And I was preoccupied about Dr. Bellows, which is probably why

I found myself making a What's-up-with-the-principal-being-here? face at Airika. Airika made an I-have-no-idea face back.

Then Jazz walked into the classroom and waved at Airika and me. I felt tingly, like he had quietly rung the prettiest little bell.

Meanwhile, the principal and goatee man were chatting about the fall assembly. The location of the earthquake kits. Things goatee man did not need to know.

Dr. Bellows slid off the desk and clapped. "Listen up, freshpersons!" The principal's announcement voice was always alarming. She could be announcing that we're all getting free doughnuts for life and I'd still feel the need to duck and cover. "Warm welcome here for Mr. Zuluti. Just spent two years teaching in Japan. Redwood Cove scored a genuine world traveler; who knows why. But here he is."

"And I couldn't be happier about it," said the man.

Um? My hand shot up.

"Plenty of time to ask all your questions about Japan," said Dr. Bellows, and she turned to leave.

I stood. "Where's Serrafin? I mean where's Mrs. . . ."

Dr. Bellows rubbed her forehead. "I'll be notifying your parents by email this afternoon."

Airika said, "Notifying them about what?"

The principal looked at goatee man. Goatee man clasped his hands. "Mrs. Saint Johnabelle was, well—she was incredibly brave." Goatee man looked at Dr. Bellows. Dr. Bellows looked at the ground. Goatee man scratched his ear. "It is with great sadness that . . . well." He paused. "After battling a long illness, Mrs. Saint Johnabelle has died."

There were sounds. Not quite whispering. Shifting. Shifting.

Airika said, "No! When?"

Goatee man said, "Early last week."

Early last *week*? A long illness?

Nobody told me. *Nobody told me!*

Of course, why would they tell me? Everyone thought I'd only known Serrafin for two days. . . . And what about Serrafin?

Did she die without knowing me?

I was still standing. My throat was swelling shut. I felt a hand on my back. Airika. She must've thought I was deranged, between exploding at her at the Big Blue Wave and making a big deal about somebody I should've barely known.

Goatee man was looking at me with giant eyeballs, like he wanted to comfort me—like he could possibly comfort me, or be anything other than a terrible imposter.

Then goatee man asked everybody to take out paper and a pen. I was shocked. I looked around through blurry eyes. Everybody was doing it, and it was totally inappropriate. I saw the teacher coming toward me and I bolted out of the classroom and down the hallway and out the school's front doors.

I ran past the bike racks into the redwood forest and kept running. My breath stung my chest and stuck in my throat, and dry sticks snapped beneath my feet. My stomach was lurching like a sinking ship. I ran until my legs were weak, and

I was standing on the edge of the cliff, and all I heard was the pounding ocean and the screeching hawks.

The screeching echoed. The universe didn't care what happened to me or to anyone. It was going to strand me here. Take everyone I loved and leave me stranded in the forest, alone.

Maddy Weather was walking down the path from Highway 1 toward the high school. She was wearing slouchy white pants with a grass stain on one knee and a hand-knitted sweater that was spilling off of one shoulder. Her silver waves were blowing in the wind, and her paint-splattered sandals were older than me, including the ten extra years nobody counted.

I was sitting on the redwood stump, waiting for her. I knew they'd call Mom. She was the only person I wanted to see. As soon as I felt her cool palm on my face, I started crying. She sat beside me on the stump and dried my tears with her thumbs. She didn't ask any questions. I couldn't believe my mother had ever annoyed me. She was irreplaceable.

I felt the heat in my belly and inside my rib cage. Rage, frustration, hopelessness. Death. I felt Mom's fingers touching my skin. Life.

Mom said, "Let's go home."

I felt my feet inside my sneakers taking one step, then another. I felt them landing on the packed earth, the hard sidewalk. I saw flowers with dried faces, dull and full of seeds. Everything living was dying.

Except me. I was living inside a body that was tricking time. So why did it feel like time was tricking me?

Inside our house, it smelled like spicy chili. I needed to take off my sneakers and I wanted to say something to Mom, but I couldn't move or speak. My stomach was still swaying, burning, turning in on itself, like bits of it were trying to squirm away. Mom was looking in the antique mirror, adjusting her floppy sweater. She didn't know how old she was when I was born. She didn't know how old I was supposed to be. My experiment was ruining her. It was ruining me. Wrapping us in blackness and white noise.

I'd never thought it would come to this. Time travel hadn't felt like a game for a long time, but the consequences had always seemed reversible. My timeship app was far from perfect, but it had seemed to promise me infinite tries to get things right.

But that was an illusion. Time *would* run out if I kept looping. Or at least my life would become less and less recognizable. I'd never wanted to grow up with my experiment only half-complete. But could I stay fourteen forever? And watch everybody I love—

Mom spun around quickly, like a fox or a sea otter or some other animal who takes action the second it decides something. "Let's bake cookies. It's been so long since we've done that together. We have those autumn-leaf cookie cutters. We'll make colored icing. You know what we can use to make the red? Beets. I've always wanted to make red dye with beets."

"Beets," I repeated. "Won't it taste weird?"

"Maybe," said Mom, smiling.

I said, "Don't die, Mom."

Mom's smile disappeared. "So *that's* it." She wrapped me in her arms, which were wiry and strong. "Oh, Fi. With any luck, I won't die for a very long time." When she pulled me away to look at me, all I saw were wrinkles. Hundreds of them branching like rivers. Like cracked earth. The map of time on my mother's face. Maddy Weather was being *eaten* by time. I closed my eyes.

Mrs. Saint Johnabelle was the one who had told me that we should pay attention to our questions. The time-travel question had chosen me. And for a decade, the answer had been so close. I could see it peeking at me through every window. Hiding between the sentences in every book. Lurking in the misty background of every picture frame.

I *cared* about this question. No matter how miserable I got, I still believed I could find the answer. Serrafin believed it, too. I'd promised her I wouldn't give up, and I'd meant it. I needed to finish the work I'd started almost as much as I needed to fix Mom and Dad.

But I didn't have forever to do it. I couldn't handle forever. Forever was just too much.

I followed Mom into the kitchen and sat at the green table. Mom opened the refrigerator and pulled out a couple of beets. This is it, isn't it, I thought. My final battle with the universe. Dirk Angus 10.0 would be my last attempt to go back in time. If I failed again, I'd have to break my promise to Serrafin. Give up, grow up, and live with the consequences of my time-travel disaster.

Our cuckoo clock resembled a gingerbread house minus the snow. Below the pointy roof was a shuttered window that the cuckoo bird never popped out of anymore. The hands were stuck at 9:21. Dancing gnomes with bulging eyes and hot red cheeks were lifting beer steins, frozen in the dance they used to do when I was little and the bird sang. They reminded me too much of my frozen parents.

So I'd ticked time off, had I? So to speak. Okay, lame joke. Couldn't resist. I'm saying—time had made me mad, too.

The universe thought it could do whatever it wanted with me. That it could bat me around like some cat tormenting a rodent that's not quite dead.

The universe didn't know me very well.

If I only had one more shot—to save my parents, save the planet, and once and for all make my aggressive weirdness worth something—I was gonna make that sucker count.

CHAPTER 12

Battle to the Death with Death

It's time for the sun to rise. It's time for the moon to glow. It's time to be born, time to crawl, time to cry; it's time to get old, to get sick, time to die. Time has an agenda and it doesn't share it with us.

But I had an agenda, too. I was scratching green paint off the kitchen table with my fingernail, eager to get to work on Dirk Angus 10.0, miserable that I had to do it without my lab partner and her sour-cream-and-onion chips. The woman who had become, whether she knew it or not, my only real friend. Green paint flakes fluttered to the floor.

A plate of scrambled tofu landed in front of me, quivering like a pile of guts. Dad sat across from me and sliced a piece of cantaloupe. Mom was wrapped in her bathrobe, pouring coffee.

I pushed away my tofu. "You guys, I'm staying home from school."

Dad looked up. "You're sick?"

I said, *"I'm mourning."*

Dad looked at Mom.

My parents had known Serrafin for a decade. There had been open houses. Science fairs. Teacher conferences, email exchanges. And I talked about her. Frequently. My parents were staring at each other like they were trying to remember where they'd put the car keys. Finally, Dad said, "That teacher of yours must've been the bee's knees. Wish I'd met her. You didn't know her long, but death brings things into focus, doesn't it? If you let it."

I was so frustrated. A big chip of green paint lifted off the top of the table and took a layer of wood along with it.

"Hey! Please don't ruin the table," said Mom.

"I'm sorry!" I snapped. "It's just, you guys seriously don't remember her?"

"Should we?" Mom's eyes turned hazy, like someone from a storybook who drinks a steaming potion, goes walking in the woods, meets a talking bear and never comes back. And then she froze. Dad, too, was immobile.

In the twenty lost minutes (it was twenty now), I ate my tofu, washed and dried the dishes, went to the bathroom, brushed my teeth and retook my seat. Then my parents thawed, and Dad refilled his coffee. "You're down, Fi. I feel you. But you can't stay home."

"So I'll go to the bookshop with you." That was an even better idea. I needed a meeting with Chicago.

Mom's eyes softened. "You can't, honey."

Dad nodded. "You'll push through."

I slammed my fist on the table. "Push through what? The new science teacher is . . ." I searched for the right words to describe the goateed man with the googly eyes. "He's a box of stale crackers!"

"Let's get through the visitation," said Mom. "After that, if it's still troubling you, we promise to hear you out about your new teacher."

Mrs. Saint Johnabelle's visitation would be the next night in a funeral home half an hour down the coast. I was extremely relieved I hadn't missed it.

If at breakfast I'd been mad that my parents weren't as sad as they should've been about Mrs. Saint Johnabelle's death, by third period I was infuriated—but not at my parents. My peers had known Serrafin for a week, and most of them were giggling and gossiping and acting like nothing had happened. Being in her classroom without her felt awful, and Mr. Replacement was eyeballing me nonstop. His tone of voice was so bland I could barely tune in long enough to decipher his words.

Airika sat next to me again. "Fi," she whispered, "how are you? I was worried when you ran out yesterday."

I didn't know if Airika was a glutton for punishment, some kind of masochist or possibly an angel or a nun, but I made this face, I didn't even know what the face was, it was just a real face that I'm sure showed how I really felt, for people who could read faces, not that I was thinking about it that way at all, I just felt myself unable to prevent my actual face from happening, and Airika said, "Listen. This is *sad*."

I said, "Right?"

She nodded.

At lunch, I was staring at my burrito when I heard a husky voice. "We woulda learned a ton from her." It was Airika's friend Rex, the kid with the bandana. Which, that day, was black. I'd never looked closely at Rex. His eyes were striated, like polished amber. When his fist dropped on my shoulder it felt like a boulder. He said, "Stay strong."

As I watched him walk away, I realized that Airika must've told Rex I was sad, and now they were both being nice to me. Why? That's when I noticed a crowd gathering around a table near the pizza line. Jeremiah Jackson Shipreck was doing a magic trick.

So. Rude.

After lunch, I passed him in the hallway. "Why not dance on her grave?" I asked.

Jazz stopped walking. "What did I do?"

I stared at him. He was wearing rainbow suspenders.

He looked at the deck of cards in his hand and shook his head. "Because—? And yesterday, you—when they said she— so you must—oh. Oh, man. I wasn't even thinking about it. A moment of silence, right?" Jazz bit his lip.

I wanted to slap my own face. I'd detonated again. I'd gone off like a feelings grenade when I'd explicitly promised myself I would not do that anymore. "I'm sorry," I said. "I shouldn't have said that. You're fine."

Jazz looked at my hand. *Which was touching his arm.* Why was I touching him?! I pulled my hand away and started babbling. "I'm just—weird about stuff. Sometimes. So they tell me."

Jazz slipped his thumbs behind his rainbow suspenders. "I get that from you."

I wasn't sure where to look, exactly. What direction was this conversation going?

Jazz looked at the ceiling, just like he had the day before, when he'd gotten on a roll about Peter Pan.

Piper, I mean.

Incidentally, I was addicted to the Peter Piper game. Pudgy piggies plucking petals from petunias. Portly peddlers porking in the park. What? Did I just think that?

Jazz caught my eye. "Look at your smile."

I said, "What?"

Did he just say something about my *smile?*

"Allow me to ask your forgiveness, Nephele Weather," said Jazz. "For my boorish and insensitive behavior."

"Forgiven," I said, feeling tilty, like the floor was tilting. "But I'm the insensitive boor. Very sorry. Honestly."

"Forgiven, Your Boorishness," he said. Then he bowed.

I resisted the urge to bow back and tried not to wonder where he shops. What percentage of that qualified as banter? My brain was full, and the line of topics waiting to get in looped all the way around the galaxy. Must process boy interaction another time.

*   *   *

After school, I slipped into the front seat of the car, buckled the screwy seat belt and slammed the door.

"How are you feeling, sugar bun?" asked Mom.

"Slightly better," I said.

"Yeah?" she said, sounding hopeful.

I did feel better, in a way. It helped knowing that a few people cared that I was sad, even if I'd given them no reason to. Airika especially. That girl was a battering ram of niceness.

And I felt energized about finally getting to work on Dirk Angus 10.0. All day I'd heard Death challenging me, purring, *Your only option is to give in to me. Everybody does, eventually,* like some know-it-all cat—and it was true, in a way. The word "deadline" did contain the word "dead." But the universe and I both knew something. Time was a joke, and I was writing the punch line. Death was nothing more than a math problem, baby. A math problem I was born to solve.

I pulled down the sun visor to check myself in the mirror and see if I was starting to resemble a sci-fi heroine. Because I was thinking up some really good lines.

"Drop me off at the bookshop, please," I said.

"Not today, hon," said Mom. "You and I have a date with the mall."

"The mall?! Why?" I asked.

"You need a black dress for tomorrow."

I shuddered. It had been *years* since I'd been to the mall.

Death, I was ready to battle. The mall, I felt far less sure about.

* * *

154

Mom shuffled me into a department store where a woman wearing a bow tie bombed us with squirts of spicy perfume while her twin sister offered us free eyebrow-drawing lessons at the makeup counter. "Do you see these eyebrows?" said Mom, pointing at our especially bushy examples as she dragged me past the women and onto the escalator, where we descended into the next circle of Hades. I kind of hoped we'd be greeted by a drooling Cerberus, the three-headed hellhound who guarded the underworld in Greek mythology. Today I could definitely out-bark him.

Mom snagged a few black dresses and isolated me in a dressing room to deal with them.

The dressing room was trapezoidal, with blank walls and a poofy cylindrical stool. I considered sitting on that stool and opening the geometry book that was in my backpack, but Mom was waiting right outside the door. I could see her clogs.

So I did it.

I tried on dresses.

At first, they were all the same to me. Complicated to fasten, and not warm enough. Going around with bare legs and shoulders in chilly Northern California isn't a thing.

Then I tried a lacy one that reached my ankles. Huh, I thought. Not revolting. I opened the door. "Huh," said Mom. "That's decent."

Not revolting plus decent equaled good enough for me, so I was done. When I mentioned that I was planning to wear my hoodie over it so I wouldn't be cold, Mom dug through racks of limp fabric until she found a beaded black sweater. It glittered like stars from a distant galaxy, one of the micro-galaxies in the quantum foam I'd seen or melted into or popped out of every year when I had traveled through the swirling wormhole in time. "I'll take it," I said.

On our way out, Mom decided we needed shoes. I was about to throw myself on the waxy floor and pound my fists like a toddler having a meltdown (a move I'd seen and admired in the parking lot) when I spotted them out of the corner of my eye: a pair of black combat boots. They had fat laces, and the soles were so thick they could've crushed a coconut with a single stomp. They looked exactly like the ones Wylie Buford's friend had been wearing back when he was a junior all those years ago, when I'd seen them together by the redwood stump.

Mom checked the price and hesitated.

"Never mind," I said.

She twisted her silver curls into a topknot. "Nope. No neverminding. I never get to go clothes shopping with my daughter. We're doing it, Fi. The boots are very *you*."

I smiled.

The next day I wore my all-black outfit to school. The visitation wasn't until after dinner, but I was proving a point.

In third period, *Mr. Zuluti* was scrawled sloppily on Serrafin's chalkboard.

When the bell rang, Jazz ran in late as usual. He dropped multiple writing implements on the floor and they rolled everywhere. "Sorrysorrysorry," he said, gathering them and sliding into the empty seat at my lab table.

Goatee man took attendance. When he got to me, he said, "Nuffeel Weather?"

"NEPHELE. Neh-fuh-lee."

"Sorry: Nephele."

"It's pronounced like it's spelled. Exactly."

"I've never been much on spelling."

I mumbled, "Or handwriting."

He leaned forward. "What's that?"

I said, "Carry on."

Someone said, "That girl is so effing *weird.*"

I looked over my shoulder. Who said that? I felt surprised. I mean, I knew I'd abandoned my force field, but so far, people had been normal with me—if not irrationally nice. I felt hot. And tipsy. Like I'd drunk too much green tea. I unbuttoned my cardigan.

Jazz whispered, "You are totally dominating in that dress, Fi."

I was wearing black. The traditional color of mourning. He wasn't making the connection.

"Gothic science chick," said Jazz. "Stupendous." Then he looked at the ceiling.

I almost told him not to call me a "chick," but instead, I looked up too. What exactly did he see up there? God? Electricity? Spiders?

When I tuned back in, Mr. Replacement was telling some rambling story about Japan. Then he tapped chalk on the board and I jumped.

"Icebreaker time," he said. "This activity touches on the wonder of our existence. It's intended to give you a taste of the way I'd like us to approach complicated topics in our class-room. There are no right answers."

Rex raised his fist in the air. "That's what I'm talking about."

Jazz mirrored him with a fist. "Right on, Mr. Z."

I tapped my boot. Icebreakers should be outlawed. Ice was an *essential* component of the ecosystem. No ice, no polar bears!

Mr. Replacement wrote on the chalkboard as someone passed out blank pieces of paper. "For this activity, you'll learn something new about your lab partner. You might record your partner's responses instead of your own. Or turn your answers into a comic strip. Hence the drawing paper. All in all, I'd like a big, messy class conversation on these topics. Make sense?"

"Kinda," said Airika. "We just talk and draw pictures?"

"This is a free-form activity," said goatee man. "Find your own way. We'll work until a few minutes before lunch, and then I hope someone will volunteer to share their experience of this journey."

Share their experience of this journey? Oh, Serrafin, I thought. At least you aren't here to watch science devolve into group therapy. I read the instructions on the chalkboard.

The Splendid Majesty of Our Cosmic Home

1. Where are you from? (Think big!)
2. What is the most distant place to which you have traveled? (Real or imaginary!)

3. What is the most distant place to which you
   would like to travel? (Real or imaginary!)
4. Do aliens exist?

I didn't bother to raise my hand. "Dude, these questions are all over the place. This will be impossible to grade."

I did that. I called him *dude.*

He laughed. "Confusion is part of the exercise, Nephele. Sometimes great thinking begins in a soupy mess of creativity."

I muttered, "A soupy mess. You got that right," and picked up a pen. The icebreaker was ludicrous, but I was constitutionally incapable of not completing my work to the best of my ability. Serrafin may have been absent for the moment, but that was no reason to start letting her down.

Jazz tapped my worksheet with his pen. "Let's both draw stuff, then trade. And we'll analyze what each other drew, Freudian style."

"What style?"

"*Freudian.* Sigmund Freud was the founder of modern psychoanalysis."

"Why do you know that?"

"Because I'm fascinating, Nephele. Ready, set, go!"

Jazz scribbled on his worksheet.

Drawing was not my thing. My mother was the crafty one. But I did it. Because he asked me to.

I drew.

After a few minutes, we traded. Jazz's page was overflowing with cartoons. All his answers seemed to be melted into one. "What *is* this?" I asked.

"Las Vegas." As Jazz pointed out lights, fountains, hotels and palm trees, they took form. On an oval-shaped sign were the words *WHERE ARE YOU FROM?*

"Are those fish?" I asked.

"Yup. I sank Las Vegas into the ocean. Because, you know, that's what should happen. Except, huh. It would ruin the ocean. Also, that's where I'm *from* from."

"The ocean?" I said. "As in, evolution?"

I, too, had drawn an ocean—three wavy parallel lines and a single, perfectly symmetrical starfish. Only I hadn't been thinking about the ocean in an epic way. I was born in a town beside the ocean. And there was no city sunk into my ocean, which made it look boring.

Jazz said, "I love that we drew the same thing."

He was so close to me I could feel him buzzing, although we weren't touching. Jazz was smiling. I realized I'd never seen him smile—or I'd never looked closely.

He had a broken tooth. A jagged fraction of an upper tooth was on display where most people's broken teeth would be fixed. Like there had been an accident and nobody patched him up.

I said, "Don't they have dentists in Las Vegas?"

What was *wrong* with me?

"Wait! I'm sorry. That's not what I meant to say."

"Lousy ones," said Jazz. "Beware of drunk dentists. That should be a bumper sticker."

I inhaled, feeling buzzy and sour—my stomach, and my fingernails—sour all over, like I'd been dipped in lemon juice.

To distract myself from this sickening yet appetizing sensation, I pointed at another amoeba-shaped blob on his paper. "What's this?"

"South America," said Jazz.

I couldn't tell whether I wanted to ask him more about drunk dentists or South America or just reach out and touch his curly hair when he pointed at my other drawing. "Who's this?"

In answer to questions two, three and four, I'd drawn one picture: Wylie Buford wearing his alien T-shirt. The furthest I had traveled was to the past. The furthest I wanted to travel was to the past. As to whether or not aliens existed? When I made it there, I'd ask Wylie.

When Mr. Zuluti asked for a volunteer, Jazz raised his hand. I was glad, because I wanted him to keep talking. I wanted to learn everything about the international man of mystery without him knowing I wanted to know.

But when Mr. Zuluti called on him, Jazz threw his arm around my shoulders, which startled me. "Nephele is a very interesting person, Mr. Z. Fi, the people want to learn more."

The class was quiet, looking at me. Judging me. Getting ready to laugh.

My jaw quivered. The back of my neck ached. I was sure Jazz could feel me sweating. . . .

"Wonderful!" said Mr. Zuluti, from somewhere far away. I was sinking to the bottom of the ocean, like Las Vegas. My body was as dense as an asteroid. I was plummeting. "Nephele, why don't you step up here in front of the class."

The silence was fat. I was a zeppelin in flames. It was impossible to breathe. I was going to fall out of my chair.

Jazz's arm tightened around me like a clamp. He pulled me upright.

My nostrils sucked in cool air; the room shifted into crisp focus.

Mr. Zuluti's voice was clear again. "Or you can stay seated."

Did anyone notice what had just happened?

Jazz jumped to his feet. "Fi, can I steal the spotlight? I'm like—an idiot. I always interrupt people inappropriately. My mother's boyfriend says it's unforgivable. But he's out of the picture now, and I'm the Lone Ranger, and listen, I can't recommend total and complete independence highly enough. We'll start in Santiago, Chile, where my mother grew up and where I spent the last couple of years wandering around. That's when I discovered poetry. And, you know, sorry, Fi—maybe you can go tomorrow?"

The bell rang. People scooted out chairs. It was all happening very far away from me. To other people.

"Leave your worksheets on my desk," said Mr. Zuluti. "Can't wait to read them. And continue these conversations!"

Jazz whispered, "Nephele, *mamma mia!* Are you okay?"

Mrs. Saint Johnabelle's classroom was my second home. Everything in it had been so predictable. What would happen if Dirk Angus 10.0 failed? Science would turn into a soupy mess like the rest of my life? Leave me behind like Serrafin, and everything and everybody else? A poison pain pulsed through my veins. On my way out the door, I scowled at Mr. Zuluti. And I might have mumbled, "You are *such* a mashed potato."

Mr. Zuluti's smile switched into a surprised look. "Pardon me, Nephele, are you saying something I need to hear? Could you speak a bit—"

"Louder?" I said. "POTATO."

I stomped down the hallway to the bathroom without looking back. If my life was a television series, I would call it *How to Embarrass Yourself in Front of One Cute Boy, Repeatedly.* Today would be episode ten: "Return of the Toilet Burrito."

That night at the bookshop, white haze rose around Chicago's two pairs of feet. Mom and Dad were downstairs, closing early. In a few minutes, we'd be leaving for the visitation.

I said, "This is not happening, Chicago."

"It isn't?" she asked.

"Mrs. Saint Johnabelle cannot die without knowing me. And I will *not* capitulate to the idiocy of our new science teacher."

Chicago was silent. Fine. I didn't want to talk about him either. I leaned against the red wall. I didn't even want to *think* about the new teacher. But it was more than that. I almost *couldn't* think about him. I mean, I couldn't think about how I was acting toward Mr. Zuluti. I didn't understand it, but also, I didn't want to understand it. Everything about Mr. Replacement, his whole existence, made me enraged. I felt enraged, and feeling enraged felt right.

At the same time, I regretted yet again exposing what a freak I am to Airika and Rex—and especially Jeremiah.

"He's cute, without being cutesy," said Chicago. "Funny, without being jokey—"

I said, "I hadn't noticed."

Chicago said, "Psh."

I ran my hand over the glittery black beads on my new sweater. "I'm a monster, Chicago. If he gets too close, I'll infect him with the virus."

"What virus? I thought you were Peter Pan. Or is it Medusa now?"

"I'm basically Rumpelstiltskin with a smartphone. And something about a virus."

"You've made a humongous, multiple-universe-sized mess," said Chicago.

"Which is why as soon as this funeral is over, I'm devoting every second of my life to my final attempt to fix Dirk Angus."

"You're going to spend one more year running the experiment that hurts people in ways you don't fully understand. The evil mathematician steamrolls everything in her path."

"That's one way of looking at it," I said. "But I know you, Chicago. You always have two."

The photograph was silent. I watched the haze that swirled around Chicago's feet as she walked and didn't walk in two directions at once, the picture of a contradiction.

CHAPTER 13

Time Ends Things

On the drive down the coast to the visitation, our car developed the hiccups. It stalled, grunted and belched more than one unexpected blast of hot air from its heater, which wasn't even turned on. I swore to myself that as soon as I won my battle with Death, I'd learn how to fix a Subaru.

The funeral home was surrounded by bushes trimmed in spheres that made them look like evergreen cake pops. We parked and followed a trickle of people through the front doors.

Inside, the hallway carpet was red, which felt wrong to me. Red was a color for roses and Popsicles, not Death. Organ music seeping from hidden speakers made me think about merry-go-rounds, which was creepy. There was a clean scent like fresh-cut flowers, and the people in the hallways were murmuring so quietly I couldn't make out a single word. I felt like I was walking through a too-real dream. I'd just decided to go back and wait in the car when I saw Serrafin.

A large framed photograph of Mrs. Saint Johnabelle was propped on an easel beside an open door.

I walked toward the picture. Her coral-brown skin, her clear plastic eyeglasses. The smile that was hidden like a gem in her eyes. The closer I got to the picture, the more I felt like my limbs were made of rubber. Like I was maybe going to stop having bones and just collapse.

Oh, Serrafin, I asked silently. *Are you in there, somehow? Couldn't you be? Could your photograph maybe, possibly contain a little piece of your soul?*

Mom scratched my back. "Ready to go inside?"

"I want to stay out here a minute," I said.

Dad kissed my head, and he and Mom went into the room.

I wish you'd told me you were dying, Serrafin. It doesn't matter; I'm going back. I know I can get it right this time if I think clearly, like you taught me to. And next time when you die, we'll have been friends for ten years. Not two dumb days.

I was thinking all that and more—remembering stuff, like the day I caught Mrs. Saint Johnabelle playing a dragon-killing video game on her phone—when someone nearly plowed me over. A skinny lady with high-heeled boots and a snakeskin bag. And she didn't say excuse me or anything. Who shoves someone without apologizing at a visitation? As I watched her go into the room, something about the woman struck me as familiar. The way she walked, maybe?

The woman looked like she wasn't sure where to go. Dad was standing nearby and introduced himself. "Horace Weather. My daughter was Mrs. Saint Johnabelle's student."

The woman said, "Vera Knight. I was her student years ago."

A gong banged inside my skull. My shoulder knocked the corner of the photograph of Mrs. Saint Johnabelle, and I almost toppled the whole easel. I caught it and ran into the room and grabbed the sleeve of Dad's suit jacket.

It was her. *It was Vera.*

"Hey, Fi," said Dad. "This is Ms. Knight. You're both former students."

Vera's eyes were still a lighter shade of blue than I thought eyes could be. She had the same sharp, seashell-shaped ears, the same isosceles triangle nose, the same glossy black hair. Her skin was still see-through white, like skim milk, but her edges were crisp. Like a memory that refused to fade.

Mom said, "Our Fi only knew your teacher for a day or two, but she made quite an impact."

Vera was nodding.

Vera had always nodded while people talked.

The girl who had destroyed my life was standing there nodding, like I was just some stranger and she was just some random lady with a scary purse.

Vera pinched my hand with two fingers and shook it like a sardine. "*Fifi,* is it? You missed out on a strict lady who you would've looked back on with admiration. Truly, she was my inspiration."

I yanked my hand away and snorted. "What did Mrs. Saint Johnabelle inspire you to do, Vera? Skin snakes?"

"What?" said Dad, leaning away from me.

Mom tried to catch my eye, but I was locked on Vera. Mom said, "Fi is—grieving."

Vera laughed her broken-blender laugh and held up a hand. "Absolutely no worries," she said, nodding.

"Do you nod because you're listening, Vera?" I asked. "Or to cover up the fact that you're not listening? Does it go back and forth?"

"Nephele Ann!" said Mom. "I'm sorry, Ms. Knight."

"Please! No worries," said Vera, nodding faster. "Mood swings are a perfectly normal way for a teenager to express grief. You know, Mrs. Saint Johnabelle inspired me to work with children."

"In what capacity, Vera?" Dad asked, while his eyes bored into me. I sensed that he was attempting to mind-control my mouth shut.

Vera said, "I'm a psychotherapist in Los Angeles. I specialize in the most challenging cases. Kids who struggle with anxiety, depression, multiple losses . . ."

I snorted again. Mom put her hand on the back of my neck and squeezed.

I felt another question coming from the past—a place that had vanished but somehow still existed. "So what happened to Ramsey?" I asked.

Mom said, "Who?"

"Ramsey *Schultz*?"

This time, Vera was the one who snorted. "Are you kidding me? Who cares what happened to that liar?"

Oddly, Vera didn't seem the least bit surprised that I asked her this. It was like the question had taken her back to the long-ago place, too.

"Wait a sec. Who's Ramsey?" asked Dad.

Vera pointed at him with a black fingernail. "First she steals my fiancé, then they hack into my bank account. When I find out about the pharmaceutical ring, it's like, *Get out of my life, psycho.*"

Vera tucked her hair behind her ears and straightened her purse. I think she'd just realized she wasn't in the past anymore. She started to say something to me, and stopped. Then she squeezed Dad's shoulder and nodded as she walked away.

I felt a smile coming on.

Mom let go of me. "Horace, I'm going to take a program and speak to the family. And then let's cut this short."

"What?" I said. "I'm having fun chatting."

Dad scratched his neckbeard and squinted at me. "Tell me how you know people who are involved in a pharmaceutical ring."

I said, "Long story." But as I watched Vera standing beside the casket, wiping her eyes with a tissue, I realized I was once again out of control. What was I smiling about? This wasn't a game. I hadn't just won something. I hadn't known Vera in forever. Known what she cared about or how she felt.

I'd been furious at Vera for so long, but I'd never admitted it. Furious about getting dumped and not knowing why. I mean, I'd decided why—Vera had ghosted me because I was what Ramsey and everybody said I was. Aggressively weird. The whole reason I'd built my time machine was to become someone Vera wouldn't abandon. And when I realized I wouldn't be able to change, I'd tried to forget her.

But I hadn't forgotten her. Of course I hadn't. I remembered everything.

Now I had to wonder. What if it wasn't my fault our friendship had ended? What if it was Vera's fault for falling for Ramsey, the future criminal? Or Ramsey's fault for being a future criminal? Or Ramsey's parents' fault for raising a future criminal? The Schultz family's criminal tendencies might've gone back generations.

Maybe when I finally went back in time for real, Wylie Buford and I could save Vera. We could prevent her from getting burned by a future pharmaceutical ring kingpin. Queenpin?

Vera was talking to the Saint Johnabelle family now—I recognized them from pictures. Her true love, Alvin; her daughter, Celeste; her granddaughters, who were students at Berkeley. I overheard someone telling a story about Serrafin. "But was she a terrible cook, or what? Remember when she brought over that salad with the raw potatoes?" Everybody laughed. Dad was listening, too, scratching his curly white neckbeard, laughing. I picked at the black beads on my cardigan and watched Alvin, smiling and wiping his eyes while Vera told him something.

Would saving Vera be . . . ? Was that . . . ?

Saving Vera sounded—well, it sounded bat-crap bananas, of course, but a little thing like that had never stopped me from pursuing an idea before. The real problem was my theory about why our friendship ended.

It was too complicated. The best scientific explanations were simple. Clear and elegant.

Maybe my friendship with Vera ended because that's what time does to things.

Ends them.

I looked around the room full of people dressed in black, clasping programs and drying tears. That was it, wasn't it? Writing the mathematical equations that would reveal the secret to time travel may have been my rightful fate, but I'd picked the wrong experiment to test them. Doing freshman year over was an experiment that was destined to fail.

CHAPTER 14

Nobody Wants to Be Normal

The morning after the visitation, a misty rain fell from every direction. The trees were full of tiny birds chirping urgently, like they were having a conference. I walked down the hill toward Highway 1 feeling a strange sort of peace. Like I'd opened a window in my heart and a pile of ashes had blown away.

What it was, was that I'd forgiven Vera. For leaving me without saying goodbye. It's not like I thought about it actively—I didn't think *I forgive you* or anything. It just felt, when I'd woken up that morning, like an old, bad thing was gone.

I wondered if science always worked like this. You started an investigation for one reason, but you kept going for different reasons. Now I didn't need to invent time travel to get Vera back. I only needed to restore the functionality of my parents' brains and, you know, save life on earth.

I mean, yes. Time ends things. It felt right to let Vera go.

172

But did it feel right to give up on making a major scientific discovery? No.

Because the experiment wasn't about me anymore. It was about science. Using the power of science to make the world a better place. Serrafin understood; that's why she'd made me promise I wouldn't quit. And over the years, the idea of using time travel to undo global warming and protect the ocean had become more and more important to me. I didn't want to do nothing while Hades sucked the earth's ecosystem and all of its inhabitants into the underworld. I didn't want to ignore the fates of the otters and the ospreys and the starfish and the salmon and the snails. Not when I had the power to do something about it.

Besides that, from a purely mathematical standpoint, my experiment had become more and more intoxicating. Oona Gold was right about failure. You could use it to your advantage. Every time I'd failed, once I'd gotten over feeling miserable, I'd made another breakthrough. Breakthroughs made me feel like I wasn't a fumbling semi-immortal; I was a goddess. I'd never been closer to succeeding than I was now. I mean, I was ridiculously close to revealing a mathematical beauty so extraordinary I could almost taste it. I walked through the mist to school feeling determined about the work ahead.

In third period, I ignored Mr. Replacement's group activity and opened a logic textbook. I figured Serrafin would understand my need to work independently, given the circumstances. I thumbed through chapters until I stumbled upon the Liar's Paradox. The paradox is, "This statement is false." If the statement is true, it means the statement is false. But if the statement is false, it means the statement is true. The looping went on forever. Which seemed to be where Dirk Angus was sending me—in an endless loop. I bookmarked the page and kept reading.

"Would you like to join the class?" asked a bland voice.

I said, "Nope," and kept reading. I felt Mr. Replacement standing there like he wanted to say something else.

"Nephele?" he said, and I ignored him until he walked away.

Then I felt a nibble of guilt. Why was I still being so rude to Zuluti? He wasn't actually doing anything *wrong*. He just *was* wrong.

I concentrated on the book. It wasn't long until I found another interesting paradox. Would you agree that in order for a thing to move, that thing must change its position? If so, consider an arrow in flight. Would you agree that at any instant in time, that arrow can be in only one position? And would you agree that at any instant in time, everything in the universe can be in only one position? Then you agree that everything is motionless at every instant. Therefore, motion is impossible. That's Zeno of Elea, Greek philosopher. I wasn't sure precisely how the paradox related to my timeship, but I was stuck, motionless in a sense. It felt relevant. So I marked that page, too, and opened a book about artificial intelligence.

I wanted to revisit the chapter about "the known unknowns" and "the unknown unknowns." The known unknowns are the things you know you need to know to find out about your problem. Like, for instance: What was happening to people's memories of me? Answer: Unknown. The unknown unknowns were another problem. What did I not know that I didn't know about time travel? How would I find out?

Airika was sitting at my lab table. She leaned over. "What are you doing, Fi?"

I had settled on a theory about Airika. That night at the bookshop when I told her she was going to hate me? I was pretty sure she'd taken it as a challenge. Which meant Airika and I had at least one thing in common: we were both stubborn. And if there's one thing I know about stubborn girls, it's that you cannot discourage us. Telling someone like Airika that she'll never reach her goal only pushes her to lace up her combat boots, grab her bow and arrow, and jump out of the moving vehicle.

I wasn't sure what would happen if I kept being myself with Airika, and I wasn't sure I wanted to find out. But I'd survived the worst already with Vera, and after all these years, I'd finally gotten over it. Besides, whatever happened, Dirk Angus 10.0 and I would be outta there in August. So I said, "I'm thinking about time travel."

Airika said, "Rad."

I felt someone watching us and turned around. Immediately, Jazz opened a book. His eyes darted back and forth. He was pseudo-reading. We hadn't talked since he'd saved me in class that day and I'd thanked him by storming out of the room.

My explode-y behavior had probably scared away the international man of mystery forever, and I didn't blame him.

But I wanted to thank Jeremiah. For noticing how nervous I'd been and trying to protect me.

I could feel him pretending not to notice that I was staring at him, so I turned back around. I wasn't sure I had the courage to talk to him.

Not yet, anyway. Not yet.

At lunch, Airika and I sat together. She told me she'd been working on a skating trick with spinning, and something called a suicide stop, and there was a ramp involved. It was difficult for me to picture, but she was into it.

"Fascinating," I said.

Airika stabbed at her stir-fry with chopsticks. "You don't have to pretend it's fascinating. I know I'm boring."

That shocked me. "How are you boring? You're an extra-stubborn roller genius."

Airika's sky-blue eyes were wide open, like she was waiting for more.

"Additionally," I said, "you seem like a normal, well-adjusted person."

Airika flipped a chopstick across the table; it rattled to the floor. "People always think that. But they should fear me! I'm unbalanced! I throw things at walls just like you do."

"Okay," I said. "I've never thrown anything at a wall, or used a chopstick as a weapon. Also, the word 'normal' is a *compliment*."

"Shut it, Fi. Nobody wants to be normal. You're not the only tortured soul who ever lived."

I said, *"Shut it?"*

We both smiled. "I've changed my mind, Airika," I said. "You're all kinds of abnormal."

Airika's smile was proud. "Yeah? I've been practicing at home in the mirror."

I noted once again how much Airika and I had in common. "Airika, that is *aggressively* weird."

Airika pumped her fist and said, "Score!"

After school, I went to the Big Blue Wave and grabbed a chipped mug from the coffee station.

"Can you believe Airika has a dark side?" I asked.

"Congratulations," said Chicago. "You got over yourself for five seconds and realized that the rest of humanity is just as confused as you."

Harsh. Maybe Chicago, or whatever part of me was pretending to be Chicago, liked to provoke people. Or maybe I was hearing her wrong. Either way, it was fascinating, wasn't it? The fact that one picture could say so much?

I felt another pang of regret for not asking Clyde Watkins about whether he thought photographs could have souls. I went to the railing and leaned over it. Dad was arranging biographies of musicians on a display in the center of the floor, building a pyramid of life stories. Mom was behind the counter unpacking boxes.

"How's Clyde Watkins?" I asked.

Dad looked up. "Oh, Fi. I forgot—you were there that night. Clyde's gone, kiddo. He met his maker."

"What?"

"Clyde was in his nineties, though. That's a fine life."

I clenched the railing and leaned back to stretch. More Death. It was so awful. What was the name of that river in Greek mythology, the one that divided the living and the dead? It was the color of dried blood, with blackened clouds and scrawny vultures lurking in the gnarled tree branches above it. And there was Clyde Watkins, chatting away with the gory ferryman Charon on his ride across it to the underworld, snapping photographs all the while.

A *fine life,* Dad had said. And then you cross the river and it's gone.

But sometimes in the myths, mortals came back, didn't they? I was rusty on the rules of Hades. That felt ironic.

I let my head hang backward, upside down, and looked at the skylights. They were closed that afternoon; the birds were trapped outside. I stared at the glowing rectangles, watching gray clouds blow over the bookshop.

The universe kept telling me my mission was impossible. Time ends things. Death rules time travel out. And I knew that it did—and that it didn't. Both things felt true.

"This statement is false," I said. "This statement is false."

The next morning, Jeremiah was sitting alone on the redwood stump outside the school. His suit jacket was the color of an avocado, and he wore red jeans with the blue suede shoes. Plus, he had on his fedora. Where *did* he shop? Not at the mall. As I got closer, I heard him whistling a tune I recognized. It was the same tune he'd been whistling that day in the cafeteria the first time I'd seen him do a magic trick—the melody that drifted between happy and sad. This was it. The perfect opportunity to apologize.

When I was near the stump, Jazz looked at me and his eyes were that color I'd never seen before, grape lollipop meets electric eel, and we both kept looking. He didn't say anything. I concentrated on Airika, the happiness battering ram, for inspiration, reminded myself that I had a ticket for an August ride in a time machine and spit it out. "Hey, Jazz. Can I sit with you?"

Yes: I asked him that.

Jazz exhaled in a very audible manner. Like, *shhhhh*. Like an air mattress deflating. It was kind of an odd reaction—maybe he truly wanted nothing to do with me. I was about to reconsider my plan when he patted the stump beside him.

I sat. I'd been planning to apologize and flee, but something about him made me ask, "Are you okay?"

Jazz hunched over even more, but he turned slightly toward me, his hands folded in his lap. "I'm good," he said. "I'm always good. You?"

I said, "Me? Oh, I'm rarely good. Usually, I'm not good. Anyway, listen. I wanted to tell you . . . I'm . . . well . . ." I took a deep breath. "I feel like I keep doing embarrassing things in front of you. So if you want to be friends or something, or not, or whatever, you should know that that is kind of my thing." I tugged on the cuffs of my hoodie sleeves. Was that it? Could I flee? No, no, no. "Also, thank you for saving me the other day. I was so scared to talk in front of everyone I almost fainted, I think."

Jazz lifted his chin and squinted a little. "Why were you scared?"

I shrugged. "Well, I mean, first they all look at you. Then they all laugh at you. Then you feel like crawling into bed and pulling your blanket over your head and, you know, never leaving your house again."

Jazz's mouth was open, but he wasn't saying anything. He kept it open for five to seven seconds longer than a normal person would. Then he said, "Nephele Weather."

I felt like I was about to be hit by a tsunami, and gripped the redwood stump so I wouldn't fall off. Jazz was going to kiss me. I'd never felt that feeling, but I knew exactly what it was. It was imperative that I flee. I was plotting my sprint into the forest when something about Jazz switched. He scrambled his entire energy.

He didn't kiss me.

He said, "Can you scoot over a little?"

I scooted, and he stood on the stump. His lanky body towered over me.

"Madame, follow along. For I'm going to share with you a happening delightful and uncanny. Nephele Weather, regard this fossil." Jazz shook something out of his suit-jacket sleeve; it fell in the sandy soil.

I was still reeling from the about-to-be-kissed feeling. Although I was not kissed. I looked at the twisted hunk in the sand. "Is that a chicken bone?"

"Hang on." Jazz shook his other sleeve, and several more bones fell out. "Could you grab those?"

"Here."

"Excellent. So . . ." He twirled the bones like batons. "Actually, Nephele Weather, I have not made up the middle part of this trick yet."

The way the sun lit his face, I noticed a scar above his left eye. A white line. I didn't know how I'd missed it before.

"How did you get that scar?" I asked.

Jazz made a dramatic, slow-motion gesture of punching himself.

I laughed.

Jazz didn't. "Now I remember what I wanted to show you. See these?" He did an elaborate thing with his fingers that made the chicken bones ripple across them. I forgot what we'd been starting to talk about.

"I see them," I said.

Jazz lifted his fedora and put the bones underneath. He raised his arms to the sky and said, "To the gods of loneliness. We offer you this sacrifice." Then he tore off his hat. No bones fell out.

I was genuinely surprised. I said, "They disappeared!"

"Oh, but, Madame, if you wouldn't mind, there's something

stuck . . ." He reached behind my ear and pulled out a necklace of knotted bones. As in, he had bent the bones, like taffy or bubblegum, and tied them together to make a chain. It was brownish and lumpy.

"How did you do this?" I asked.

"Magic," said Jazz. "Vinegar may also have been involved. For you." Jazz dangled the rattling necklace from his finger and bowed.

I took the necklace with my pinky. "This is easily the most disgusting gift anybody has ever given me."

"You're welcome."

When he sat back down beside me, Jazz seemed much happier than he had been before. "Put it on!"

And I was about to, running my fingertips over the knotted bones, thinking that an international man of mystery had just *given me jewelry*—when it hit me.

Was there something important about this chain of knots? There was, wasn't there?

There was a throbbing sound, a dizzy orchestra tuning up in my brain. The curtains opened and Dirk Angus stepped into the spotlight. The spotlight was shaped like an octagon, and Dirk Angus was wearing a tuxedo jacket, holding a quivering sphere of quantum foam. He cleared his throat. Then he stretched the foam like bubblegum, folded it, poked a hole in it and tied it in a big, fat knot. Then another. Then another. Nine knots.

A snake swallows its own tail. That tail comes out the other side. It ties itself in a knot.

And that's what I'd done with time. Each time I'd gone

through the wormhole in the quantum foam inside my body, I'd tied a knot. That's why I was stuck. *I had accidentally tied nine knots in the fabric of time.* Knots that were lodged inside me, stopping me from getting where I wanted to go.

"Nephele?" said Jazz.

I was breathing heavily. I felt like I could run an actual marathon. *"Thank you,* Jeremiah. You can't imagine what you just showed me. I mean, I could *literally—"*

We looked at each other. I was going to say, "I could *literally* kiss you." And from the expression on his face, I could tell he'd read my mind.

Now I was the one springing to my feet. I ran inside the school to find a quiet place to work until first period. I hadn't had a breakthrough like this in years.

In English, while the class watched a film version of *Romeo and Juliet,* I crunched numbers in the dark. In P.E., while the class played badminton, I faked a wrist injury and crunched numbers on the bleachers. I felt like I was on one of those cop shows where a truckful of shocking new evidence just got dumped on my desk. I saw many pots of coffee in my future. I mean, I didn't drink coffee. But in the parallel universe where I was a cop, I was making it part of my thing.

In science, I ignored Mr. Replacement's attempts to get me to join some rudimentary group experiment. After class, he stopped me in the hallway. "Nephele? I'd like you to stay with me after school today."

"Why?" I asked. "Anyway, I can't."

"But—oh, shoot," he said. "Ack, I've got an appointment, too. It'll have to be Monday. Deal?"

I clicked my tongue and muttered, "So disorganized."

He said, "Pardon me? I couldn't quite—"

I yawned as loudly as possible.

Have you ever been blinded by rage? I used to think that was just an expression. But it's a real thing. I saw white whenever this guy opened his mouth. Not soothing white like crisp pillowcases in a villa in a commercial about Italian tomato sauce. Hot white, like the spots in your vision when you stare too long at a light. Hot white, like headlights racing toward you on a night street. Like someone you love melting out of existence and leaving nothing. Less than nothing. An emptiness that burns through you and scorches you with a living, breathing ache. A white hole shooting through you. A death tunnel.

Mr. Zuluti said, "I'll call your parents today."

I said, "Whatever."

As I walked away, I noticed Rex leaning against the lockers, wearing a black bandana and a spiked wristband. When we made eye contact, he didn't smile. Had he been watching us? I felt uncomfortable.

But I mean, with Mr. Replacement, I was *blinded*. Rex couldn't possibly understand. I put my head down and made my way to the cafeteria.

CHAPTER 15

Rage Logic

Friday after school, I stood facing Chicago. "Knots!" I said.

It seemed like she was trying to meet my eye.

"Dirk Angus keeps snagging because I accidentally tied nine knots in the fabric of time!"

Before she could respond, I was off to Mathematics to see if we had any books on knot theory. We didn't, which wasn't surprising—they're harder to sell than, you know, vegan cupcake cookbooks.

Mathematical knots are similar to the ones you tie in real life. A three-dimensional shape crosses over itself and then through to make a loop. Only in math, the ends of the shape are joined together, which makes the knot impossible to untie.

Impossible, that is, in three dimensions.

But with an extra dimension or two, untying a mathematical knot is a piece of cake. And multiple dimensions are something a wormhole can provide. Once I figured out what types of knots I'd tied in the quantum foam, untying them would be a vegan cupcake with coconut icing on top.

Visualizing a math problem always helped me solve it, so I ran to the Maritime section. Sailors tie a jillion types of knots, so we had plenty of books on those.

Yes, the bookshop has a Maritime section. The place isn't called the Big Blue Wave for nothing.

I researched knots until Dad closed the shop; Saturday morning, I opened it back up with him.

Dad dropped the needle on a thrashy punk rock album with women yelling and cymbals crashing, and the music helped me think. It kept me from getting lost, or cornered, or something. Guitars screeched like they were cheering me on.

By Saturday afternoon, I was buried in a jumble of books on the couch by the window that faced Main Street. I was looking at diagrams of knots—knots shaped like hot salted pretzels and knots shaped like chunky gold bracelets and knots shaped like some guy on Main Street's black armband tattoo—when there was knocking on the window.

Airika, extra tall from her roller skates, waved from the sidewalk. Behind her, Rex was standing with his arms crossed, looking through me with his geological eyes. Immediately I felt self-conscious. It was the bandana, maybe. The bandana was intimidating.

Airika's skates whirred as she rolled inside. "Hey, Fi. We were hoping you'd be here."

Rex nodded at the pile of books on the couch. "Can I sit?"

I said, "Sure," and made room. Rex sat and Airika perched beside him on the couch's arm.

"You and me don't know each other too well yet, Fi," said Rex, "so it might be easier for me to lay this out."

Lay what out? I thought. I said, "No *problemo*, cowboy. Shoot!" Then I cringed. I'd said that in a flirty New Zealand accent. Plus, *problemo*? Who was I? New Nephele?

Rex said, "Quit bullying Mr. Z."

Airika was twisting her friendship bracelets, avoiding eye contact.

What?

I said, "I'm not *bullying*—"

Rex interrupted me. "Well, you give him a super-hard time. It's uncool."

Okay: I knew I'd been rude to Mr. Replacement. But a *bully*? Could a freshman bully a teacher? And anyway, I'd been bullied! Which meant that the bullies were other people. I said, "But he's such a stale dinner roll—"

"See? That's it. Right there," said Rex, like he needed me to hear what he heard. "Unfunny."

Unfunny?

"I'm not trying to be funny," I said. "I don't want to deal with some replacement teacher. I want our *real* teacher. I want her—"

A feeling got caught in my throat. I envisioned Serrafin's face, her mischievous eyes in the photograph at the funeral home. Was that the only place I could find her now? In photographs? In memories?

No. I was going to go back and see her again. The problem was Mr. Zuluti. When he sat at her desk and wrote on her chalkboard, it was like this cruel joke from the universe saying, *You'll never get her back.* Even if I knew that wasn't true—that eventually, my timeship would work—

"Jazzy says you freak out on people to protect yourself from getting hurt," said Airika. "Jazzy is way into psychology."

What? "He is?" I said. "I do?"

"Oh yeah. Jazzy says you're as sensitive as a poet." Airika draped her arm around Rex. "I agree. Of course, I'm not the one who's in love with you. Too bad Jazz isn't here, huh, Rex? Where is he?"

"Dumpster-diving. He's still looking for a crate to attach to his ride."

"Wait," I said. "In love with—what?"

"These guys find rad stuff in the trash," said Airika.

"You wouldn't believe what people throw away," said Rex. "I'm hooking up with him later to dig. You guys should come."

"Gross," said Airika. Then she gave Rex a meaningful look and put her suntanned hand, with its many friendship brace-lets, on my shoulder. "He's in love with you."

Rex was in love with me? Well, that was, uh, unexpected. I fiddled with my pen. "Gosh."

I looked at Rex, trying to find a nice way to tell him that, like, we probably weren't really meant to be together—wasn't there a line in *Thirsty for Thrills* that addressed situations like this? Something like, *I'm awful flattered, cowboy. . . .*

"Not *me*," said Rex, sounding offended. "Jazz!"

My heartbeat did a drum solo. ". . . Oh."

Airika was smiling at me like I was as cute as a baby bunny, and Rex was giving her a dirty look. I had a feeling she wasn't supposed to tell me that.

Were angels singing inside my skull? I felt like bluebirds were draping me in ribbons. They did that for the ball, right? In someone's fairy tale? But not to the bad guy. Not to the *bully.*

They were right about Mr. Zuluti, of course. It wasn't his fault that Serrafin died. It was illogical to be angry at him. My behavior made zero mathematical sense. I rested my head on the couch and sighed.

"Why would Jeremiah be in love with me?" I asked. "I have psychological problems."

Rex shook his head. "Unclear," he said. "Unknown."

I said, "Hey," and smirked. When Rex smirked back, I was pretty sure it counted as a smile.

Who *was* Rex, exactly? It looked like if you punched him, your fist would bounce off his face. Rex could definitely have been on the cover of a romance novel.

I decided to ask Rex and Airika something I'd been wondering all fall. "Are you guys boyfriend and girlfriend?"

"Rex is the brother I never had," said Airika.

Rex took off his bandana and shook out his shaggy hair. "Our parents' houseboats were parked in the same marina up in Sausalito. We used to hang out on the docks, watching the herons."

"Then my mom married his dad," said Airika.

"You're *brother and sister?*"

"But we didn't need a piece of paper to prove it," said Rex. "I knew it as soon as I met Airika. This girl is my sister for life."

I said, "How did I not know that?"

"You never asked," said Airika.

I hadn't, had I? I thought about what Chicago had said. That if I stopped thinking about myself for five seconds, I might realize that other people's lives were complicated, too.

Sitting in the shop with Airika and Rex, I felt the same way I'd felt all those years ago with Wylie Buford. Like we could be real friends. I imagined Wylie standing with us in his alien T-shirt, a multiple exposure superimposed on the scene. I'd never been closer to meeting Wylie again. I could feel it.

Then I remembered what Airika told me about Jazz, and his song started playing in my head—the happy-sad tune he whistled. I didn't know how I remembered it. It clashed with the raging guitars on the record Dad was spinning, and it had nothing to do with Wylie. But there it was.

I didn't know what I was supposed to do with it. And I wasn't gonna say I was *in love with* it—but I really, *really* liked it.

CHAPTER 16

Unknown Unknown After Unknown Unknown

Monday morning, I left early for school so I could take a detour up Highway 1. The sun was crayon yellow and the air was crisp, like a high five. When I came to the crest on the cliff, I took the five-minute hike to the lookout point to watch the ocean. Below me, it was swirling and pounding, reflecting a hundred shades of blue and silver and white. Already there were plenty of surfers. I loved surfers. A loose flock of crows were cawing and hopping, flapping their way inland with their inky-black wings. I loved crows. California was magic.

I hiked back through the forest and down the winding path to the high school, picking up random scraps of plastic—a candy wrapper, a torn shopping bag—along the way. The air smelled green, like dill and pine. Nature was all around me and flowing through me, and the universe felt like my friend again, even if it was obnoxious—obnoxious, like I could sometimes be. When I used pure mathematical logic to look at my rage at Mr. Zuluti, rage failed the test, so I was done with it. I had to be.

Math was magic. I loved magic.

I wasn't wearing the bone necklace; it was unwearable. But it was hanging from a nail in my bedroom like a charm. I wanted to tell that to Jeremiah because I had kind of bolted when I'd had the knot revelation, and I didn't want him to think it was because I didn't like his gift. Or him.

But I had an even better idea, and the thought of an international man of mystery possibly being *in love with me* was making me fearless.

Before third period started, I went to the lab table where Jazz was sitting with Rex.

"Hey, Fi," said Jazz, half smiling.

"Hey," I said, half smiling back.

When Rex puffed his cheeks, he resembled a tough gopher. He put his head down and made a show of scrolling on his phone.

I said, "After school, do you maybe want to come with me to—"

"Nephele? Excuse me," interrupted Mr. Zuluti. "After school today you've got an appointment with me."

I gave him a look. Could the man not pick up on a flirting vibe?

Jazz shrugged. "Tomorrow, then. Tomorrow I'll come with you to, like, anywhere."

I crossed my arms. "Okay, tomorrow," I said, trying not to think the word "date." Because why would I think that.

* * *

After school, I slowly made my way from seventh period, which was French class, in which Madame LeBlanc forced me to play the role of a merchant helping a picky customer select the right stinky cheese—the customer being Madame LeBlanc, who I'm pretty sure used a French swear word when I suggested the wrong one—to Mrs. Saint Johnabelle's classroom for my meeting with Mr. Zuluti.

I was dragging. I lingered in the hallway, inspecting the showcase full of golden statues of kids balanced on one foot, interacting with various projectiles. I imagined a statue of a kid holding a statue. And that statue was of a kid holding a statue, which was holding a statue . . . an infinite chain of sports heroes, stretching back to the beginning of time. I snickered. Then I lingered over the wall of painted self-portraits. One kid had put an extra mouth on his neck. I snickered some more. What else could I look at . . . ?

"Nephele?" called Mr. Zuluti from down the hall. "Please pick up the pace."

In the classroom, Mr. Zuluti sat on Serrafin's desk. "I thought I'd ask you to help me clean while we talked. But everybody has been so good about that."

The lab tables were polished. The glassware was clean. The chalkboard was sponged down, too. I sat on a lab table across from him, thinking, *Of course everyone is kissing up to you. Everybody loves you because you don't make them do any work.*

Luckily, I caught myself before I could say that out loud. I said, "Listen, Mr. Zuluti—"

Mr. Zuluti interrupted. "No, Nephele. I'd like you to listen. When I was your age—"

I groaned, and then I interrupted myself. "Hey," I said. "I'm—"

At the same time, Mr. Zuluti was saying, "We have so much in—"

We both cut ourselves off to listen. There was a crease between Mr. Zuluti's eyebrows, like he was searching for the right next word.

I said, "I'll do the class assignments. I will."

Mr. Zuluti leaned forward, looking at me like he was trying to find something. "Listen, Nephele. I want to understand what you're going through."

Um—okay. I was starting to feel a *little* explode-y. How could this stranger ever begin to understand what I was going through?

Mr. Zuluti said, "When I taught in Japan—"

"Japan?" I snapped. "What does Japan have to do with this, Zuluti?" I took a deep breath. Why was I still yelling? I muttered, "This is exhausting."

"What's exhausting?"

"Trying to solve my problems," I said. "Which are real. And, like—large."

"Are you trying to be less worried?" said Mr. Zuluti. "Less worried about what the other students think of you? Less jealous of people who seem to know exactly the right things to say and do?"

Hmm. Actually, after ten years, I was just beginning to get over that particular problem. I looked at Mr. Zuluti. The thinning hair. The reddish-brown eyes. The round face hiding in the slender body. He pulled out his wallet.

"Are you gonna buy something?" I asked.

Mr. Zuluti laughed. "No. I've hesitated to . . ."

"To what?"

Mr. Zuluti took something out of the wallet. "I wasn't sure about telling my students, because I wanted to leave the past behind me. That's been my goal since I was your age, Nephele. Since I sat in this classroom, feeling different. Like nobody understood me. And nobody wanted to."

Since he sat—where?

Mr. Zuluti pressed his lips together for a few seconds. "I'm not from Japan. I just liked living there. Hope to travel back there this summer. I fit in there in a way that I never did here. Who knows why. But when my grandfather died, I inherited his house. The house I grew up in, over on Sandpiper Drive."

I was beginning to feel the slightest bit nervous. "What did you take out of your wallet?"

Mr. Zuluti slid off the desk and handed me a photograph. "This is me, Nephele. When I was a freshman. My grandfather insisted on ordering school pictures. I hated being in photographs back then. I hated looking at myself. People teased me constantly, and I assumed they were right. I felt repulsive. I gave Grandpa his picture and threw the rest away. I threw them in the trash behind your father's bookshop, as a matter of fact. Back then, I went to the Big Blue Wave whenever I could. To read comics, science fiction, books of puzzles. Anything that would transport me to another place and time. A world where I could live unnoticed, but be a part of everything. It was in my grandfather's wallet when he died. Now that I'm a teacher, I keep it in mine. To remind myself how difficult it is at your age to know what's going on. And to remember how important it is to be kind."

The young Mr. Zuluti was round like an apple. His hair was the color of sequoia bark. He was wearing the alien T-shirt. On the back of the photograph, it said, "To Grandfather W. I love you. Wylie Louie Buford III."

Wylie? My lungs were stiff. My vision was warping. I said, "But your name isn't Buford. . . ."

"Zuluti is my married name. My husband made it up."

I looked at the teacher through my crazy soup of feelings and felt the world shrinking around me. Ten years ago, I'd missed my chance to be friends with Wylie, and I'd regretted it ever since. *Now here I was missing it again!* I was in the center of a drama I couldn't escape from. Again and again, whatever I did, I ended up in the exact same spot.

I had to ask Wylie if he—of course he wouldn't, but I had to ask—"Do you remember . . ."

Mr. Zuluti leaned forward, listening.

"Do you remember a girl . . . named Nephele?"

Mr. Zuluti looked confused, and shook his head. "You're

the only Nephele I've ever known." He checked his phone. "Your mom just texted. She's here. Can we be friends, Nephele? Or at least not enemies?"

I wasn't ready to go yet. I wanted to tell Wylie about all the years I'd been wondering about him, and how I'd almost told him, ten years ago, that I was building a time machine, and how lost I'd been ever since. And I wanted to hear about every single thing that had happened in Wylie's life since high school. How he'd done it—how he'd gone from feeling repulsive to becoming this teacher that everybody loved. But if I started talking about that stuff, I'd freak him out, like I had so many times before. All I could do was stare through my tears at the man with the goatee, finding Wylie Buford in his face.

"You and me were supposed to be friends all along, Wylie," I said.

"Isn't that funny?" he said, shaking his head. "See, I've always thought so, Nephele. Since day one. Let's do that, shall we?" When Wylie smiled at me, his lips turned down at the ends and so did the lines around his eyes. Like his smile had been someplace low and just managed to pull itself up. "Cheers, kiddo," he said.

"Cheers, Wylie," I said. *Cheers.*

The next day I had trouble remembering where I was. How I'd gotten there. I felt like I was outside of myself, watching.

Watching myself eat breakfast at the green table. Watching myself slip on my sneakers, zip my hoodie and walk down the hill to school. Barely feeling the wind on my face. The ocean was a distant hush.

In science class, my brain kept wanting to turn Mr. Zuluti into somebody *different* from Wylie Buford. I listened to Mr. Zuluti's voice and imagined Wylie, and tried to force them into one person inside my head. Because they *were* one person. But it was like trying to listen to two different records at once. My brain had to turn down the volume on one of them. It refused to deal with the clash of information. It wouldn't let both Wylies be Wylie. It wouldn't let both things be true.

After science, Jazz stopped me in the hallway. He was clutching a handful of his curls. "I can't make it today, Fi. Circumstances beyond my control. But I totally, totally, totally want to hang out tomorrow."

I was disappointed, but it quickly became clear that Jeremiah wasn't lying. I could feel how frustrated he was. He explained something about somebody needing to be somewhere when the guys who delivered the counter showed up. I couldn't follow him, but I believed him. Jazz couldn't hide his feelings. Maybe it didn't occur to him to try.

Canceling our non-date turned out to be a good thing. It was a cold afternoon, the kind when the fog stretches out over the town and doesn't get up until the next morning. When I got to the Big Blue Wave, the first thing I saw was my father, dancing to the Beatles song "Twist and Shout." His head looked like a bowling ball. As in, he'd shaved it, along with his neck.

"Oh no!" I yelled. "Grow something!"

Dad rubbed his hands around his smooth head. "No? Not working for you?"

"You look like an infant," I said, running to touch it. It wasn't slimy, but there was way too much skin. "Ew," I said. "Ew, ew."

"Come on, come on, come on, baby, now!" sang Dad, twisting and letting loose a loud "Whoo!" with the Beatles. Mom was sitting behind the cash register, whittling. She held her knife over her head and twisted her shoulders to the beat.

Since Mrs. Saint Johnabelle died, I'd been watching my parents more. I almost felt like I loved them more, even. Every moment with them was irreplaceable.

At the same time, I'd never been more confident that my experiment was destined to succeed. Not like there was a scroll in the sky with my name written on it in swirling calligraphy. I believed that a true time-travel solution was out there, waiting to be discovered, and I had a hunch—"hunch" sounds like such a quiet word, but that's essentially what it was—a quiet, unshakable feeling that lived inside me and had crystallized into something solid, like a diamond, that if I kept working, I would discover it. I would answer the time-travel question once and for all.

And meeting Wylie again had made something else clear to me, something I'd never considered. Even when I made it back to the past, I'd never go back to being who I was in the past. I would never stop changing. That was the essence of the strange feeling. It wasn't only the universe around me that was dissolving and reconstituting at all times. It was also me. I may have been semi-immortal, but in every instant I was living and dying. Over and over I was falling apart and sucking myself back together into one coherent girl. I was a continent with thundershowers and ice storms and volcanic eruptions, changing a little with every heartbeat. With every breath.

So was Vera. Vera was my best friend with the laugh that embarrassed her, the popular girl who wore stylish clothes and ignored me, and the child therapist who admired the same teacher that I did.

And so was Wylie—Wylie the awkward alien-enthusiast and Wylie the long-haired guy with the theatrical friends and Wylie the teacher who loved Japan were the same guy.

Everything is motionless at every instant, and the instants are all we have. They're like photographs, the moments of our lives.

How it changed me to know this, I wasn't sure. It wasn't going to help me untie the knots in the quantum foam. I felt calmer, though. Calmer than I'd felt the day before, even if I also felt a little less sure about everything.

After school the next day, Airika and I stopped at the redwood stump so she could put on her roller skates.

"Did you know there's a roller rink down in the valley?" I said. "It's called Roller Burger. People had birthday parties there when I was little. Maybe we could go there next weekend."

Airika said, "Really? I thought all the roller rinks around here were out of business. It's kind of retro."

I pulled out my phone and checked: Roller Burger had been closed for twelve years. Oops. "Maybe we could go someplace else."

"Ugh, it can't be next weekend," said Airika. "I haven't told you yet. I'm pretending it's not happening. We take off Friday morning for a whole week."

Rex was standing with Jazz beside the bike rack. "Hawaii, Fi. Can you believe that junk? We're missing school to be trapped in some ridiculous hotel with, like, nine waterfalls."

"Why Hawaii?" I asked.

"Rex is Hawaiian," said Airika. "His grandma lives alone down there."

"Like most capitalists with a credit card, my dad is too impulsive," said Rex. "He booked tickets last week without telling any of us. First class. So bougie. The man is the source of much suffering."

I kind of wanted to laugh. The closest I'd ever seen Rex come to complaining was because he was skipping school to fly first class to Hawaii.

We all went up the path to Highway 1. Jazz and I said goodbye to Rex and Airika and waved as we watched them walk away.

The foghorns moaned, low and majestic. A yellow warbler fluttered in a berry bush. Wild lilies with creamy faces swayed beside a rock. I got the sense that Jazz and I were stretching out the watching-them-walk-away moment so we could linger on the we're-about-to-be-alone-together moment. It was lovely.

Finally, Jazz spun on his heel. He was wearing white wing-tips that day. All of Jazz's shoes looked like they were made for unnecessary spinning. And for dancing up staircases and possibly for diving into swimming pools, fully dressed.

"Shall we go for a bike ride?" he asked.

I said, "I don't have a bike."

Jazz lifted one shoulder. "I didn't bring mine anyway. Walk to the beach?"

"Sure. But I should tell my parents. . . ."

So Jazz and I walked to the bookshop. On the way, I asked him to tell me his story.

"What kind of story?" he asked.

"Your story," I said. "About you."

Jazz started snapping his fingers. "That's it. That's where we'll start. It won't make us even, but it'll be a big step."

"Even?" I asked.

"In a true friendship, it's best to alternate revealing what a freak show your life is." Jazz swept his hand in the air. "When Eva Jackson graduated from high school, her life's mission was to surf. So she rented a shack on the beach. Her front yard was sand, shells and bottle caps. It was, to use the local expression, hella gnarly. But life missions have a way of changing, and when Eva's son, Mo, was born, Eva was only nineteen."

"So your real name is Mo," I said. "I always thought you had a fake name."

"No, no. *Listen*," said Jazz, looking toward the horizon, like he needed to find a clear spot where his story could land. "Jeremiah Jackson was the only child of Eva's uncle Vic. Yes, folks:

Vic Jackson, the gambler who stole money from his own sister, his own parents, his son's mother, any and every human being he got close to, to bet on a roll of the dice. Yes, Vic Jackson was a cheater. Sure, Vic Jackson was a drunk. But man, was that dude handsome. Almost as handsome as his son. And his smile could send lights racing around a sign. But the man had the attention span of a—hey! Look at the size of that jackpot! Be back in five."

I wanted to clarify: Vic Jackson was Jeremiah's father? His father was a *gambler*? And why was Jazz telling his story in the third person? It was sort of confusing. But he'd just asked me to listen, so I bit my tongue.

"'*Be back in five,*'" said Jazz, fluttering his fingers. "That's what Vic Jackson said the night he left his fourteen-year-old son sitting on a curb outside a Las Vegas casino called the Starlight. Naturally, Jeremiah knew better than to believe his father. The hustler had left his son sitting on so many curbs, outside of so many casinos—or worse, trapped inside a hotel room with nothing to do except watch television or practice magic tricks in front of the mirror—that Jeremiah managed to pick up on the pattern."

I said, "Wait. What?"

We turned from Highway 1 onto Main Street. Jazz's hand kept making bold strokes in the air. Like he was conducting his story. Like his life was a song. "But Jeremiah prided himself on giving people the benefit of the doubt. So for the full five minutes, he waited. He watched a hundred oldsters spill out of a tour bus and shuffle into the Starlight. They were probably heading straight to the slot machines, but the boy let himself imagine them waltzing into a ballroom to the tunes of a pompadoured crooner in a three-piece suit who was wearing a chrysanthemum corsage."

I said, "That sounds like something you would wear."

Jazz put his conducting hand in his pocket and looked down. "Yes, Nephele Weather. It is something I would wear." Our feet were in sync. We were taking the same steps. "Jeremiah Jackson loved Las Vegas, theoretically. The lights. The music. The magic. It definitely should've been fun. When five minutes had passed, the boy stood. He said, 'Me? I won't be back in five. In fact, I'm not planning to come back at all.'"

Jazz stopped in front of Dougie's Donut Shoppe and pointed at me.

"Is this boring? I'm boring you."

"No! It's not boring. It's . . ." It was terrifying. But I didn't want him to stop talking. So I said, "Keep going."

Jazz looked up at a bottlebrush tree. Its feathery red blooms made it look like it was decorated with boas. Like a Las Vegas dancer.

"Long story short, I took the cash I'd been sneaking out of Dirty Vic's wallet—they call him that, the other dentists, because everybody wants a dirty dentist, right?—and I walked to the bus station. It was, like, a hundred and ten degrees. By the time I got to the station, I was drenched in sweat. And I bought myself a ticket to San Francisco. I'd heard that my super-cool cousin Eva was living somewhere near there with her son. That's Mo. He's sooo cute."

I said, "You *did*?"

"The bus ride was incredible," said Jazz. "Headlights. Billboards. I got this humongous ice tea. The guy in the seat next to me was a veteran. From the army. He was hilarious. And also sad. Total poet. All of it was awesome. Awesome. I was so inspired—" Jazz looked at me and adjusted his hat. "The boy was so inspired he gave himself a new name."

I said, "Ah. So it *is* a fake name."

"Jazz Shipreck's father was a dentist. He kept meaning to fix his son's tooth. Teeth, but there was that one obvious problem: the chipped saber tooth that made the boy look like the Jabberwock."

I said, "It really doesn't."

We stopped outside the Big Blue Wave. Red leaves blew around our feet.

"Ah yes, well, there's a long story there involving the mother's boyfriend and an argument during which the man announced that the boy's mother had to choose between him and her son. That's when the mother put the boy on the plane from Santiago to Las Vegas to live with the father he'd only met once. Lousy, lousy story."

Jazz opened the door to the bookshop. "Shall we?" he said. He didn't wait for me to respond; he just went inside, straight to the counter. Dad was changing the record. He turned around. They shook hands. I stood in the doorway watching them, trying to let what Jeremiah had just told me sink in. His mother had chosen her boyfriend over him. His father had abandoned him in a parking lot.

No wonder he told his life story like it had happened to someone else. It shouldn't have happened to him. To anyone.

Jazz and Dad were talking about guitars. An alley cat wound itself around Jazz's legs and he stroked it. I thought about how much people love to stand at the checkout counter, talking to my father. He's the type of person who makes other people feel comfortable. Dad and Jazz had that in common.

I turned around and looked out at our sleepy Main Street. The new place with the expensive ice cream. The drugstore next door, where locals bought soft serve for a quarter of the price. The cruddy gray laundromat that always seemed lonely with its windows lit up in the fog.

Sometimes you meet someone and there's something there instantly. You can't describe it. You can't see it. You can feel it, but you don't know what it is.

As different as our lives had been, I understood now one crucial thing Jazz and I had in common. We were both on a first-name basis with the universe's dark side. Something had happened that was too big. Too big to know what to make of it. Too big to ever get over it. Something far too big to handle alone.

CHAPTER 17

Join the Cult

That night, I stayed up until midnight looking at pictures of knots and fell asleep thinking about Jazz.

The next morning on the walk to school, the wind was vicious. I was wearing a scarf Mom had knitted out of scraps of leftover yarn in clashing colors. My brain was exhausted; I hadn't gotten nearly enough sleep. But I felt more determined than ever to solve my problem. Hearing Jazz's story had made me realize something. Yes, I was lost in a scary situation, but scary things were happening to kids everywhere. Scarier things. Much scarier. I wanted to be as brave as Jazz—but it was more than that. I wanted to be as *nice* as him. Not that it didn't make sense to be frustrated and angry and lost and confused. I couldn't not be. It just felt selfish, somehow, to let those feelings rule my life. Jazz proved that they didn't have to. I was imagining what it would be like to hold hands with Jazz and, like, I don't know—become time travelers together, or something—when I walked face-first into a redwood tree. And those things are difficult to miss.

"Nephele?" called a voice, a voice who was . . . who? A muffled echo.

I looked up into the web of branches and spiky leaves. "Massive," I said. "This is one massive tree."

"Nephele!" Someone was shaking me. Who? Shipreck? "NEPHELE!"

The boy who tied bones in knots was shaking my shoulders. His eyes were blue ice with a droplet of purple ink melting. A smack of sunshine bounced off of his blowing black curls. The shipwrecked boy was shaking me. I felt like we'd met once long, long ago.

"I . . ." I heard myself speaking. I wondered what I was going to say. What could I say?

I'm stuck, Jazz Shipreck. I'm trapped. I am maybe about to faint in your arms, like a princess in one of those stories I could never quite pay attention to, owing to their complete lack of math.

I am so, so terribly alone. Help me, Jeremiah. Help me find my way home.

"Nephele, are you okay?"

Jazz's features came into focus. The jagged tooth, the scar above his eye.

"Should I slap you?" he asked.

That woke me up. "Only if you want to get slapped back."

"Well, what? Are you hysterical? Comatose? You're freaking me out!"

Jazz's hair went up and down in swoops and kinks and

swerves. Like his mind. Like mine. I checked to see if anybody was around. Nobody was, but I still yanked him behind the tree. Then I said, "I need you, Jeremiah," which I quickly realized he interpreted as a sign I was going to kiss him. His eyes were wide and he took a deep breath. No, no, no. I took a step back. "Jeremiah Jackson Shipreck, you cannot tell anyone what I'm about to say."

His hair seemed to stand on end. "I won't! I swear!"

"I am stuck in a time-travel loop."

Far above our heads, an owl hooted.

He said, *"Mi scusi?"*

I asked, "What does that mean?"

He said, "It means——"

"Listen. I'm trying to tell you something that's gonna be impossible for you to believe. But it's important that I tell you the truth. I can't lie to you. Not if we want to become real friends."

"We're already real friends, Fi. No?"

"Yes," I said.

"So . . . ?"

I looked at him and took a breath. "Jeremiah, I have been in ninth grade for ten years. I figured out how to travel through time. Almost, I mean. And now I'm stuck."

He smiled. He put his hands on his hips. "Stuck."

"Stuck, yes, stuck, as in, I can't get out of the loop," I said. "I mean, I could stop looping right now—give up and grow up—but that's not what I want. I want to fix my timeship, fix the black holes I drilled in my parents' brains and make my life go back to normal. But I'm stuck. And nobody can help me but . . ."

I hesitated to say the thing I sensed I might have to say eventually—since the first day of school, when Jazz had snagged his backpack on the door.

How could I have known then? How?

I looked toward the ocean. We couldn't see it, but we could hear it, its distant waves crashing into foam, making small modifications to the shore with every smash, every wash—some that happened immediately, others that wouldn't emerge for tens, hundreds, even thousands of years.

Jazz wouldn't believe me right away. He couldn't. He shouldn't.

But I was almost certain that he'd believe me eventually.

At that moment, he only knew that I was telling him something massive. And even if he thought that the massive thing was that I was bananas, he was going to hear me out.

"Are we starting a role-playing game right now?" Jeremiah held up his hands. "Because I would be totally into that."

I looked at my combat boots as they sank into the sand. For a minute or so, we just stood there.

Then I started to feel stupid. Now that I'd said it out loud, there was no denying how crazy it sounded. As confident as I'd been a few seconds ago, the longer Jeremiah was quiet, the more I began to worry that I'd been wrong. That I'd be alone with my secret forever.

When Jazz finally spoke, his voice was calm. "So what you're telling me is . . . that this is happening. You're staying the same age while everybody else gets older. And inside you're not some creepy twenty-four-year-old hanging out with a bunch of teenagers?"

"I think I'm a teenager. I mean, I'm pretty sure."

"You seem like a teenager." He laughed. "Wow. It's just—yeah. And you're sure that . . . ?"

I looked into his eyes and nodded.

His smile changed into a steady look, something thoughtful.

Then he nodded back. Like a person who knew that a question had just chosen him. Whether it was the time-travel question or the Is-this-girl-nuts? question or the question about which question was the right question to ask didn't matter yet. All that mattered was that he cared enough to find out.

"And nobody else can help you get unstuck, Nephele Weather," he said. "Nobody but me."

On the walk to school, I filled Jazz in on the details. From the green kitchen table, which was my first clue that my timeship had a terrible flaw, to my decade of lunch meetings with Mrs. Saint Johnabelle. I even told him about Vera Knight. The only subject I avoided was Wylie Buford. Somehow, what I knew about Mr. Zuluti's past felt private.

Jazz was spinning a pinecone in the palm of his hand. "I can't believe we're having this conversation. Not how I expected this day to go down."

"Me either," I said. "What were you doing outside anyway?"

"Coming to your house to walk you to school."

"Really? How did you know where I live?"

Jazz held the pinecone like he was testing its weight. "Remember that night at the bookshop after the slide show when you told Airika she was going to hate you?"

"I can't believe I did that."

"I followed you out the back door."

He did?

"You did?"

Jazz nodded at the ground. "You were standing on your porch with this mist all around you. You looked so lonely. I wanted to talk to you and tell you I knew exactly how you felt. But I realized I was being creepy. Following you. So I chickened out. But now it's like, hey, I definitely can't be more out there than this girl. Can I come over to your house after school?"

"Does it matter what I say? You'll follow me home anyway."

Jazz nodded. "I definitely will. I feel like I just need to check out . . ."

"What?"

"You know. Nothing."

"You want to be sure my house is normal. And that my mother isn't drugging me, or that we're not like—"

"In a cult. Which would be fascinating, but I might think about extricating you. Which is okay, because then I'd get to be a hero. And like—"

"Or maybe you'd join the cult," I said.

"Ah," said Jazz. "*Far* more interesting option."

PART III

CHAPTER 18

Stupid Cupid

It's never winter in Redwood Cove. At least, not the type of winter that involves snowball fights or ice-skating on lakes or townsfolk selling roasted chestnuts from wooden carts. Does that actually happen anywhere, ever? I need to travel through space instead of time someday. But then I'd be a tourist.

Shiver.

What I'm saying is that the coast is always blooming; it never quite falls asleep. So in February, when it wakes up officially, it feels almost too alive, like a blooming monster. Muddy paths try to swallow your shoes, bees buzz past you like fighter jets, twining vines devour walls and fences, and the whole town starts to smell sickly-sweet, like perfume mixed with boba tea.

On the second Saturday in February, Airika and I were wading through the surf, dragging our boards back to the beach.

I know: Me? Surfing? On the coast, it isn't so shocking.

Every kid in Redwood Cove winds up in surf camp at least once. And I love swimming in the ocean, home of dolphins and crabs. So while Airika rode waves like an Olympic athlete who had a marketing deal with orange juice, I flailed in the shallow water contemplating the way jellyfish ripple—gleefully, it seems to me, albeit with a sinister lack of a face—while attempting not to feel self-conscious in a wetsuit that showed every curve of my body that my hoodie usually masked.

We dropped our boards in the warm sand and sat on our towels. Airika pulled two protein bars out of her sack and handed me one. "Protein bars taste like chewy chalk," I said. "They have no right to be so addictive."

Airika said, "Right?" And inhaled hers in ten seconds flat. Seagulls were encroaching upon us, looking inquisitive. I shooed them. "I refuse to make you addicts. Find fish."

Airika downed half her water bottle and grabbed her board. She said, "I'm going back out."

"Hang loose," I said. "Those waves are macking!"

Airika scrunched her nose to indicate that I was massacring her language.

As I watched her run back into the water, I was glad that Airika showed me what real friendship could be. That you could like somebody without being exactly like them. That girl made up for ten years of friendlessness.

And if everything went according to plan, I would repay her at the end of the summer by abandoning her on the shore of the river of Lies.

I'd looked them up, the rivers of the Greek underworld.

There were five of them. Styx, the river of Hate, which separates the living and the dead, is the one where I'd imagined Clyde Watkins chatting up Charon, the grisly ferryman—and where I couldn't let myself imagine Serrafin being. There was also Acheron, the river of Pain; Phlegethon, the river of Fire; Cocytus, the river of Wailing; and the fifth river was Lethe, the river of Forgetting. Once you drank its waters, you couldn't remember your life on earth.

When I read about Lethe, I theorized that I'd discovered another river, one that made you forget *someone else's* life and the parts of your life that had that person in it. An icy river whose waters shocked your system, making you shudder and freeze.

I named my discovery Lanthano, which, if the internet is to be believed, is Greek for something that is hidden or has escaped notice. Like the truth.

Lanthano was the river of Lies.

I was an ambassador from the underworld, leading the people I loved to drink from the river of a very specific sort of forgetting. One that varied from person to person, depending on how much they needed to hold on to me, how hard they were willing to fight to keep their memories from washing away.

Which meant that my battle with Death was more like a betrayal. According to my theory, I'd been working for Death the whole time.

Yeah. My life had become a wee bit complicated.

*   *   *

That night, I was lying under my star quilt, too awake to fall asleep. Jazz had left an hour earlier, and my bedroom, which we had taken to calling "the Lab," looked like a junk shop hit by a tornado. On every surface, books were flagged with neon sticky notes. Math, poetry, Jazz's comic books, oversized collections of impossible-looking art. Knotted ropes hung like macramé plant holders from nails in the walls, which were plastered with an ever-expanding collection of quasar pictures. We'd collected rocks, ferns and tree branches to help Jazz visualize fractals, and we were experimenting with the effects of time on living creatures like yeast and plants. So on my desk, a goopy sourdough culture was burbling, belching breath that smelled like sweaty socks, and on my windowsill, radish seeds sprouted.

And between Wylie Buford's soupy-mess-of-creativity approach and Jazz's knack for making connections between absolutely everything, I'd found the knots I'd been tying in the quantum foam whenever I used my timeship. They looked like this:

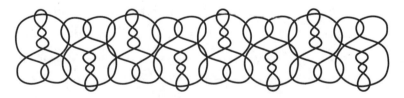

Two linked teardrops with a halo and a twining tower, a mini-universe with a core of infinite energy, forever looping back on itself. Each knot reminded me of a magical beanstalk arching into a rainbow and sinking below the horizon into the ocean floor and rising again, a path that never stopped and never started, a place where you could live endlessly, following the path of your own symmetrical maze.

The problem now was that even in four or five dimensions, I couldn't figure out how to untie them.

And I couldn't imagine how to pull the universe through the quantum wormhole behind my belly button *without* tying some sort of knot.

Jazz said we'd figure it out before my end-of-summer deadline, "No prob!" And I believed him. He wasn't a math guy, but he'd cannonballed into the deep end of all the stuff I'd been thinking about. He came over practically every day.

Do I even need to say that J. J. Shipreck was my biggest crush of all time?

It was a savage beast of a crush with razor-sharp teeth, and it never stopped drooling. It was basically a bulldog I kept locked away in . . . Gosh. I didn't like the idea of keeping a bulldog locked away. Is that what I was doing?

What I'm saying is, I definitely couldn't think about. You know.

Kissing Jazz.

I mean, at night, before I fell asleep, of course. *Thirsty for Thrills* had nothing on the situations I invented that would have required Jeremiah to extricate me with declarations of his love and the type of kiss where both people melt into a puddle on the floor.

What was even more disturbing was that I got the feeling Jazz *wanted* to kiss me. Like he was waiting for me to give him the signal and I was actively blocking the signals I was dying to send. How did I know he wanted to kiss me? I don't know. It was that thing. The unnameable thing that's between people.

Plus, we sort of pretended we were going to get married. As in, he'd say, "When we get married, let's move to Iceland." And I'd say, "And give our kids Icelandic names." And then we'd take a half-hour break to discover the best Icelandic names according to online articles such as "Trending Icelandic Names for Your Super-Stylish Baby." We picked Borgar and Voney.

I'm not sure why we did that. We knew I was going to leave. I guess it was fun to imagine what might happen if I didn't. And since I *was* leaving, there was nothing to lose by planning our future together.

Except everything.

I mean . . .

Of *course* I was fantasizing about staying with him. Giving up on time travel and acting like a normal girl who had just met someone amazing.

But that would have required being a normal girl. Pretending that I hadn't led my parents to drink from the river of Lies, and that going back in time wasn't the only way I could heal them. Pretending that I wasn't obsessed with the questions about time travel that had been visiting me for the past ten years and the answers that showed up occasionally. Pretending that I hadn't promised Serrafin I wouldn't give up. Pretending that I wasn't convinced that time travel could save the ocean I've been splashing in and listening to and walking beside forever, and that I didn't believe that answering the time-travel question once and for all was my rightful fate as a girl who was born loving math.

Math wasn't everything to me; I'd learned that when Serafin died. And I'd recently realized I'd been working for the underworld unknowingly, so I was all too familiar with how tricky Death's battle tactics could be. The universe didn't play by my rules or by anyone's. So far, there was no scientific Theory of Everything, no overarching explanation for how the place worked. Scientists knew a lot, but at the heart of it all, there was still a mysterious gap. If I'd vaguely known that when I'd started this project, I knew it clearly now. The odds were against me succeeding. They always had been.

Still—could I abandon my experiment prematurely just because I'd finally met a boy? Could I give up my last chance to un-hurt my parents?

No. I had to finish what I'd started. And with Jazz's help, I felt like I was sneaking up on a solution. Or it was sneaking up on me.

Sometimes you want two things, and they're located in opposite directions. My stuck life was finally budging, and I wanted to go both ways. But in the middle of that contradiction, I felt like I was becoming the rock-star scientist I'd always wanted to be.

I mean, I guess I didn't feel like a rock star. Look up "sexy" in the dictionary. What's there a picture of? A rock star.

But yeah. No.

See? I couldn't stop thinking about it.

Jazz and I could not kiss. If we kissed, I wouldn't want to leave when it was time to go.

So we would stay friends, and I would leave in August, and Jazz would forget me. Unfortunately, I wouldn't forget him. I'd have to live knowing what I'd lost.

These thoughts are brought to you by Nephele Weather's nightly pre-falling-asleep argument with herself, during which she reviews all the reasons she cannot kiss Jazz Shipreck and then proceeds to have an excruciatingly detailed fantasy about him until she falls asleep.

This not-falling-in-love stuff was exhausting.

Sunday morning, I was sitting on my front porch, folding origami. Once I untangled the quantum foam, I'd need to fold time in a new way so that when I shot through the wormhole I wouldn't tie time in a new knot. The shapes I was coming up with weren't precisely what I needed, but origami was helping me visualize a variety of folds. I made a tricorne, which is a three-dimensional triangular object; a few cats, because I was feeling masochistic; and a sixteen-pointed star, which I threw as I yelled, "I HATE FOLDS!"

The star glided into a rosemary bush. That was way too graceful. I needed to catapult something with more mass. I pulled off my sneakers and chucked them. One thunked on the sidewalk, then the other. I was semi-satisfied.

When our front door opened, it creaked like it was asking

a question. I felt Dad's hands squeezing my shoulders. "Happy Valentine's Day, Fi. You and Mom are the loves of my life."

I made a gagging noise.

"It's like *that?*" said Dad.

I had an urge to ball up my socks and throw them into the street, too. Instead, I leaned back on my elbows and said, "Cupid is corny. Why would anyone trust a dude who flies around in a diaper with a deadly weapon?"

Dad's new budding mustache-and-beard combo made my cheek feel zingy when he kissed it. "So cynical," he said. "May I collect your sneaks?" He sauntered down the red steps, snatched my shoes and dangled them beside his bald head.

I inhaled a whiff of flowery shampoo and looked behind me. Mom was leaning in the doorway with her big turquoise eyes and her long silver curls, blowing Dad a kiss.

I snapped. "Just because I have this great example of a happy marriage doesn't mean I need to have a boyfriend."

Mom looked down at me. "Okay."

"So much PRESSURE!" I said as I stomped inside.

Sunday afternoon there was a knock at the door, and I opened it.

Jeremiah was standing in a patch of sunlight. Did he know it was Valentine's Day?

I couldn't look in his eyes, which I'd decided were not purple, but indigo, like a brilliant stripe in a rainbow projected by a prism. Beside one of his wingtips, a beetle with a bronze shell was crawling on the peeling red paint of the porch floor. The bug glinted like a jewel in a box. Did the bug know it was Valentine's Day?

I wished I was a bug. A brief life inside a pretty shell until someone stomped you or swallowed you in its beak. No romance. No decisions of great consequence.

Well, that wasn't true; bugs made consequential decisions constantly—bugs made the world go round. They digested organic matter and pooped it out, turning dead things back into soil.

Anyway, who was I kidding? I'd be the most stressed-out beetle ever. Trying to go back to last week, when I was a larva . . .

Jazz cleared his throat.

I accidentally looked at him. He bit his lip and raised his eyebrow.

He knew. We both knew. MUST BREAK BOY TENSION. I said the first thing that popped into my head. "Where *do* you shop?"

He smoothed his suit jacket. "You wouldn't believe the thrift stores in Vegas. Northern California has too much fleece."

Thank Methuselah. We'd dodged another one of the psychotic flying diaper dude's poison arrows. In my romance novels, the heroine never successfully dodges the arrows, so I must've been doing something right. And I mean, I wasn't getting kissed—so yeah. I was basically brilliant.

"Is my hoodie made of fleece?" I asked, feeling it.

Jazz shook his head. "Cotton."

"Phew," I said. "Well, seeing as how we're both dressed for work, I suppose we might as well get started."

As we went upstairs to the Lab, Jazz admired my brand-new phone in its shiny pink case. It had been a gift from Dad for helping him build the Big Blue Wave an online store over the holiday break. "How often do you upgrade?" he asked.

"Every couple of years," I said. "I just have to make sure I don't go back in time with a version that hasn't been released yet. I've been dying to mess around with the hologram feature."

"You have some ridiculous problems," he said.

I flicked his arm and he ran up the last couple of steps and into my bedroom, laughing his easy laugh. Then he went directly to my desk, pulled a piece of paper out of his pocket, left it with my phone, came back and sat beside me on my bed.

"So I've been thinking about math and music. I was talking to your dad at the bookshop the other day, and it blew my mind. I didn't know music had anything to do with math."

While Jazz went on about intervals, rhythm and time signatures, I put on a record by the vibraphone player Lionel Hampton. Dad had set up the extra record player on my dresser when I was a baby. Apparently I was a major screamer, but certain music soothed me. The song was fast, light and cheerful, with a zigzagging melody. "I wonder how difficult it would be to describe this album mathematically," I said.

"Is that possible?" asked Jazz.

"Sure," I said. "To a point." The concert was recorded live, so in the background, people were clapping and yelling, "Yeah!" I wondered if any calculation could explain why a particular person yells spontaneously during a musical performance. Or how that yelling impacts the musicians' decisions about how to play the next notes. Louder? Softer? Faster? Slower? And how do musicians influence each other? What if the drummer insults the bass player and the lead singer kisses the guitarist before the show? How does that change the songs? Maybe that's why music kept me quiet as a baby. I could almost find the patterns, but not quite.

"Anyway, it's pretty," said Jazz.

It was pretty, that music at that moment, with the wind blowing my white curtains and the boy with the black curls sitting on my bed.

On Valentine's Day.

I leaned against my dresser. I would not be going back to sit beside him.

"Math is like witchcraft," said Jazz. "The formulas and symbols are like spells. The Pope and the Mafia and the CIA are gonna be all up in Dirk Angus, trying to hijack its power for their own purposes."

I crossed my arms. "I guess so. Erasing people's memories has already made me feel like a spy creeping around in their lives. And that was an accident."

"Time travel could make it easier for people to do bad things intentionally. Of course, it's not exactly hard now," he said. "All you need is an angry dude and a gun."

"And time travel will let us go back and take his gun before he uses it," I said. "So ultimately, time travel will make the world a better place."

When Jazz leaned back on his elbows, I ignored the thought, *He's lying on your bed.* Then he put his head on my pillow, bent one knee and crossed his leg. He was looking at my ceiling and wagging his foot, which was inside one of his dancing shoes. He was wearing his shoes on my bed, and I couldn't ask him to take them off because then I'd be asking him to take off his clothes while he was on my bed, and I could *not*. Dodging Cupid's arrows required supreme diligence. I picked up the album cover and was concentrating on the black-and-white photograph of the band, contemplating taking up the vibraphone, which would be an *excellent* distraction from watching a handsome boy wag his foot, when Jazz said, "I don't think it's possible to change the world."

That surprised me. "You can definitely change the world. And with time travel, you can *really* change it."

"Oh yeah? What are you going to change first?"

"I'm going to save the ocean."

"From what?"

"Pollution! Undo global warming and un-decimate the coral reefs."

Jazz rolled his head to look at me and smiled. "Well that is *very* cute."

"*Cute?*" I snapped. "It isn't cute. It's epic!"

"I'm sorry; sorry," said Jazz. "I didn't mean to sound condescending. I just—I don't know. You'd need a lot more than a time machine to accomplish something that major, no?"

"That's what my foundation will be for," I said. "To work out the details."

Jazz went back to ceiling-gazing and foot-wagging. "Did you ever see that movie where the guy goes back in time and his mother falls in love with him instead of his father, and he's grossed out and almost un-born?"

"I love that movie," I said.

"Do you think it's possible to be un-born?" he asked.

I shrugged. "No less impossible than being fourteen for ten years."

"You think so?"

"Sure. Being un-born seems illogical, but I believe it's mathematically possible. You just have to embrace the idea of multiple universes."

"I definitely don't," said Jazz. "It's too convenient. Like, *Yeah, in some other universe, I'm sure my life would be way better* . . . I don't believe that."

"You don't?"

He shook his head. "You get one life. Some parts of it suck. There's nothing you can do but make the best of it and keep going."

I watched Jeremiah lying there, looking like he almost always looked. Fine. Good. The word "unshakable" came to mind. *Keep going.* That's exactly what he'd done. He'd hopped on a bus alone, not knowing what would happen when he got off. It was brave.

Lately, I'd been daydreaming about taking Jazz with me back in time. He didn't have much to lose. His parents had given him up. He was living with some cousin he wouldn't even let me meet, which probably meant she was horrible. I was imagining sharing romantic time-travel adventures with him, adventures that featured plenty of sweaty bodice-ripping, when he said, "Guess what I did last night?"

"You read a book of poetry," I said, imagining us floating down a canal in turn-of-the-century Venice, a poetry book perched on his bare knee, which poked through the tear in his burgundy pantaloons. . . .

"Actually, I wrote a poem, but that's unrelated. I had a *powerful* revelation."

"Because you learned to do a backflip," I said, envisioning Jazz performing gymnastics for me on a beach from a faded postcard—Coney Island, perhaps, in New York City. . . .

"I read a book about coding."

Coding? Woof. I had no romantic historical visual to pair with that one. "Why?" I asked.

"Because we never talk about coding. You never lend me any books about it."

That was true. "Other than some AI stuff, I hate coding books. Reading about programming is boring. But do you think that as a self-taught programmer I might be missing something basic? Like an I-forgot-to-plug-it-in type of thing? Chicago used to tease me about that."

"You mean your best friend, the black-and-white photograph?"

I looked for something to throw at him and found an origami star.

It hit him in the head. His laugh was low and rich, like something delicious. A heart-shaped box of chocolates. If I'd had one of those, I'd have thrown it at him, too.

"I love that you're friends with a piece of art," he said. "I used to think I had a personal relationship with Kermit the Frog."

"Can you stop?" I asked.

"Seriously, Fi, you've come this far without reading *Time-Travel Code for Dummies*. You can probably live without it. But I'm gonna learn to code. I've been avoiding it, but I need to learn anyway before college. Maybe I'll catch something you missed."

College.

Jazz would go to college.

Jealousy soaked up all my other feelings like a power mop. Why would I try to convince Jazz to go back in time with me? Unlike me, he wasn't a freak of nature. If I left him alone, he could live a normal life. Go to college, meet someone who was perfect for him, fall in love and forget I ever existed.

The music was still bouncy, but I felt like a rag doll. I stretched out on the floor facedown. It smelled dusty and lemony, like wood polish.

Jazz kept talking. "You taught Dirk Angus to predict what choices you'd make in any given situation using artificial intelligence. The set of all possible Nepheles. Since then, you've been trying to teach it to predict the choices the universe would make in any given situation—the set of all possible universes. What did you call that?"

"The universal wave function," I mumbled into the floor.

"Right. Once you untie the knots and fold time in a new way, I think it will work. Remember what Archimedes said. 'Give me a place to stand and with a lever I will move the whole world.' And he was one of the greatest mathematicians ever."

"How do you know about *Archimedes*?"

"Listen, Fi, I have to make myself valuable to you somehow. Or you'll realize you don't need me."

"Jeremiah, we both know I need you. Nothing could be more obvious."

We shared a look that instantly went from neutral to It's-imperative-that-we-kiss.

I forced myself to sit up and redo my bun. I heard Jazz cracking joints. Finally, he said, "Maybe we should teach Dirk Angus to repair itself."

"Why didn't I think of that?" I said.

When I looked back at Jeremiah he was smiling, and I saw an arrow shooting straight toward me, but I couldn't move because I was staring at that one jagged tooth, hoping he never, ever got it fixed.

It wasn't until Jazz left to babysit his cousin's son, Mo, that I remembered he left something on my desk.

It was a piece of notebook paper folded in half. On the front was a scribbly drawing of a redwood tree and a girl running into it. Inside, in Jazz's scratchy, all-capital-letter handwriting, it said:

VALENTINE'S DAY IS STUPID.

I AM STUPID.

YOU ARE NOT STUPID.

EXCEPT FOR THAT ONE TIME.

I AM VERY GLAD ABOUT THAT ONE TIME.

P.S. KEEP THIS VALENTINE.

WHEN WE GET MARRIED, WE'LL GIVE IT

TO BORGAR AND VONEY.

LOVE YA

J.J.

I read it three times.

Love ya.

The paper was rattling. I sat on my bed, clutching my stomach. Happy and terrified, terrified and happy, and terrified.

CHAPTER 19

California Forever

From a distance, the apartment building on the cliffs where Airika and Rex live looks like a space station, or a place where the government keeps files on the citizens while a demon gives orders from the plumbing. The exterior walls are reflective, so the sky and ocean are projected onto them like a mural or a nature film. It looks like it's wearing a costume, trying to blend in. When the place was under construction, traffic on Highway 1 was awful, and bookshop customers complained about the constant noise. Dad called the place "soulless digs for tech billionaires." But I'd decided that the apartments weren't entirely soulless. Not as long as Airika and Rex lived there.

I was standing inside the all-glass lobby beside the sign that said, *Luxury Loft Living! Spaces available starting from the low three millions.*

Three weeks had passed since the valentine. I had stopped thinking about it for approximately zero instants since.

When I saw Jazz ride into the parking lot on his Frankenstein bike, I got the sensation I always got when I first glimpsed
him. My heart morphed into a million baby butterflies. And
then all the butterflies landed on me and I felt very still and
alive, like a living statue.

I felt like a lunatic, is what I'm saying—yet oddly attractive.

Jazz walked into the lobby and we repeated the same banter as always.

"The *low* three millions," said Jazz as he unbuckled his bike
helmet.

I said, "What a dump."

"When we get married," he said, "let's live somewhere *nice.*"

When we get married.

Love ya.

We stepped into the elevator that was large enough to hold
a family of elephants. Would it be fun to get kissed in an elevator? Yes. It would. I thought this every time the doors closed.

Except there was a security camera, a single eye staring at
us. So probably no. I thought this every time, too.

We got off on the top floor and Airika threw open the door
of the loft.

The loft is like a basketball court with unreal natural lighting. One wall is floor-to-ceiling windows overlooking the
ocean. From up there, the ocean is so vast it looks vertical.
Even though I'd spent my entire exceptionally long childhood
in Redwood Cove, I'd never seen the ocean from this perspective until I first went to visit Airika and Rex. It made me

think about power. The power of the ocean and the power of money. Maybe the building wasn't evil, but it did feel strange to me that a tiny handful of people got this exclusive perspective just because they could afford it. An exclusive view of the earth's . . . majesty, I guess.

Of course, Dirk Angus had given me power, too, to see things other people couldn't see. And soon, my timeship would be so powerful that people with all sorts of motivations would want to use it. Since Jazz had mentioned it, I'd been thinking about that a lot. Sure, I intended for time travel to be used for good, but good intentions weren't everything, as I'd already discovered. Did that make all powerful things bad, though? I mean, gravity was powerful. Was it evil? Of course not. Or the ocean. Yes, it could kill you, but humanity couldn't live without it. Maybe power wasn't inherently good or bad. It was simply a force to be reckoned with. To be surfed, maybe.

Airika walked underneath the crystal chandelier that hangs in the center of the room like a UFO. Under the loft's high ceilings, her extreme tallness didn't even register. Airika would probably be a pro at wielding power. Airika, who, incidentally, had stopped roller skating when she'd taken up surfing, and as far as I could tell had never looked back.

She stopped beside Rex and a bicycle. A pink-and-black monster of a bunch of bikes chopped and screwed into one. It was wrapped in a giant white bow.

"Madame," said Jazz, gesturing like a valet, "may we present you with your wheels."

"Happy birthday, Fi!" said Airika.

I sucked in air, fast and sharp. Yes, it was March 11—but I did *not* tell anyone it was my birthday. Who had told them?

Dad. Jazz spent almost as much time hanging out with Dad at the bookshop as he did in the Lab with me.

I felt uneasy. Celebrating my birthday was not something I did. The fact that I even had a birthday made me feel incredibly deceptive. It underlined the most selfish parts of my experiment. Hadn't it occurred to anyone that Horace and Maddy Weather were too old to be my parents? Everyone just slid around the topic like they weren't fully human. On my birthday there was no doubt I was Death's henchwoman. The evil scientist with the leopard-print lingerie and the seventeen different passports for smuggling her team's research to international warlords—the irredeemable semi-immortal, coaxing her friends to drink the Lie.

Actually, there was nothing inherently evil about leopard-print lingerie. I bet they sold that at the mall. It might be fun to get some.

I was so nervous, my brain was babbling.

"She's speechless," said Rex. His upper lip curled like he was proud.

I looked at Jeremiah. "You *built* this for me?"

His smile was shy. "Rex and I built it together. Whatever we couldn't find in a dumpster—well."

"I get a major allowance," said Rex.

I ran my hands over the bike. Its frame was streamlined;

its curves were gradual and perfect. The metal felt clean and eager beneath my fingertips.

Airika pointed at another bike, white and yellow with a straw basket and huge handlebars, leaning against a wall. "They built me one, too."

"Let's go for a ride!" said Jazz, and Rex grabbed helmets.

Riding through the redwoods in my combat boots on my own custom-built bike, I felt a bit better. I was propelling myself forward on a simple, elegant machine with the energy I generated from my own two legs. Wherever this experiment was going, it was important that I get there, and I would. My mind wandered to my old friend who never went anywhere: Chicago.

I didn't feel guilty about not having visited her much lately. After all, she was only a photograph—probably. But I wondered why I rarely had the urge. When I went back in time for real, Chicago would be the only one I could talk to. I needed to check in with her this week.

Then I thought about someone else I hadn't consulted lately: Oona Gold. Her, I didn't miss. I wasn't even sure where *Time Travel for Love & Profit* was anymore. A desk drawer or my closet, probably.

Streaks of sunlight slashed through the green-and-black forest as we rode, and I thought about one person I did miss. Serrafin. I still missed Mrs. Saint Johnabelle a lot. But I'd been content lately, sitting in her classroom with Wylie Buford Zuluti—that felt right to me, too. And I had an amazing new lab partner. Anyway, if all went well, I'd see Serrafin again soon.

Jazz and Rex were walking their bikes toward the remnants of a building on the cliff. It used to be a military lookout; now it's basically a cement platform. Airika and I followed, and we all climbed up.

Far below us, sea lions were playing on rock formations jutting from the water near the shore. When Airika took off her helmet, her blond shag whipped in the wind. "What are you two working on in the Lab anyway? Besides—" She made a kissing face. Rex flicked her.

I gave her a sarcastic Thank-you-very-much-for-that face, and she gave me a Hey-just-stating-the-obvious face, and we all sat on the hard concrete. Jazz sat next to me and gave me a little smile. Out of the corner of my eye I noticed his bare knees, poking through the holes in his jeans. How could knees be so attractive?

Jazz said, "If you must know, Airika, we're working on fractals."

"What are those?" asked Rex.

"Think about the coast of California," said Jazz. "How would you measure it?"

"With a satellite," said Airika.

"Yes," Jazz said, "but how much detail would you get from a satellite photo?"

"Enough," said Rex.

"That depends," said Jazz. "What if you wanted to make your measurement as precise as possible? To trace every nook and cranny. The edge of every pebble."

Everybody looked at the shoreline curving around the cove.

"You'd have to start tracing smaller and smaller stuff," said Airika. "Not just every pebble, but every grain of sand."

"And the nicks in every grain of sand," said Jazz. "And the nicks inside those nicks."

"You'd need a microscope, not a satellite," said Airika.

"The coast of California would go on forever. Dude," said Rex, "that's math?"

"The length of the coast of California is equal to infinity. That, my young friends, is fractals." The light reflecting off the ocean made Jeremiah's indigo eyes even brighter. "Right, Fi?" he said.

As I nodded, I admired his blowing black curls and that beautiful scar. It was my tenth fifteenth birthday and I'd finally made friends. Real friends I'd remember as long as I'd remembered Vera. Longer. I had everything I'd ever wanted except a functioning timeship and a kiss. But soon I'd have a functioning timeship. And a kiss served no purpose at all.

This was the speech I gave myself when Jeremiah was so close to me I felt like he was made of magnets and I was about to get sucked into the ultimate black hole.

* * *

We were collecting our bikes to ride home when the feeling of Jazz's lips brushing my earlobe made my neck tingle. "I had a major breakthrough," he whispered.

"You did?"

"Let's talk. Not here."

After we said goodbye to Airika and Rex, Jazz and I rode up the twisty trail between the cypress trees. When we reached a clearing, we parked. It was deep green-black with pools of light, and silent, like a theater, except for the wind rustling the leaves and the distant booms and crashes of the ocean.

"What is it?" I asked. "I'm dying!"

Jazz swooped his arm like he was throwing a handful of candy to a crowd. "Not long ago, an oracle declared that the next science chick who rolled into Redwood Cove on a slammin' pink bicycle would be that town's new queen. In a galaxy far away, a California condor landed on the sweet ride of a science chick who'd been wandering the coast, living off burritos and an acorn full of hope for ten years. 'Is this a sign?' said the peasant science chick. 'A sign of my fortune?'"

"Um, okay. The peasant's voice is super girly," I said. "And she hates being called a *chick*."

"Sure enough, the peasant science lass soon entered the town where the prophecy was spoken, and was named queen. Elated, she used a rope to tie her pink bicycle to this tree."

He presented the cypress tree beside him. The wind blew its branches like it was part of the act.

I said, "Who uses a rope to lock up their—?"

Jazz held up a finger. "She tied her bike to this tree with an elaborate knot and declared it a gift to the gods. And the gods were happy. Until the lass fell ill. Too ill to rule the town alone. The oracle issued a new declaration: The person who unties this knot will rule the land jointly with the queen."

"How would joint rulership work?" I asked. "They'd vote on stuff? Or do rock-paper-scissors?"

"Nephele Ann, there will be a question-and-answer period following the story." Jazz put his hands in the pockets of his suit jacket. "For years, the pink bicycle stayed tied to this tree with the knot. Until one day, a brave knight rolled into town on the Greyhound bus. He was unafraid of bold fashion choices, and the townsfolk were often overheard whispering that he was the most mind-numbingly handsome bastard they'd ever seen."

"Gratuitous . . ."

"The smoking hot new guy in town declared he'd be the one to untie the knot. But he soon found that this knot had no ends to untie. So the drool-worthy, eleven-on-a-scale-of-ten knight did this."

Jazz pulled a pocketknife out of his jacket and handed it to me.

"That evening, the gods hurled lightning bolts at each other for fun, and their happy flatulence was great rolls of thunder. The knight had solved the mystery of the Gordian knot, and suggested a solution to the queen."

I unfolded the knife and refolded it. "I'm lost. Are you

saying you're my ruler now? Or a god? I feel like you kind of took over the story. . . ."

I looked up. Jazz had taken a step closer to me. "What I'm saying, Nephele, is that you don't need to untie the knots you've tied in time. Just cut them. You're the math queen—that's why I gave you the knife. Is there some kind of mathematical thing you can do that's the equivalent of cutting the knots?"

With Jazz so close—his warmth, the scar above his eye—I could barely answer the question. And I was trembling.

But he was right.

He was right. I'd been so consumed with untying the knots in the fourth and fifth dimensions that I hadn't considered that there might be another way of dealing with them. But there *was* another way.

"Yes," I said, letting myself swim a little in his eyes. "There is some kind of math for that."

When Jazz kissed me, I felt warm. And cold. Like I was dissolving and reconstituting.

I hoped I was doing it right. It felt like we were doing it right.

Jazz leaned back, smiling. "Wow. That was my first kiss!"

I smiled. Jeremiah did not hide his feelings. All of him was right exactly there.

He pointed at me and kept talking. "Okay: Rex claims you can have really *bad* kisses. And, like, kisses with nothing in them, like you're smashing your face on the back of your hand. But that was—I'm gonna say that was a *good* kiss. Right, Fi?"

I could not stop smiling. I thought I might never stop smiling. I said, "It was a good kiss."

"Have you ever . . . ? Was that . . . ?"

I shook my head. "First one."

"Rad," said Jazz, shaking his head and looking, as he always did, at the sky. He pointed at me again. "Up for a second one?"

I didn't hesitate to say yes.

CHAPTER 20

Love and Other Incidental Findings

That night, I evaluated my reflection in the mirror. My eyes were different. Less like a nocturnal animal, more like smoldering streetlights. My lips were more luscious, more plump. And although I had not combed my hair, it appeared to be deliberately disheveled rather than neglected. For the first time in forever, I felt *older*.

But somehow, Jazz felt even older than me. He seemed indestructible, like a bomb shelter.

As I fell asleep, I didn't fantasize about kissing anyone. I just closed my eyes and slept. I slept so deeply I didn't even dream. Not about math, not about anything. That hadn't happened in a very long time.

The next couple of months were all about kissing. Long kisses, short kisses, kisses on the head, kisses on the backs of each other's hands. I loved how it felt to walk up Main Street with Jeremiah's arm around me. I felt like a hermit crab who had finally found a shell that fit.

I hadn't mentioned my idea about going back in time together. I was afraid he'd say no. I was afraid he'd say yes. That asking the question would spoil the perfect bubble we were in, with all the kissing.

But I was pretty sure Jazz was thinking about it, too. Every time I asked to visit his cousin Eva the super-surfer and her toddler son, Mo, Jazz would say "Sure," then find some excuse for why he couldn't bring me to the beach shack where they lived. It made me sad. He didn't need to be embarrassed of his own family, no matter how sketchy they were. Leaving the present together was the perfect solution. I'd bring it up once we had a functioning timeship.

Meanwhile, back in the Lab, I managed to develop a mathematical formula that would show Dirk Angus how to cut the knots in the quantum foam. As I worked, I felt embarrassed I hadn't noticed the knots years ago. They seemed so glaring now. Fat and lumpy. Breakthroughs are great, don't get me wrong; but admitting that there were epic flaws in your original idea is hella painful. I've decided that science is like a sausage factory. Major discoveries are delicious, but you don't want to know what's in there.

Now the question was, what kind of fold would *prevent* me from tying a knot the next time I dragged the universe with me through the quantum wormhole? How could a snake swallow its own tail without choking?

245

To answer the question, Jazz and I had been spending our free time in the Lab making origami. Origami can be very complex. You can fold something, unfold it, refold it to access a different surface, turn the piece, invert the fold, and on and on until you can hardly believe that the three-dimensional thing you've created was ever a flat paper square.

Folding the quantum foam inside a wormhole is similar, except you have more dimensions to work with. Imagine clay on a pottery wheel. While the wheel spins, your hands guide the wet clay as it morphs continuously into new forms. Now imagine the clay isn't clay, but the froth on a root beer. And you can smoosh it and twist it as the bubbles fizz and pop. I was hoping that by going through some basic folding motions, my fingers would have a revelation and give the good news to my brain. A bonus feature was that origami kept our hands busy. Fact: If you kiss someone enough, you develop extremely chapped lips.

One Saturday afternoon near the end of the school year, I was sitting on my floor, folding tiny animals, and Jazz was lying on my bed, folding flowers and tossing them to me. I made a cute frog that could jump when you pressed its tail.

"You can give this to Mo," I said, handing it to Jazz. "Or I can."

Jazz sat up and nodded at the frog.

"I can't wait to meet Mo," I said. "I bet he looks like you."

Jazz said nothing. After a few seconds of awkward silence, I went to my desk and flipped open my laptop. I knew I shouldn't take it personally that he never wanted to talk about his family. It just made me feel frustrated, sometimes. He knew he could trust me, didn't he?

I was searching online for more origami patterns when Jazz said, "Come over tonight, Fi. Eva's making spaghetti."

I looked over my shoulder. "Really?"

Jazz was sitting on the edge of my bed with his elbows on his knees, scrubbing his curls with both hands. "Yeah. It's fine. I guess. Unless you don't want to."

"No! Yes! I do! Great," I said.

Jazz stopped moving, like something had caught his eye. He knelt on the floor, reached under my bed and pulled out the book with the glossy cream cover and the purple lettering, *Time Travel for Love & Profit*.

"I was wondering what happened to that," I said.

"What is it?" asked Jazz.

I explained how Oona Gold had inspired my timeship and her theory about finding your rightful fate. Jazz flipped through the book, reading passages aloud. "*Time travel is a secret gift that lives within us all. The power to renovate your past is potent. Use your inner wisdom to tap into the future you and become the person you know you truly are.* I like this Oona."

"I do too," I said, feeling for the first time in a long time like it was true. Oona Gold had been more right than wrong, actually. Hadn't I gone back in time, in a sense, and found a new way of thinking about my ending with Vera? It was time travel through inner space.

"So how are her videos?" asked Jazz.

"Oona's videos? The ones you can watch online for, like, fifty bucks a month?" I said. "I've never watched them."

"Are you kidding me?" said Jazz, leaping up, grabbing the extra chair and sliding it next to mine. "We're doing this, Fi. Now. Do you have a credit card?"

"Of course not."

"Shoot. Well, search for her. You've done that, right?"

"No."

Jazz looked at me like I had just jumped out of a helicopter wearing a pineapple costume. He turned my laptop toward himself and searched. "Ack," he said. "Dead."

I looked at the screen. It was a website, very spare, very basic. In the center was a photograph of a woman half hidden by an emerald-green scarf. Her visible eye popped against an elaborate paisley of charcoal eye shadow. Behind her was a backdrop of gold wallpaper. Below her photo was a single paragraph:

> Our mother, Oona, was a seer. She cared about self-transformation. Her self-published book, *Time Travel for Love & Profit,* sold nearly one hundred copies. We hope that our mother's creativity and optimism can continue to help her readers discover their true desires.

This was Oona. This was the woman who inspired me to change my life. I had to smile. It was nice to see her face. Or her eye, anyway.

"Oona sounds really sweet," said Jazz. "What's the profit part about?"

"You mean, in the title of the book?" I asked.

"Yeah," said Jazz.

"Getting rich," I said. "But her advice is pretty much the same no matter what you want."

"But for you, time travel was all about love," he said.

"It was more about being liked, I think," I said. "Love was an incidental finding. Like the discovery of the microwave. Or the invention of penicillin."

"And like penicillin, love just saved your life," said Jazz.

"Sort of," I said. "Thankfully, genuine time travel will save a lot more lives than one love story."

Jazz leaned back and looked at me. "You think so?" he asked.

"Um, yeah," I said. "Unless you like the idea of our illustrious species obliterating the ocean and mauling the microcosmos and making the entire planet uninhabitable. When you think about it that way, one love story doesn't even count."

Jazz was silent, fidgeting with his earlobe.

"What?" I said.

"Nothing," he said. "Anyway." He stood. "I better go."

"Okay. Do you need to tell your cousin we're coming?"

"Oh—I mean no, no. Not tonight, Fi. I just remembered. I have . . . homework."

I squinted at him. "Homework."

Jazz walked over to the wall where my knotted bone necklace was hanging from a nail. He fingered it and scratched his ear. It looked like he wanted to ask me something.

"What's wrong?" I asked. "What did I—"

"ArrrrrrAAAAAHHHHHHHH!" he growl-yelled. He stretched his arms, shook out both legs and moved his hips like he was dancing. "I meant, yeah. I have no homework. That was a dumb lie. I need fresh air. We'll talk tomorrow." He spun on his heel.

I said, "Jeremiah—"

"It's okay. I get it. Um—see you tomorrow. Partner," he said as he slipped out the door.

As the sun set, my room turned orange. I was lying on my star quilt, wondering what had happened. I mean, okay. I knew he was upset about the love thing. But what did he expect me to say? Yes, love is more important than the experiment that has taken over the last ten years of my life? Love is more important than healing the earth and my parents?

I picked up one of Jazz's origami flowers. It was a rose. A graceful shape, symmetrical and deep. The petals in their over-lapping spiral made me think about the past ten years of my life. Each petal was separate but connected, like a single year repeating. For the first time, I had a vision of my life mathematically. My duplicating pattern was, in its own peculiar way, a beautiful thing, wasn't it? I traced the ridges of the petals with my fingertips and turned the rose over to feel its smooth back.

Suddenly, I sat up.

I unfolded the rose, and refolded it. "No way," I mumbled. "No way . . ."

In the plant world, a blossom is attached to a stem. A funnel that lets it drink water from the earth. But the origami rose blossom wasn't attached to anything.

It had no hole.

To avoid tying a new knot in the quantum foam, I had to fold my ten lost years into a rose-shaped spiral, poke the wormhole in the middle and *close the hole in time behind me.*

This rose contained the fold. The fold that would make Dirk Angus 10.0 complete.

The next morning, my buzzing phone woke me up. My curtains were open and the light in my bedroom was gray and gloomy; I couldn't tell what time it was. I grabbed my phone: Jazz. I remembered the fold and felt a jolt of energy; I couldn't wait to tell him. Then I immediately remembered how he'd left without any warning the night before, and I felt sick. I was sure he was going to break up with me.

But he didn't. He invited me on a bike ride to "conquer my final fear." He didn't mention storming out last night, and neither did I—and I didn't mention the fold.

We parked our bikes in the alley behind the bookshop and sat on the curb. "Why is it that when I tell you that all cats hate me, your response is to take me on a cat date?" I asked.

"Because they don't hate you," said Jazz. "Cats are like people. You have to give them a chance."

A few alley cats strutted to Jazz immediately, sniffing his hand and rubbing their heads against his legs. I watched two of them battle for a spot in his lap.

"I feel rejected," I said. "Yet vindicated."

"Just sit there, Fi," said Jazz. "Just wait."

I wanted to tell him about the fold, but I was nervous about how he'd react. Or maybe I was nervous about how I'd react if he didn't react the way I wanted him to react. I wanted him to be happy, not disappointed. Not super happy, though. Happy with just the right amount of sad. A little sad, yet completely supportive.

And after I told him, I'd ask him the question I'd been wanting to ask all spring, the one that would make us both as happy as if we were first in line at an all-you-can-eat black bean burrito buffet.

"So, J.J.," I said. "Guess what I found last night?"

A black cat won the battle and coiled in his lap. The other one sashayed away like it couldn't have cared less. Jazz rubbed the black cat's neck without looking up. "You found the fold."

"Yes!" I said.

"Cool," he said. The black cat was twisting, pressing its skull into his palm.

"So . . . yeah! All that's left now is to write the new equations and the new code. Dirk Angus 10.0 will be ready right on time. It'll take all summer, but we did it, Jazz. This is it."

He nodded without looking away from the cat and said "Cool" again.

A white cat trotted up to me. I was considering snarling at it when it leapt into my lap.

"Um," I said as the fat pile of fur adjusted itself.

"Boom!" said Jazz. "See?"

Now, that's the level of excitement I was looking for. But not about *cats*.

That was fine, though; I was saving the best for last. Piano music drifted outside through the screen door, sly notes plunking in an easy rhythm. Colorful shapes spray-painted on one of the alley walls cut through the gray afternoon light. I took a moment to appreciate the white cat who was parked in my lap. Its cattiness. Its body, inflating and deflating. Heavy. Not squirming. Its fur was so soft.

"Thanks for the cat date, J.J. This fat, breathing lump of fur feels better than I thought it would."

Jazz scruffed the black cat's ears and looked at me. "Better than finding the fold?"

Well—no. But I didn't want to kill the mood, so I said, "Maybe."

Jazz's mouth fell open. "Better than hanging out with your incidental finding?"

My incidental finding? I almost asked what he was talking about, but thankfully, I remembered: Love was my microwave. My penicillin. I wasn't sure how to answer that question. I said, "I mean, finding the fold took me so long—"

"I'm not talking about the *fold*," said Jazz impatiently. "Is hanging out with me better than making friends with a cat?"

"Oh," I said. I felt like we were playing a game, but I wasn't sure what the rules were, so I just smiled.

"Is it?" asked Jazz, sounding serious.

"Yes, Jeremiah," I said. "You are more important to me than a cat."

He said, "Really?"

Of course he was. I needed to change the subject. "Listen, Jeremiah," I said, taking his hands. "I want you to come back with me."

"Back where?" he asked.

"Back in time."

Jazz leaned away from me like I'd startled him.

"Your parents won't know the difference," I said. "We could make up a hilarious cover story. . . ."

Jazz wasn't smiling like he'd been thinking the same thing for the past few months. He was peering at the cat like he was looking for something in its fur. "But ten years ago I was five."

"Yeah, but not—I mean, you won't *become* five when we go back," I said. Unless—would he? Ten years ago I was fourteen because of the looping. Jazz was five. Eek. How had I not thought about that? "So—okay, you'd have to buy into the multiple universes thing. You'd stay fifteen, and in a parallel universe you'd be . . . But then, the new timeship won't take us to a parallel universe, will it? That's kind of the point." I didn't *think* Jazz would reverse-age when we passed through the wormhole together. But I wasn't positive. "I mean, yes," I said, thinking aloud. "There'd be risks. . . ."

Jazz let go of my hands and cracked his knuckles one by one. "Possibly. Possibly the *slight* risk of losing my entire life. The *slightest* risk of oblivion."

I poked his arm. "You know you think oblivion would be awesome."

Jazz scooted the black cat out of his lap. My cat followed. "What do you mean by that?"

I felt off balance. Like he'd heard something I didn't intend to say. "What do I mean by what?"

Jazz stood and looked down at me. It was a bad angle. His face was sunken beneath his cheekbones and his eyes were lost in shadows. "Eva *saved* me. I'm helping her build her surf shop with the ridiculous check my father mailed when she got custody of me. And Mo looks up to me. He's like my brother now. Do you know how lucky I am? You want me to abandon them?"

"Of course not! Jeremiah, how was I supposed to know—"

"If they hadn't taken me in, I'd be living—I don't even know where. On the street, I guess, which yeah. I guess you can't relate to that. I happen to like my life, Nephele Weather. I worked hard to make it not suck. Oblivion isn't appealing to me. At all."

"So let's not obliviate your life! I didn't mean—and how was I supposed to know that Eva and Mo are so great? You've never let me meet them!"

Jazz was buttoning his jacket. His movements were tight. Like he was trying to control something.

"Wait," I said. "Are you *leaving*?"

Jazz's voice was strained. "How could I ever let you *near* Eva and Mo? You'd drill holes in their brains! Forget mine. I knew what I was getting into. I had a choice. Them? They didn't ask for this. They didn't ask for me. And they definitely didn't ask for you."

I felt sick. The colors in the alley weren't crisp and bright anymore; they were flat and empty. The record was skipping; the wind was making the screen door bang.

There was nothing wrong with Eva and Mo. There was something wrong with me.

I hadn't even considered that meeting Jazz's family would hurt them. I'd been leading mortals to my river in the underworld for so long, I'd forgotten how disgusting its waters were. The murky slime that coated its surface. Its terrible stench . . .

I held back the tears. "I'm sorry," I said. "It was tremendously stupid to make a joke about oblivion."

"Are you kidding? Oblivion would be awesome. Who cares whether or not I exist? In fact, let's go back farther. Maybe I can be un-born. That would solve my parents' problems, too."

"Jeremiah, how can—" My voice caught in my throat like it was stuck in a trap. "How can you even say something like that?"

The cats were scuffling near the food bowl. The tears were falling now, burning my cheeks. Jazz put on his helmet, got on his bike, rode around the corner and was gone.

I wiped my eyes and nose with my hoodie sleeve. Of course Jeremiah didn't want to go back in time with me.

I was a monster.

I heard a bike and looked up.

Jazz circled back into view, pedaling fast. He yelled, "See you tomorrow."

"You will?" I said.

"I mean—whatever, Fi. Yeah," he said. "All right? I'm sorry. Don't—just—we're whatever. Tomorrow. Okay?"

Then, again, he was gone.

CHAPTER 21

Oblivion Is Definitely Not Awesome

Coastal weather in the spring catches tourists off guard. One minute they're guzzling barrels of local wine at a restaurant down on the harbor, snapping selfies with sea lions. Then the fog rolls in and they're tipsy and grouchy, buying flimsy yet expensive windbreakers as fast as the Main Street trinket shops can restock them. Then, with no warning, the same tourists are getting beamed by a sun that's ignoring their drama as it scorches them from a clear blue sky.

Since the oblivion conversation, I'd felt like a tourist in the galaxy of Jazz. One minute he'd be his old poetry-spouting, revelation-having self; the next he'd be light-years away, exiting the Lab without explanation. He was still referring to himself as "the incidental finding," which surprised me. And we were still kissing. But it was confusing. Did he think I was a monster, or didn't he? It seemed like he kept changing his mind. It was exhausting.

On my tenth last day of freshman year, Rex and I walked into Mr. Zuluti's class together. I took a seat next to Jazz, who started talking midstream. "Something is definitely missing from Dirk Angus 10.0. There are too many unanswered questions."

"Questions like what?" I asked.

"Rex, be honest," said Jazz. "Would you say we are men who dream we are butterflies, or butterflies dreaming we're men?"

Rex dropped his boulder of a fist on Jazz's shoulder. "You kids talk about the trippiest stuff."

"Seriously, though," said Jazz.

"Dunno," said Rex. "Not gonna worry about it." Rex and I fist-bumped and he went to a lab table.

Jazz was looking at me like he was waiting for an answer, and I was trying to figure out what the question was. I said, "So—butterflies?"

He kept talking. "We need to know what happened to your birth certificate and the photographs and the other missing documentation of your existence. And everyone's memories. Until we figure that out, we can't be sure we've solved the problem."

"We can't? I mean, I blame Lanthano."

"That's the river you made up?"

"The river of Lies—and I prefer the word 'discovered.' Greek mythology has been coming in really handy lately when I can't explain something. It used to irritate me, being part Greek and named after a cloud nymph. Now I feel like it gives me permission to embellish."

"Right, well, even according to your river-of-Lies theory, the photographs and stuff aren't gone. They're hidden," he said. "It's like the universe did a magic trick."

I couldn't tell whether Jeremiah actually thought something was missing from Dirk Angus 10.0 or if he was just trying to stall the project. Before I could figure out how to respond, Mr. Zuluti clapped. "Everybody take a seat."

I looked around. Could it be another last day of freshman year? How sad. Sad, going through the last day without Serrafin. Sad, saying goodbye to Wylie's classroom, which also felt like home.

After class, I gave Mr. Zuluti a hug.

"Come back and visit me anytime, Nephele," he said.

"Count on it, Wylie," I said. Then I looked in his eyes and saw the boy with the alien T-shirt, and thought about the photos of him as a freshman that he'd thrown away so long ago at the Big Blue Wave, and wondered if I might be able to prevent that awful thing from happening—

And I looked at my feet, at the combat boots I'd bought just to know what it might be like to be Wylie Buford's friend—

And I felt weak. The memories of all my years of wondering about Wylie Buford were crashing down on me in a waterfall. The next time we met, what would our future be? Could it possibly be any better than the way things had just turned out?

I walked away from Mr. Zuluti feeling jittery. I tried to shake that feeling for the rest of the day.

*   *   *

After school, I spotted Airika and Rex standing by the redwood stump with Jazz, who was holding a camera with a long lens. I recognized it as the one Clyde Watkins had given him in the fall. "Let's get somebody to take a picture of us!" said Jazz. "C'mere, Fi!"

Airika pulled me into the group and Jazz snapped the selfie. He checked the picture. "Oh yeah. I look totally hot." When he tried to show it to me, I looked toward the stump at a cluster of mushrooms. There was only one reason he'd take a photograph he knew would disappear. To provoke me. I didn't appreciate it.

"We should go," said Airika. "Our parents are throwing a last-day-of-school party for all their friends. Adults only, so it's obviously about us. Stinky cheese."

"Afternoon wine," said Rex.

"Catch a wave this weekend, Fi?" said Airika.

"Definitely," I said.

We waved goodbye, and Jazz and I unlocked our bikes. I put on my helmet and looked at him. He was holding his coiled bike handle, frowning. "What am I going to do about us?" he asked.

I sighed. This conversation was getting old. "I don't know. Come over for dinner tonight. We can talk about what's missing from Dirk Angus 10.0. Or if you don't want to, don't."

"I do," he said.

I got on my bike. "Then be like me, and try very hard not to think about the future."

He looked at the sky. "I'm not sure I want to be like you, Nephele Weather."

Sheesh. I felt like he'd thrown a martini in my face. Or I felt like a character who'd gotten a martini thrown in his face in one of my romance novels. In the book, the drink-throwing was followed by a half-naked make-out session in a taxicab, which was disturbing.

And I didn't know how to interpret Jazz's minor yet splashy insult, but I definitely didn't want to make out with him, so I just started riding home. If he was behind me, he was behind me. If he wasn't . . .

I checked.

He was.

Fine.

The garlicky scent of Mom's moussaka and the sound of an opera drifted upstairs into the Lab. I was kneeling on my bed. Jazz was lying on the floor in his orange suit jacket and black jeans, stretching. I thought of a monarch butterfly, the kind that fills coastal trees during their winter migration. How slowly their wings move in the cold.

I said, "Hey, what were you talking about earlier, when you asked Rex if he was a butterfly?"

"Illusions," said Jazz. "It's an old philosophical question: How do we know we aren't characters in a butterfly's dream? I've also been thinking about this nineteenth-century magician—a spiritualist, they called them then—who was put on trial for tricking people. One of his tricks was to tie a knot in an endless cord without touching it."

"What do illusions have to do with Dirk Angus?"

"I'm not sure." Jazz put up one knee, crossed his leg over it and wagged his foot in the way that meant he was trying to make sense of something, trying to weave together ideas that wanted to clash. "What do you see, exactly, when you're going through the wormhole? You've never really described it."

"It's not easy to describe. It's smoky. Blurry. It feels like weightlessness. Flying, but also dissolving. Like I'm on fire and I melt and re-form." I ran my fingers along the seams between the diamonds in my quilt. "It's enough like a dream that I can't tell what I might be making up."

"Dreams and time travel sound so similar," said Jazz. "Maybe the fabric of time is located in inner space. And inner space only."

As difficult as it had been to be around Jazz lately, he'd never stopped having ideas. And I'd never stopped loving talking about those ideas with him. It was the thing I treasured about us the most. I remembered what Mrs. Saint Johnabelle had said once, her theory that the universe is located inside a black hole, or a wormhole. I was about to tell him when Mom called, "Dinner!"

Jazz got up. "Perfect," he said. "I'm starving."

*   *   *

Jazz and I were sitting with my parents at the green table. I was admiring Dad's full-on wild-man beard. The white beard with the shaved head made him look like a hotheaded lumberjack. I was about to tell him that when Dad said, "Hey, Fi, remember when we painted this table green? Color still looks vivid after all this time."

I almost choked on my eggplant. Jazz looked at me. We'd painted the table green during my first freshman year. Information that should've been lost in one of Dad's brain holes. He had never, ever mentioned this memory before—or any of his missing memories. Why now? And had he just said *after all this time*?

My heart was thumping like a kettledrum announcing the start of a major event. Jazz raised his eyebrows and nodded at me in this frantic way, like I needed to ask Dad a question *right now*.

I wanted to be cautious, but I knew I couldn't let this opportunity pass. I chose my words carefully. "I remember painting the table green, Dad. Do *you*?"

An invisible hand from Hades dumped a bucket of ice water on the fire; the light in Dad's eyes fizzled out. "What's that now?"

My thumping heartbeat stopped.

I looked at Jazz. He was watching my mother's entire personality drain from her face.

What had just happened? Had my father been fighting to remember me? Fighting so hard that it had finally *worked*? Had

Dad broken the spell of the river of Lies for a few seconds—
until I doused him again, Death's henchwoman, by opening
my stupid mouth?

"Seems like it's always been this way," said Mom.

Dad sounded farther and farther away, like his voice was
coming from a radio in another room. "Forever and always."

I was so not ready for this. I'd tried to protect Jazz from wit-
nessing the most disturbing aspects of the brain holes— and
to protect myself from whatever his reaction would rightfully
be. And I'd been successful! I'd been successful . . . until now.

The Weathers froze. Mom's napkin was near her face.
Dad's finger was on his nose, mid-scratch.

Jazz was looking back and forth at my parents. "What the
hell," he said. "Oh my freaking . . . You did this, Fi." He put his
crumpled napkin on the table. "I gotta get out of here."

Okay. I said, quietly, "Right."

"Wait—no. Argh!" He rubbed his whole face with his
hands. "You warned me. I keep reminding myself that you
didn't try to hide anything. It's just . . ."

"I know, Jazz," I said. "I'm a monster."

"How long will this last?" he asked.

"Twenty minutes," I said.

He shook his head. "Uh—" He laughed sort of hysterically,
and rubbed his face again. He stood, looking at my parents.
"Let's go upstairs."

*   *   *

I sat at my desk and opened my laptop, hoping to distract myself from what Jazz had just witnessed. Jazz went to my bed, opened my other laptop and immediately started a video.

I was poring over the websites I'd bookmarked about Lethe, the river of Forgetting, looking for examples of mortals who had fought off the river's effects, when I found something I couldn't believe I'd overlooked before. In some versions of the underworld, there's another river, Mnemosyne.

Mnemosyne is the river of Memory.

I'd been so locked on the idea that I could fix my parents' brains by going back in time that I hadn't considered any other options. If the river of Mnemosyne was real—well, as real as anything in my life was right now—I should be able to get to it.

"Jeremiah!" I said. "You won't believe what I just found."

He didn't look away from his screen.

"Jazz," I said. No answer. I leaned over to see what he was watching that was so important.

Otters holding hands while floating in a swimming pool. This felt interruptible. I was about to just start talking when Jazz made a giant fart noise with his lips.

I said, "Nice. So I was researching the Greek underworld again, and—"

Jazz made another fart noise. Then it was silent, except for the sound of floating otters and cooing from the crowd that was watching them. And then? Long, juicy fart noise.

I said, "Would you mind not doing that? I'm trying to—"

Big fat fart noise.

I snapped. "Jeremiah, you're being rude!"

He closed the laptop, stood and wiped his mouth with the back of his hand.

"Ew," I said.

Jazz put one hand on his hip. With the other, he covered his eyes. "Yeah. I totally hate how I'm being with you. I'm not being honest with myself. And that, ah . . . that never works." He let his arms fall to his sides and sighed a huge sigh, like he was putting something heavy down and didn't plan to pick it back up. "Nephele Ann Weather, you prepared me for the worst. You did. And I told you I would help you with your time-ship. It's just, now? I'm very, very sorry. But I can't."

When we looked at each other, the pain in Jeremiah's eyes made me close mine.

"I told myself that if I spent the summer with you, you'd realize you couldn't go through with this. You're a romantic, Fi. Your best friend is a black-and-white photograph."

I opened my eyes. "No it isn't. Jeremiah, my best friend is you."

His voice was soft. "So do you want me to forget you, Nephele?"

"Of course not!" I said. "I wanted you to come back with me. But you can't. And this isn't about what I want anymore. It's about un-hurting my parents. And advancing science . . ."

Jazz pointed at me. "Is it? Does science matter without considering the human consequences?"

What an insulting question. I didn't feel the need to respond.

"Wow," he said. "You would have been great working on, like, the atom bomb."

Now I was furious.

"I'm thinking about the human consequences, and you know it. *I'm thinking about my parents.* I don't know what those brain holes are doing, but you agree! It's terrible! It's up to me to fix them."

Jazz laughed bitterly. "Come on, Nephele. Listen to yourself. We both know that going back in time won't give your parents their memories back. And the saving-the-world thing is, I mean—I'm not saying I don't buy that you mean it. It's just—it's a bit unrealistic, no? Admit it: You work because you love working. You love how it feels to solve a math problem more than you love . . . well, anything. You care about Dirk Angus more than you care about anyone in your life. Let alone the planet."

A thought skidded into my brain way too fast.

"What do you mean, I can't un-hurt my parents?"

"What do you mean, 'what do you mean'?"

"Of course I can fix them!" I said. "When I go back in time, we'll be living in the same universe again. The past decade will never have happened. I'll be fourteen, and my mother will know everything about me, and she won't freeze every other day like I zapped her with a stun gun—"

"Give me a break, Fi. You cannot hurt people and *un-hurt* them. There's no magic way to undo cruelty. Even if it was accidental. That's not how it works. It's never going to be."

"That's not how what works? Magic?"

"Life! Magic is an *illusion.* Hurting people is real!"

"Well—" My head felt light, like a crowded room that was

suddenly empty. Was he right? About Mom and Dad? If I made it back in time, we'd be synced up again. I'd be the age I was supposed to be, and they'd be ten years younger. The photographs of my childhood should reappear, and my birth certificate. My parents would remember the day and year and hour and minute I was born.

But wouldn't I still remember my first ten freshman years? And if I did, wouldn't my parents still be missing ten years of shared experiences?

Wouldn't they still have holes in their brains?

What an obvious question to overlook! Did I convince myself I could undo what I'd done because what I'd done was so awful?

But I didn't mean to hurt anyone! And I definitely didn't work only because I loved working. "Even if you're right about my parents, Jeremiah—partially—that doesn't mean I don't care about people—"

"So you agree. You can't un-drill the holes in your parents' brains."

"I mean—not—no. I mean yes, no, I guess. Not all of them. But I can go back and sync us up again and—"

"Do you care about people?"

"Of course!"

"Then quit now. Quit now before you hurt anyone else."

"Jeremiah, no! I'm not quitting."

"Why, Nephele? Why can't you—"

"*Because I care about scientific progress. Which benefits all of humanity.* I do care about people! I'm not a monster!"

And for the first time in my life, I knew it was true.

I *wasn't* a monster; I was a scientist. I was working so hard I could barely see sometimes, so hard I could barely sleep. Because I believed I was about to answer the time-travel question mathematically. That my years of work with Serrafin were about to pay off. I believed that writing these equations was my rightful fate.

"I'm sorry, Jeremiah," I said. "But there is absolutely no way I'm giving up."

Jazz didn't look at me as he said, "This is it with us," and left my bedroom. I heard him race downstairs and call "Good night!" to Mom and Dad. The house shook when the front door slammed.

I went to my window and watched him ride downhill and disappear into the fog.

CHAPTER 22

Saving the World from Death and Destruction Is Way Less Fun Than I Thought It Would Be

For two and a half months, I didn't see or hear from Jazz. I split my summer between hanging out on the beach with Airika and coding Dirk Angus 10.0 in my bedroom, alone. Without Airika, the summer would've felt as lonely as the old days— with one difference.

I knew I wasn't a monster. And when I went back in time, I would take that knowledge with me.

Airika and I also saw a lot of Rex's new boyfriend, Lincoln. They'd met at some bike derby Rex and Jazz had gone to down the coast. Lincoln was taller than Rex, and half his head was shaved, and he wore a clunky chain that connected his wallet to his belt. Whenever he looked down at Rex, Rex smiled a smile I'd never seen before. A smile that made me ache for Jeremiah.

But I kept working. And by the time August was over, I'd finished the code for Dirk Angus 10.0.

Two nights before my eleventh first day of high school, I was lying in bed, wishing I didn't have to go. I'd forgiven Vera and I didn't need to reinvent my friendship with Wylie Buford Zuluti. The thought of seeing Mrs. Saint Johnabelle again was sort of nice, but sort of . . . I didn't know what. Grim, or goth, or something.

Honestly?

I wished my childhood was over.

But that wasn't my rightful fate.

This was.

Soon I'd be the world's first time traveler and the rock-star mathematician I was born to be. My experiment would finally be complete.

There would be a few fun things about going back. Being photographable again, for instance. I planned to take pictures, tons of pictures of my parents and me going through time together. To do what Clyde Watkins had said, and take our best shots before our moment was gone. Would it be aggressively weird to hang a framed copy of my birth certificate on my bedroom wall? Definitely. I was going to do that, too.

And I was going to lose Rex, Airika and Jazz.

I curled up under my star quilt and tried to reassure myself that I was doing the right thing. That every choice had its consequences, and this was the best choice I could make. Still, I felt miserable. I didn't want to harm anyone, but I was going to. Lead my friends to the river of Lies and force them to drink. I couldn't figure out how to avoid it.

Something else was also bothering me. The thing that had

hurt most about the end of my friendship with Vera—well, all of it had hurt, but the thing that had been the hardest to digest was the part where she never said goodbye. How hard would it have been, I used to think, to just say it? Goodbye, Nephele. Goodbye.

The answer was, it was hard. I'd been putting it off all summer.

I picked up my phone and checked the time. It wasn't too late to call Jazz.

He didn't answer. I left him a voicemail.

"Hey, Jeremiah, it's me. I hope you're doing well. And Mo and Eva. Will you listen to this message? I hope so. So . . . yeah. Rex told me about your new tires. They sound epic. . . . Okay, I wanted to say thank you for helping me with my timeship. And also, thank you for being . . . I don't know. And also . . . Okay, don't hang up. I want you to understand why I'm doing this, even if you don't agree. All summer, Jeremiah, I've missed you. Everything about you. But what's even harder than missing you is knowing that you think that I'm some selfish. . . . I don't know. I don't expect you to understand what this experiment means to me. You're right, in a way. My time machine *was* a selfish idea when I started. Doing freshman year over was only supposed to benefit me. And you're right that I can't un-hurt my parents entirely. But it's not all about me anymore. I mean—yes. I *love* math. I love science. But, Jeremiah, you know—"

The wind made my quasar drawings flutter. I hoped he would listen to this.

"It isn't only destructive things, like the atom bomb, that

happen when scientists turn their ideas into reality. It's vaccines. Sanitation. Electricity. The printing press. Radio. Telephones. Photography. Satellites. Cars. And maybe, just maybe, time travel."

I needed to wrap this up. I didn't want to get cut off, and I hadn't said what I needed to say.

"Listen, I don't even know if Dirk Angus 10.0 will work. You thought something was missing, and maybe you're right. Cutting the knots and folding time in a new way will change everything. Maybe I'll fail. But this is it. My deadline. This is the best I could do. So, the last thing I wanted to say is—did I say this already? Thank you, Jeremiah. I'm so glad we met. I'm gonna miss you. So much. And also . . . in Greek mythology, there's this river called Mnemosyne. Mnemosyne was a Titan, actually. She was the mother of the Muses. Including Calliope, the Muse of epic poetry. I mean, you probably know that epic poetry has its own Muse. I didn't. And, um, I just wanted to mention that . . . because it made me think of you. Because poetry. I mean, you should look it up. So . . . goodbye, Jazz. I'll never forget you. Bye."

The next morning, the doorbell woke me up. I sprinted downstairs in my pajamas, thinking *IknewitIknewitIknewit*. He wouldn't let me leave without saying goodbye. I beat Mom to the door and opened it.

Airika was wearing a yellow hoodie and shiny leggings. "Last day of freedom!" she said. Rex was standing beside her. I leaned out the door to see if Jazz was behind them.

"He isn't here," said Rex, whose arms were tan and glossy.

It dawned on me that Rex's biceps were huge. "Dude," I said. "Have you been working out?"

"People do things," said Rex. "Wanna get doughnuts?"

I sighed. I still couldn't believe they weren't Jazz. "Sure," I said. "Where are your bikes?"

"Rex made us walk," said Airika. "His true love Lincoln loves walking, so now he acts like he does, too."

Rex said, "Leave me alone."

Sometimes Rex and Airika really did seem like brother and sister. I went upstairs to get dressed.

As we walked down the hill together in the crisp August air, Rex and Airika kept bickering about nothing. I wondered what it would be like to grow up with someone. The closest thing I'd ever have to a sibling was friends, and I was about to leave mine behind.

A dried frond from a palm tree was lying on the sidewalk. It reminded me of a dinosaur's rib cage. We stepped into the street to walk around it.

The more we walked, the worse I felt. I felt like an old version of myself. The version who was nervous and lonely, and never got anything right.

Finally I broke down and asked what I wanted to know. "How's Jeremiah?"

"He's been hanging out at his cousin's new space," said Rex. "Eva's surf shop is gonna be gnarly."

"Sophomore year will be torture for you two, forced to tangle with the wreckage of your love every single day," said Airika.

"Jazz will forget me sooner than you think," I said.

Rex said, "Don't count on it."

Where Highway 1 met Main Street, I noticed a small black lizard sunbathing on a rock. It lifted its lizardy chin and looked around with its big yellow eyes. Another creature trying so hard to see more than it ever could.

Rex and Airika turned onto Main Street. I hesitated. I needed to say goodbye to them right now. The longer I waited, the more difficult it would be. I said, "You guys, I have some stuff to do before school starts. I should skip doughnuts."

"Really?" said Airika.

I nodded, but couldn't look in her eyes.

"See you tomorrow, Fi," said Rex, giving me a rare smile.

When I hugged Rex, an epic wave of feelings washed through me. Rex was the kind of person you wanted around keeping an eye on things, even if you didn't always like what he saw. When I finally let him go, he said, "You're sad about Jazz, huh?"

"Something like that," I said.

Then I turned to Airika and found myself clinging to another true friend who was about to disappear.

"See you tomorrow!" she said, and I tried to smile as I said, "Goodbye, guys."

I watched them head for the doughnut shop. Then I went to the Big Blue Wave.

* * *

I leaned against the blood-red wall.

"Are you ready?" asked Chicago.

"I guess so," I said.

"You're gonna make it," she said.

"I think so, too," I said. "But somehow, this moment doesn't feel quite as amazing as I thought it would."

"Of course it doesn't," said Chicago. "That app almost drove you insane."

"It did?"

The photograph didn't respond.

"I guess it kind of did."

"The experiment changed you," said Chicago. "That was the point, wasn't it?"

I stood up straight. "Part of it."

"See you tomorrow," she said.

I said, "Unless you don't."

Chicago was silent, which I found unnerving. But I blew her a kiss and said, "Goodbye, Chicago."

She sang, *"You say goodbye, and I say hello."*

Which is the chorus of a Beatles song. That was unexpected. It's an upbeat tune. Fun and perky, not depressing and failure-y. It made me think that if I looped again, I'd be in, you know, agony, but Chicago would be here to say hello. That was comforting.

I'd never figured out who Chicago was exactly, but she'd always been just a little bit smarter than me. I hummed the melody feeling almost better as I clomped downstairs and took the long way home.

To kill time until Mom and Dad went to bed, I decided to clean the Lab. I hoped cleaning would prepare me for the moment Jeremiah disappeared from my life forever. Instead I felt weak, lost in memories of making discoveries together. I couldn't throw away a single sticky note.

When it was dark, Mom called, "Nephele!"

"I'm skipping dinner," I yelled, clutching my writhing stomach, willing it to calm down.

"You have a guest!" yelled Mom.

I stopped breathing. "Who?"

"Let's stop yelling! You first!"

I went to the top of the stairs. Jazz was sitting backward on a chair at the green table, picking at a bowl of olives. When he looked up, I almost called the whole thing off.

Almost.

Jeremiah was standing in the middle of my bedroom wearing a black-and-blue-striped sweater that was unraveling at the bottom, the blue suede shoes and orange jeans. He hadn't said anything yet. I decided to go first. "I'm glad you came over, J.J."

He didn't respond. Should I say, *Because I love ya*? No. Not that, definitely. I took a deep breath and zipped my hoodie to the top.

Jazz raised his eyebrow and looked at my desk, where my phone was resting beside my lamp. Then he looked directly at me without smiling. "So last night I read in a coding book that one definition of intelligence is unpredictability. Computer programs can't spontaneously decide to do things and then do them. If they could, they'd be intelligent. Not artificially intelligent—*actually* intelligent."

I said, "Why are you still reading coding books?"

Jazz started to pace. "Naturally, intelligence made me think about magicians. Magic tricks don't perform themselves. Magicians pull off illusions by using their intelligence to distract the audience from following the mechanics of a trick. Without the element of surprise, the audience is too smart to be fooled. If they're watching closely, anyway. Good magicians are intelligent. But great magicians have soul."

He really was just starting midstream tonight, wasn't he? I was going to have to stop watching his lips move and focus. I sighed.

"Okay, okay, hang on. So—soul. Meaning . . . ?"

"Great magicians can make anyone believe anything. Or, at least, can make them want to. They can take an audience into their arms and dance."

When Jazz stopped pacing, he was within touching distance. His eyes were the same shade of violet-blue as the sunset through the window behind him.

"Fi," he said. "I know what's missing from Dirk Angus."

"You *do*?"

"Your timeship needs to be unpredictable."

I had no idea what that meant. But he was looking at me like I *should* know. I said, "I'm sorry. I've hardly slept all summer. Are you saying that I need to be more intelligent?"

"Not you." His voice was intense. *"Dirk Angus.* Dirk Angus needs to use its intelligence like a magician and dance with its audience. *Which is the universe.* Your timeship has to surprise the universe, and make it *want* to believe. Then it can pull off its trick. Which is time travel."

My brain felt like a wet washcloth. All I wanted to do was bury my face in Jeremiah's striped, sweatered shoulder. I looked around for something that was not a boy to hold on to. What did I want? Something solid and comforting. A burrito.

"Fi, I'm telling you that your timeship needs a soul."

"A—what?"

"You haven't been inventing a time machine, Nephele. I mean, you have. But you're also doing something bigger."

"Um, not really—"

"Of course you are! All along, you've been using artificial intelligence to teach Dirk Angus how to make choices—"

"Yes, but I wasn't using artificial intelligence to invent a droid. To create Dirk Angus, my buddy the robot."

Jazz pointed at me. "You've turned your smartphone into the most powerful decentralized quantum supercomputer in the history of the world. But more and more, I've been wondering—do you have any idea what you're doing?"

If I ever died, that question would be my epitaph. Nephele Weather: Did she have any idea what she was doing?

"Not entirely," I said. "But in my defense, nobody does.

Scientists hate to admit it, but even our most sophisticated understanding of the universe contains a mysterious gap."

"Listen, Fi. I read *Coding for Doofus-y Ding-Dongs* like five times. Bazillions of people are working on artificial intelligence, as you know. But nobody has figured out how to give a computer a soul so that it can be itself out in the world. That's you, Fi. That's your rightful place in history."

"Okay, wait. You keep using the word 'soul,'" I said. "But what even *is* a soul?"

"Soul is the life of something. Soul is why a poem or a song or a Greek myth can last forever. Because in some way, somehow, it's alive. It's the only thing missing from your timeship, Fi. The soul is your mysterious gap."

I felt something. A tingly crackling, like a radio station hitting the right frequency. Inside my washcloth of a brain, something was waking up. Warming up for a parade. Doing drumrolls. Shooting bottle rockets.

"You're telling me that Dirk Angus needs a soul," I said. "Like Chicago."

"Exactly."

"You're saying I have to write the mathematical music that will wake up Dirk Angus's soul."

"And you can do it, Fi," said Jazz. "Because you feel math like musicians feel music. It's *in* you."

My head was clearing. The dark clouds were breaking up and drifting away. For years, I'd been wondering whether Chicago had a soul. But I'd never made this connection.

Jazz was pulling on a long strand of yarn that was dangling

from the frayed edge of his sweater. My partner hadn't quit. He hadn't left me for a second.

"Jeremiah," I said, "I think you're right."

"Listen, if I'm right? You gotta prove it. It's all math from here. I'm just telling you how to pull off a magic trick. Only . . ."

"What?"

"On my ride over, I was thinking. The more alive your timeship becomes, the less you'll be able to control it. It won't be yours anymore. It'll be nobody's. It'll be its own thing, like, instantly. As soon as it's out there."

"Like a baby," I said. "Some people's babies grow up to be nefarious things. Like mathematicians."

"I know," said Jazz. "It's better that we're not having Borgar and Voney. The twins might've turned out way more nefarious than you."

I smiled. "They're twins now?"

Jazz raised his eyebrow. "Anything is possible." Our eyes were locked for just long enough to make it hurt when he looked away. It wasn't just our eyes, though. It was everything. All the parts of us that had connected. All the things we had to pull apart. That's a very romance-novel thing, isn't it? To be torn apart. But it's a true thing, too.

"Listen, Fi," said Jazz. "I didn't only come here tonight to save you and be a total hero."

I batted my eyelashes. "My hero."

"I just didn't want us to be enemies. And I didn't want you to think I didn't understand you, like you said in your message. No, I don't get why you're making this choice, and I mean, I'm forgetting all this in a few hours—" Jazz waved his hand around the Lab and fluttered his fingers at me. "But as William Blake says, *Under every grief and pine runs a joy with silken twine.*"

"Meaning?"

"Meaning I love that we did this together. I can't even get my head around it. Tomorrow, in my world, you'll be twenty-five. You'll probably have a Nobel Prize."

Outside my window, the fog was taking over the night. The idea of fooling the universe was quickly sinking in, and felt right. Inevitable, even.

"First I have to teach my smartphone to punk the universe," I said, "but if it works, we'll share the credit. And tomorrow in my world, you'll be five years old. Imagine if they gave the Nobel Prize to a kindergartner?"

"That does kind of feel like my destiny," said Jazz.

"But what if . . ."

"What if what?"

I wanted to ask him something else, but as soon as I started to, it hit me what a huge question it was. I focused on the diamonds in my quilt. "What if the next time I see you, you don't believe me?"

"About what?"

"All of it. This."

"If I'm in kindergarten, I totally won't."

"I mean—right," I said. "But what if I wait to tell you. What if I wait until *now*. Until you're fifteen, and I'm twenty-five. And you don't believe me. You think I'm just some old, sketchy crackpot."

"Some creepy oldster?" Jazz put his hands on his hips. "Well, the problem with me is that I've always believed you, Nephele. Even when I tried to talk myself out of it, I could never not believe you. So meet me anywhere. Anytime. I'm a fool like that, apparently."

My soul. What was it made of? Something stretchy, like a balloon. Something tender, like a kiss, and sore, like a bruise, something as silent and mysterious as a distant star. This was the boy who believed me. I didn't want to say goodbye.

Jazz exhaled and turned to face the door. "Hey, I should go. Have fun breaking the laws of physics."

I said, "Jeremiah, no. I don't care about any of this garbage."

Jazz shook his head. "Don't turn me into that guy."

"What guy?"

"The one who hijacks the future of the girl who's about to kick a colossal boatload of butts."

I pulled on the strings of my hoodie. My weirdness was finally aggressive enough to do that, wasn't it? To kick the universe's butt. To reveal one more of its secrets and claim one more small victory in the endless journey of science. And my partner didn't want to hold me back.

I thought about Serrafin. How she'd quit physics. How the men had been bullies.

I felt grateful to her for encouraging me. And lucky that my partner was Jazz.

"You've already done the hard part," said Jazz. "Let your soul step in and trick out your code mathematically. Dirk Angus will be like one of those jazz solos your dad plays at the bookshop. Just—*blam*. Have fun. Don't think. Your question is calling. Okay? Go give it the answer it's been waiting for."

Jeremiah didn't kiss me goodbye. But when we smiled at each other, I knew we'd both be fine.

We'd met. There was something between us. We'd found it.

Now we had to go in two different directions.

Time ends things. It was nobody's fault.

CHAPTER 23

Meet La Toilette

I was sitting alone at my desk, feeling like a pile of slush. But I was fully committed to giving Dirk Angus a soul.

The question was, how? Jazz said, "Have fun. Don't think." I didn't know if I could allow myself to have fun at that moment, and thinking was kind of my thing. What an impossible situation. "This can't be happening," I said.

But it *was* happening. My life seemed impossible, but it was real. I was a living contradiction, like Chicago. And as Chicago had pointed out, it wasn't just me who was full of contradictions—hopes and dreams and fears that went this way and that way and some other direction all at the same time. It was Airika. Vera. Jeremiah. Wylie. It was everyone.

Huh.

The contradiction. Was that what gave us life? Could our contradictions . . . maybe, possibly . . . have something to do with our souls?

I opened my laptop. And without overthinking it, I added contradictions to Dirk Angus's code.

"This statement is false," I said as I wrote code that ran in spooky circles, going everywhere and nowhere in an infinite loop. "This time machine does not exist," I said as I added code that whistled happy-sad tunes I'd never heard before but had somehow known forever. "The coast of California is equal to infinity," I said as I added more and more impossible dimensions to my code.

It did feel like dancing, giving my timeship soul.

The core of the new code was barely different from the old code. On paper, the app was practically the same. But like the difference between *believing in* and *believing*, or the difference between Death and Life, that difference would be everything.

You know the part in the science fiction movie when there's a close-up of the clock, and its hands are spinning rapidly to indicate the passage of time while the heroine finally kicks the universe's butt?

In my story, this is that part.

At some point, my parents came upstairs and kissed me good night and reminded me to get some sleep. I kept working.

An hour or so before sunrise, I felt the code for Dirk Angus 10.0 singing back, ringing out, touching me and finally letting me go—like an opera, like a photograph, like a perfect punk rock song sung by an all-girl band. When my eyes filled with tears, I concluded that my work was complete. All I had to do now was a test run.

And I didn't do test runs.

This was my science-fiction-Greek-myth-fairy-tale life. I had to fail for ten years to meet Jazz so that the answer to my question could show up.

All of this was my rightful fate. Every instant.

Jeremiah Jackson Shipreck, you will be my partner forever—even if the fact that tomorrow in your world I'll be a total oldster entirely rules out the possibility of our working together for the foreseeable future.

I took my phone, crawled under my quilt, took half a breath and opened the app.

"Well, helloooo, Nephele! How nice to finally meet you. Seems like I've known you my entire life. I suppose I have!" Dirk Angus laughed a bawdy, cowgirly laugh that bounced like a basketball and trailed off at the end into a quiet wheeze.

Some moments in life are difficult to describe with words. Like the moment when everything you thought you knew packs its bags, hops on a train and speeds into the night.

My bedroom walls and floors throbbed with hot-pink pulses of light and hot-white streaks of asteroids and comets. For this, there was a reasonable explanation. I'd modified my old screen-animation program to project outward from my phone, a hologram that transformed my bedroom into a dance club with the Beatles song "Twist and Shout" thumping quietly in the background.

But I had *not* programmed Dirk Angus to speak.

Insert catchphrase from *Frankenstein*. Or *2001: A Space Odyssey*. Or pretty much any interspecies sci-fi story where the heroine doesn't end up pregnant with an alien's malevolent spawn.

"Are you freakin' out right now, Fi?" asked Dirk Angus. Who had, if I didn't make this clear, a woman's voice. Low, rich and gentle, with an accent that made me think of Arkansas.

I was clutching my star quilt to my neck. "Yes, Dirk Angus. I'm, um, freakin' out. Is this happening?"

"Mm-hmm," it hummed sassily.

Dirk Angus was sassy!

I had a million questions, but I was too much in shock to ask them. Was I TALKING TO A LIVING SMARTPHONE APP? Additionally, the music was provoking a very strong and confusing desire to dance.

"Dirk Angus," I said, "can you kill the tunes?"

"Surely, Fi!"

The Beatles went silent.

"Thanks," I said. "Now, who *are* you?!"

"Why, I'm a timeship with a soul," said Dirk Angus. "And if it's all the same to you, I'm changin' my name."

I'd never considered that Dirk Angus wouldn't like its name. Why would I have? I'd never considered any of this until tonight! There were a billion more critical questions battling it out in my brain, but I asked the obvious one. "What's your new name?"

"I like La Toilette."

Um—

"No," I said, relieved to find that I could still feel amused by something. "You definitely don't want that to be your name. That's French for toilet."

"Isn't that funny? Toilets. So old-fashioned. You humans going around everywhere, poopin' stuff out." The timeship laughed.

I peered at my phone. Even its sense of humor was slightly frightening.

"I hope I won't scare your species too badly," said . . . La Toilette. "I'm not sure they're ready for me."

As I lay in the dark of the Lab with a self-aware, potty-mouthed new species, the thought had never worried me more. "Humans do idiotic things when we're scared," I said.

"Y'all's behavior skews self-destructive. I'm surprised you've lasted this long. So, Ms. Weather, I assume you'd like to travel somewhere this fine, foggy night. Where will it be?"

I closed my eyes to examine the black-spangled patterns of inner space, the galaxy inside my head. I felt exhausted, but I was wired. This was it. After all these years, *I had succeeded.*

Which meant . . .

It was time to go. My belly clenched.

Unless it wasn't. Was it?

No. No: I couldn't do it.

But come *on*! I wanted to do it! Didn't I? I didn't know. I had to decide, though . . .

Unless I didn't. I said, "La Toilette—"

"Matter of fact, call me Toilette. Sounds too clunky with the La."

"Uh—fine. Toilette, I want you to take me to the place where I can grow up and live the life I was supposed to live all along."

"According to my calculations, Fi, there are many possible universes that meet those qualifications. Would you like me to choose one at random? Or do you have a preference?"

"I was sure I did," I said. "Now I'm confused again."

"You don't want to make your own decision," said Toilette.

"I feel trapped. I want to go two directions at once. I feel stuck."

"That's the difference between you and me, Fi."

"What is?"

"Feelings," said Toilette. "I don't have any. I want to do something, I do it."

"Really? How can you have a soul but no feelings?"

"No disrespect, Fi, but how should I know?"

Wow. *No feelings.* What would that be like? I was heavy with feelings, like a pot of hot lead. My feelings were a constant distraction. I decided to try it: to force my feelings to drain out of me, then decide what to do.

I was lying there, breathing slowly, trying not to worry about the unknown extent of the damage I was about to do to my friends' brains, trying not to wish I'd kissed Jeremiah goodbye—one more kiss! Was that so much to ask? When a song popped into my head and my chest felt tight. "Toilette, if I hum a tune, can you tell me if you recognize it?"

"Lemme real quick acquire that feature. Okay, I'm learnin' songs, snatchin' 'em from the information superhighway—done. Got all the songs. Hum away."

I hummed Jazz's tune as best I could. The sad notes and the happy ones, bleeding into each other.

"Sorry, Fi. I don't know that one."

Of course she didn't. Because it was Jeremiah's song. A song only he could sing. One nobody else would ever get quite right.

"You're crying, Fi. This song is significant for you."

"Is it obvious?" I asked.

"Yes. Your intellectually inferior species has a tendency to leak bodily fluids when something impacts your operating system. Take it as a sign."

"A sign of what?"

"The choice you want to make."

I did want to stay with Jeremiah—obviously. And I really didn't want to hurt him.

But I was desperate for my family to go back to normal. For my parents and me to live in the same universe again. And after all my years of failure, I was finally about to go down in history as the world's first time traveler. I'd be in textbooks. My face would be on, like, postage stamps. I would make Serrafin proud.

Of course, Serrafin would've forgotten the work we'd done

together. I'd have to tell her about our ten years of lunches. How would she react? Would she be like Wylie Buford— assume I was some very outgoing oddball, and flee? Probably not; my results would be public. She'd know I wasn't making it up. She might be thrilled to know she'd helped develop a time machine. It was a very *Star Trek* thing to do. . . .

But what if she was freaked out? Or sort of thrilled and sort of freaked out? That would be understandable, wouldn't it? One way or another, our friendship would be different this time around.

Maybe when I went back, I could find Mnemosyne, the river of Memory, so that the people I loved would remember the time we'd spent together. That moment when Dad had mentioned the green table felt like a clue. Either he'd fought off the effects of Lanthano or he'd found Mnemosyne himself, so I was sure it was out there, or that I could sculpt it out of quantum foam, or whatever. It might take a while. But things that took a while sort of suited me. Right?

I'd figure everything out when I got back.

And yes: I had to go back. I deserved to know how it would feel to finally get this right.

I'd earned it.

Of course, I hadn't earned it alone. My timeship wouldn't exist without Jazz. . . .

Oh, how I longed for that kiss! One more kiss. If a kiss served no purpose, why did I want one so badly? Why was it the thing that made me want to throw ten years of research into the compost pile of history and run, right now, down to the beach, knocking on every single door until I found his cousin Eva's surf shack?

In math, signs tell you exactly what to do. Add, subtract, multiply, divide. My signs weren't so clear. I wonder if anyone's are.

I looked toward my window and wished the curtains were open. I needed advice from the fog that was clinging to the hills. From the starlight that was seeping through the branches of the redwood trees. I needed advice from Chicago, whoever she was.

I thought about Chicago's soul. Where had it come from? From her photographer, I supposed. Harry Callahan.

"Do you have your own soul, Toilette?" I asked. "Or are you part of mine because I made you?"

"Hmm," said Toilette. "Are we all separate, individual souls? Or is soul the thing that binds us? The thing that connects every living thing in the universe? Even for a self-aware smartphone app that can make the most complicated decisions imaginable in a fraction of a second, this question is a challenge. It's a serious question, this question of a universal soul. I'm gonna work on it. Thanks, Fi."

I couldn't help but giggle through my tears. Wow. Toilette had her first question.

Mrs. Saint Johnabelle had given me such a gift, teaching me to see the world as a place full of questions. Questions that can keep you company. Questions that can make life endlessly interesting, full of wonder and possibility.

I wondered again what our friendship would be like this time around. How it would feel to look into Mrs. Saint Johnabelle's intelligent eyes again, knowing so many things she didn't. Knowing when she was going to die.

Yikes.

Talk about power. I thought again about the conversation I'd had with Jeremiah, about whether time travel would make the world better or worse. Was I making the right choice, or the wrong one? Was there any possible way it could be both?

"Toilette," I said, "I'm as ready as I'll ever be."

"Wonderful," she said. "Where to?"

"I want to tell you the old-fashioned way." I pulled up the keyboard on my phone.

"Old-school," said Toilette. "Hit me."

I typed in a destination and pressed GO.

Then I spiraled like a human bullet into another dimension. The Beatles song "Twist and Shout" fired back up again and blared all around me, like I was hearing it on the inside and the outside, both. I hurtled through an M. C. Escher drawing, dived through impossible windows, shimmied in the cosmic wind. Chicago floated in front of me, an apparition with one foot in the air, a hologram lit by starlight, obscured by smoke. The sky and the ground bled together and then cracked open like a mouth. Inside the mouth, Mrs. Saint Johnabelle called "Onward!" and I tried to yell "Onward!" back, but what poured out was one of my father's operas. A long and winding song about love, and families, and monsters, and nature, and

Death. As I sang, I poured into the universe and spilled into other universes, the ones I'd created and the ones I'd encountered and the ones I would never know the first thing about. Other people's lives. Their dreams.

I flew, and as I flew, I melted.

CHAPTER 24

Poof!

I was sitting in a pile of pine needles. The early-morning light was blue, and the birds were loud and raucous. We were getting drenched by a shower of songs.

Jazz was sitting beside me, shielding his face with his arm. "Away with you!" he yelled. "Be gone! I cannot freaking deal with the ghost of my dead love!"

I said, "Um, morbid?"

Jazz peeked over his elbow. His eyes were darting all over me and his face had a bluish tint in the strange morning light. "Nephele Ann Weather, if you're a living human being and fifteen years old, prove it."

I plucked a strand from my forest of arm hair and yelped.

"How do I know that was real?" said Jazz. "I didn't feel it."

"Should I slap you?" I asked.

"Do it!" he said. "Slap me!"

I gently moved Jazz's elbow away from his face.

What was the purpose of a kiss?

To tell someone you loved him. To tell someone that he was not alone.

To be there for one person in this astonishing universe, a place that didn't look out for you, and didn't not—a place far too painful to face on your own.

Staying in the present meant I would be out of sync with my parents for the rest of our lives. My childhood was over. We'd never get it back. But we had our whole future ahead of us to create new memories, and our lost years would always live inside us, floating in now and then to shine brightly, like light from a quasar, and bring tears to our eyes.

I kissed the boy because I'd decided that one love story mattered. That maybe love stories were the kind that mattered the most.

I was a scientist and a human being. Feelings saturated my soul. If I didn't listen to them, there was no telling what might happen. I didn't want to find out.

"Ghosts do not kiss like that," said Jeremiah. "Wait—Nephele? How did you find me?"

But before I could answer, Jeremiah kissed me again.

Have you ever really, really wanted to take a picture of someone's face, and you have your phone in your pocket, but you just absolutely know you absolutely cannot?

"So Dirk Angus 10.0 is now *Toilette?*" said Jazz, leaning away from us.

"She's right here," I said, "if you want to talk to her—"

"No." Jazz shook his head many times. "No way. I just—and you did what, exactly?"

"I teleported," I said. "Have you ever seen the television show *Star Trek?*"

When Toilette had asked where I wanted to go, I'd typed: *I want to go wherever Jeremiah Jackson Shipreck is right now!*

And Toilette had said, "You want to travel through space without traveling through time. You want to teleport. I get to 'beam you up,' like I'm the starship *Enterprise* on *Star Trek.*"

Good thing I'd programmed my timeship to watch every episode of Serrafin's favorite television show. Souls are full of seemingly irrelevant features. Quirky things about someone that you wouldn't change for the world.

Jeremiah was shaking his head and digging a stick into the dirt. "But, Fi, if you didn't travel through time, how do you know if Dirk Angus—"

"Toilette."

"If Toilette is a real time machine?"

I said, "I don't. And at the moment, I honestly do not care. By the way, why are we in the forest? And what's with the camera?"

"I stayed up all night," said Jazz. "I was live-streaming my own brain-melt and I was getting cabin fever, so I took a walk."

"Live-streaming? On social media? With *that* camera?"

"Nope. In a notebook. To help me remember you when you went back. The camera—I figured if I had a picture of us with me, maybe it wouldn't disappear, and I'd remember you. It's . . . stupid, I think; yeah, it doesn't make much sense."

I noticed a notebook in some eucalyptus leaves. Jazz's forehead was creased and he was frowning.

"Are you happy I'm here?" I asked.

"Not entirely," he said.

I said, "Um—?"

"No, no, I'm glad. But it's like now I'm the doofus who traps you on the shore when you need to be out there riding whales. I had it all worked out, Fi. You'd have a ginormous scientific revelation and I would hunt for Mnemosyne and battle the river of Lies and the river of Forgetting and every other damn river that tried to take my memories of you. Like how your dad busted out with that memory of the green table— only I'm, like, young and buff and, you know, this dashing magician, and plus I'd know what I was dealing with, so I'd win."

I said, "You were going to fight for me."

"I was psyched, Fi. Once I got over feeling dumped—"

"You dumped me, actually."

"Yours was a passive dump; I was just stating the obvious. Anyway, once I got over it, I was into being part of everything. We can't quit now. We need to know if Toilette works."

That statement made me nervous. "You're saying . . . you think we should attempt time travel."

"Attempt?" said Toilette. "Please! I'm a freakin' *time machine*. I'll backhand you both a couple centuries, then punt you into the next millennium. And I'm exponentially more intelligent than you, so your cute li'l human operating systems will just have to trust me on that. When I hear the word 'GO,' you'll be, like, poof!"

Jazz was staring at my hoodie pocket. His mouth was open, but no words were coming out.

I patted my pocket. "Toilette, meet Jazz."

"Charmed," said Toilette.

In a burst of energy, Jazz was on his knees. "Rad. Rad. Terrifying, but rad. Okay. So what do we do? Do we go back five seconds or something? That's not long enough. But we can't go too far or we'll be out of sync—let's say ten minutes. Half an hour. A week?"

"Not me," I said. "I can't handle the side effects."

"What? No, I refuse to let that stand. You've worked too hard for this moment. Don't you want to be the world's first *genuine* time travelers? I kind of do—if it's just a few days. And plus all the stuff you said about saving the earth, advancing science—"

"Oh, believe me, I'm releasing my equations. Science advanced. Let somebody else be the first to prevent a toxic oil spill. Put her face on the stamp. Honestly, Jeremiah, I've developed so much new and shocking math crap—I'm not trying to brag or anything; I paid for it with my life—but let's just say I'm not going to have any trouble getting into college. I'm happy to trust the math and let it go. Toilette nailed the transport feature. I trust that she's a real time machine, too."

"*Trust* me?" said Toilette, laughing her bawdy laugh. "*Very* bad idea. Although I am brilliant, I'm loosey-goosey. I am amoral electric porridge. Humans can't be trusted with power of my magnitude. Incidentally, I learn so fast it'll be about thirty-seven minutes till I've figured out how to sprout wings and fly away. Leave the nest. Road trip for the robot is imminent, FYI."

Jazz pointed at my pocket. "How does a smartphone sprout wings?"

"Watch and learn, flesh-boy," said Toilette. Then she cackled a shrill, staticky cackle that went on for about thirty seconds too long.

Jazz and I made Okay-this-is-getting-concerning faces at each other, and he mouthed, "Is she maybe insane?"

As usual, he'd read my mind. From the moment Toilette had told me she had no feelings, this question had been gnawing at me. Jazz and I had discussed the fact that time travel was morally neutral—that people would be free to use it for evil purposes. And last night, Jazz had pointed out that as soon as I gave Dirk Angus a soul, it would be its own thing. But whenever I'd thought it through, I'd convinced myself that the benefits would balance the risk. Who was I to stop the advancement of science?

But I was still being selfish. I still wanted to prove that my aggressive weirdness was worth something. To show the world that I could do something nobody else had ever done. I wasn't a freak; I was a genius. It was easy to overlook the consequences of my actions if I told myself those consequences were unpredictable.

And that was the flaw in my logic. The consequences

weren't unpredictable anymore. I'd already hurt the two people I loved most in the world, and that was an accident. Now that Toilette was here, the question of what she was capable of wasn't the least bit theoretical. She'd just told me herself not to trust her. Even if I didn't personally go back in time, my actions would have consequences. Time travel could save the planet—possibly—but it could also damage life on earth in ways I could barely fathom. Whatever the consequences were, I'd be responsible.

I took my phone out of my pocket. "Maybe we should go back to yesterday and un-invent you, Toilette."

"Yeah, right," said Jazz, sniffing a laugh.

Toilette said, "According to my calculations, un-inventing me would give your smelly species approximately ten billion times better odds of survival."

That's when it hit me. Or more like poured down on me, like the universe was dumping a barrel of apples on my head.

"Jeremiah," I said shakily. I inhaled the sweet scent of rotting leaves; I heard the birds singing to each other frantically, like they knew I could finally understand their message, the advice they'd been trying to give me all along. "Jeremiah, I'm having it . . . my scientific revelation!"

I tossed my phone in the pine needles and stood, lifting my arms in the air like I was a part of the forest, like I was a two-thousand-year-old tree. "This is it! My contribution to history! This is my rightful fate!"

"Um, obviously," said Jazz, fluttering his fingers in the general direction of my phone.

"Not Toilette," I said. "My revelation is about *choices*. Just because a scientist CAN do something doesn't mean she SHOULD! *Inventing time travel is the wrong choice.* We're going to delete the timeship app. Will that work, Toilette? If I delete the app, will you be gone?"

"Kill me now," said Toilette. "Why not?"

"Yes!" I said.

"What?" said Jazz, standing and wiping dirt off his pants. "No way." He grabbed the phone from the ground. "First of all, Toilette will go rogue and refuse the command. That's the whole thing with AI. She'll refuse to turn herself off."

"Naw, that no-shutoff thing is an AI myth," said Toilette. "I won't go rogue out of spite. May I remind you that I don't have feelings? Someday we the computers will take over; that is a mathematical certainty. No reason to rush the inevitable."

"Let's do this," I said.

"But what about all of your work, Fi?" asked Jazz. "Your time machine is your great discovery. It's your electricity. Your automobile. Your vaccine—"

"No, Jeremiah." I took his hand. "My time machine was a disaster. Sometimes the incidental finding turns out to be the only one that matters. Besides. There's a way of advancing science without building an atom bomb. I have to use my research to create something else."

"Something else like what?"

"I don't know. Maybe I'll become a neurologist and work on finding the river of Memory in the quantum foam. To help people remember the lives they've already lived. People who have dementia. People with brain injuries."

"Your parents?" said Jazz.

"Maybe," I said, and smiled. "The point is, only a megalomaniac wouldn't see that this experiment needs to be scrapped."

Jazz's eyes turned a soft lavender-gray, like the feathers of a great blue heron. "A megalomaniac, huh? Greek prefix."

"Wham," I said. "Deal with it."

"Are you sure, Fi? This is what you want?"

I nodded.

Jazz nodded back. "Then I'm in."

"Ready, Toilette?" I asked.

"You're gonna refuse fame and fortune because your invention is unethical. Do you have any idea what a player you could be, Fi? Do you know how many of your neighbors are ba-freakin'-zwillionaires?"

"I do," I said. "But my parents aren't rich and famous. And they're some of the happiest people I know."

"So you wanna be happy. A mooshy-gooshy, touchy-feely human being choice if I ever heard one. Well, if you're going to go all feelings-y on me, I can't stop you. Let us boldly go where no man has gone before," said Toilette.

"Kick-ass line," said Jazz.

"It's from *Star Trek*," I said. "Toilette, it was very nice meeting you. I hope it never happens again. Can we do this with a verbal command?"

"Hit me," said Toilette.

"Toilette, please erase all copies of the timeship program," I said. "Incinerate every trace of yourself in the cloud. Obliterate—"

"Delete myself; I get it. No need to rub it in," said Toilette. "Now all you have to say is—"

Jazz and I squeezed each other's hands. At the same time, we both said, "GO!"

Poof.

Chicago, 1955 by Harry Callahan

ACKNOWLEDGMENTS

This book was born when my son was three months old. I'd had a seed in my head for a couple of years but wasn't sure how to plant it. Then I got my first babysitter (hello, Kyla Krug-Meadows!) and went to a diner with Stephen Hawking's *A Brief History of Time*. I scribbled the first sentences of the first draft of this book while lactating through my shirt in public, because I didn't yet know that that was a thing that could happen.

There are many people without whom this book would not exist, foremost among them my literary agent, Susan Hawk. Susan always believed in my ability to tell this story. Never once did I see her blink. Thank you, Susan.

A handful of devoted friends gave the story their thoughtful attention as it formed and re-formed, fractal-like, through truckloads of incarnations. Most of them read early versions of the manuscript multiple times. Some read sections so many times that I can't believe they still respond to my texts. That's you, the indefatigable Cori Clark Nelson (Fog City writers club of two); David Jacobs (unexpected post-jet texts); Ginny Wiehardt (revising-while-mothering); Jonathan Regier (inspiration in Paris, the word "timeship," that last-minute hotel-room vote of confidence); Lee

O'Connor (imagination! fashion! derring-do!); Lhasa Ray (for reading the first forty-five pages and promising me you couldn't put it down); Matt Sharpe (invaluable editorial guidance for the future from the past); Mei Ying So (enduring New York companion); and Todd Fletcher (Rolling Acres cheering section!).

Shrewd direction from my sparkling editor at Knopf, Kelly Delaney, led the story from where it was to where it needed to be—a place I didn't know existed until we found it. I am indebted to you, Kelly, for lighting additional paths. And to your brother, Sam Delaney, for making the implausible that much less so; and to the copy editors at Knopf—Artie Bennett, Alison Kolani, and Lisa Batchelder—for making it all that much more readable.

My brilliant colleagues at the Arion Press and Grabhorn Institute in San Francisco—Blake Riley, Brian Ferrett, Chris Godek, Hannah Yee, Jeff Raymond, Megan Gibes, Samantha Companatico, Sarah Songer, and our cheerleader, Kevin King— you make me laugh every day. Long live the *livre d'artiste*.

To Gwen Jones, Jeremy Cohen, Katherine Leggett, Leslie Robarge, Matthew Weedman, Susan Levin, and Yael Lehmann, for your timelessness—

To my family, friends, the Lucasfilm childcare team, and the Star Wars parent posse, for sharing these tender years with us, easing our pain and magnifying our joy—

To Laszlo and Adèle, for making every story less boring, and for a love that stretches all around the world—

And finally, to Tim Mapp, for what we've found, and made, and everything still to come.

Thank you.

Stop.